No Space for Love

A North Korean Defector Story of Love and Survival

ELLEN MASON

BOOKBABY

New Jersey

NO SPACE FOR LOVE

A North Korean Defector Story of Love and Survival

A Novel

By Ellen Mason

Published by BookBaby, Pennsauken, New Jersey

www.BookBaby.com

For information, please address Ellen Mason

Ellen@EllenMason.com

Print ISBN: 978-1-66789-657-1

eBook ISBN: 978-1-66789-658-8

Printed in the United States of America

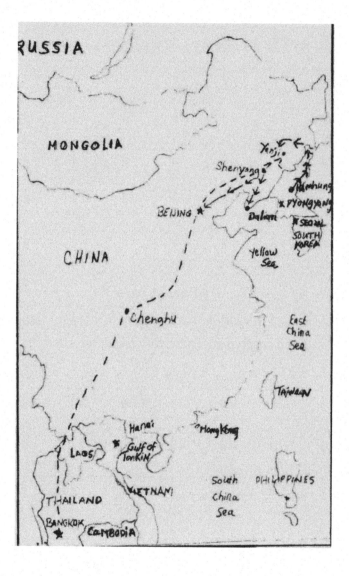

------- Ha-.na's Journey

→→→ Seng-il's Journey

CONTENTS

PART I

January 2020

"They don't give you the space to love in North Korea. I don't know what love is—is it a bowl of rice?"

—Seng-il Park

CHAPTER 1

Phoenix, Arizona

❋

Adam had a funny feeling as he pulled the car into the garage. Something was just not right. No lights were on in the house, and when he called an hour ago to see if his wife needed him to pick anything up from the store on his way home, Sophia had not answered the phone. At the time, he thought it was a beautiful evening and presumed she was outside playing with the kids. Now he was sure something was wrong. It was just a feeling.

Grabbing his jacket while glancing into the backyard, he made his way into the kitchen. He could see Kimi attempting to pull Elayne out of a little wagon. "Kids," he thought, "can't they play together without fighting?"

"Hey, play nicely with each other!" he yelled to them as he turned on a light and waited for them to stop and look at him.

"Appa!" (Dad), they responded almost in unison.

"Where is your Eomma?" (Mother)

Kimi stopped pulling on Elayne's shirt and without looking up, said, "Sleeping. She's been sleeping a lot."

3

"Appa, we're hungry," four-year-old Elayne whimpered. Now Adam was genuinely concerned! It was not like Sophia went to bed at midday, leaving the kids outside alone. Where was she? What was happening?

"You kids play out here for a few minutes longer, and I will make sure dinner is ready," he tried to make his voice even and not sound an alarm. He needed to find out what was wrong with Sophia.

He opened the bedroom door as he rushed through the house, turning on the occasional light. Entering the dim room, his eyes swept the bedroom looking for his pretty young wife. No Sophia. He ran into the bathroom and turned on the light, expecting her to be there. Perhaps she was sick. Not seeing her there, he turned back. That is when Adam saw Sophia curled in the fetal position, half leaning against the wall, and crying in a corner. Hustling to her side, he leaned down on one knee and touched her shoulder. "Sophia, are you OK? Do you need a doctor?"

Sophia simply turned further away from him and continued to cry softly into the blue cloth she was tightly grasping in her hands. When she did not respond but cried even harder, Adam gently shook her shoulder, placing his hand around her hand holding the piece of cloth. "Sophia, talk to me. We need to talk," he whispered, but with firmness in his voice. As he was saying this, he lifted her to her feet and sat her in the chair by the bed. Then pulling on the blue cloth she was holding, he said in a forlorn voice, "It is Yoon-ha, isn't it? You have been missing Yoon-ha today?"

Sophia sniffed but did not answer his question immediately. Instead, she let out a low, mournful cry: "I want to go home. I just want to go home and see my baby."

Adam immediately stiffened and stood straighter. "Home. You are home, Sophia. You are home with me and our children. You can't mean home to North Korea, can you? You don't have any family there; everything is hard to get, and you would probably starve there!" While they had never had a discussion quite like this before, he was exasperated and could hardly contain himself.

"No, not North Korea! I meant China!"

"China! Oh, for...." He paused briefly, then continued with renewed vigor, "China! Sophia, we could never make it in China! You know how it is there! No one wants us there—the jobs are hard and pay so little! Some people are nice, but others are downright mean!"

Adam was pacing by now as he was becoming more agitated. "Sophia, do you remember how often they beat you—the humiliating work they forced you to do? Do you want to do that again? What about me, Kimi, or Elayne? How could you want that life again?" He was almost pleading by now. All this time, Sophia continued to cry, with big tears rolling down her cheeks.

She looked up at him, her eyes brimming with even more tears. He could barely hear her as she creaked out, "Yoon-ha.... Su-lin."

"Yes! Yoon-ha! I understand, but we have two babies here too—two hungry children who need us!" Exasperated, Adam spun around and stomped out.

Going into the kitchen, Adam slammed a pan down on the stove and began to rummage around in the refrigerator to see what he could throw together for dinner. How could Sophia forget their beautiful life in the United States? Had she completely forgotten the hardships they had both been through in both North Korea and China? How they both had nearly died? Would she want to give up everything they had worked so hard for in the United States and go back to China? He had no answers to that. He did know they were surviving fine here. He felt sick to his stomach thinking about it.

Getting up early the next morning, Adam went to work at the small convenience store. He knew he had work and responsibilities. Yet, all he thought about was Sophia and their children. Over the next week, he worked extremely long hours, but when he was not directly interacting with a customer or his boss, Adam was thinking about Sophia and remembering how they had met and had come to live in Arizona. He remembered how they had had long telephone conversations, getting to know each other. It had somehow been easier to talk and tell their stories over the phone. Strangely, he had felt protected and knew shy Sophia also felt safer and less threatened as she told him the awful truth about her life. They had bonded. Did Sophia want to give up their life together? Did he?

PART II

Ha-na/Sophia's Story

CHAPTER 2

North Korea

❀

Ha-na always knew that her father loved her older brother more than he loved her, but that had never bothered her. After all, they lived in North Korea, where men and boys were always more prized than women or girls. Her brother, Chang-hee, was two years older than Ha-na and had always protected her. They had shared their chores and their deepest secrets. Chang-hee was always exceedingly kind to her and had never allowed the neighbor kids to say one bad or derogatory statement to Ha-na. For this, Ha-na loved and looked up to her brother.

"Here, Ha-na," my mother said as she scooped over half of her meager portion of rice onto my plate, "I am not so hungry tonight, and we cannot waste the food. You eat what I can't eat."

"NO!" My father angrily shouted at my mother as he reached for the plate. "If you can't eat it, give the food to Chang-hee. She is nothing but a girl."

But Mother surprised me this time when she pulled the plate back and softly said, "But Ha-na is my daughter, and I love her too. It is my food, and this time I am giving it to Ha-na. Chang-hee has gotten it every night so far this week."

Father surprised me even more when he did not object and only grunted as he got up and left the table, letting me have the rest of Mother's food. Such a small thing, and yet it simply demonstrated once again how little my father regarded me. I was, after all, "just a girl" and was clearly inferior to my brother's status in the family. In a highly patriarchal North Korean society with deeply entrenched Confucian values, a woman's principal role is to maintain a family's household and since I was not yet a woman, I was of even less value. Father had always doted on Chang-hee and he was the new favorite child, holding all the hopes and dreams of the family. My parent's firstborn was a son who had unfortunately died in infancy. I never knew why he died but knew that my father blamed Mother for depriving him of his son. Mother accepted the blame (rightly or wrongly placed) and was deeply apologetic and remorseful, even though she knew there was nothing she could ever say or do that would right this wrong with Father. Mother did, however, partially redeem herself when the next year Chang-hee was born. I called it "partially" because while Chang-hee was the beloved boy, he also had a club foot, which meant he was considered disabled. Under Kim Il-sung, all disabled veterans enjoyed a high social status if they said their wounds were the result of American aggression in the Korean War, but it had not been so good for disabled children. It was widely whispered down through the years that when a baby of either sex was born with physical defects, he or she was quickly put to death and buried. But my parents had worked hard to have a boy and did not see Chang-hee's deformed foot as all that bad. They did not want him to be sent away from Pyongyang, the showcase capital, for any reason, and they were afraid that Chang-hee might even be taken to an area camp for the disabled and they would never see him again. Secretly, Father paid a local man handsomely to make Chang-hee special shoes that concealed the fact that his left foot pointed inward and was shaped oddly. At home, Chang-hee wore a special, handmade brace that forced him to walk normally even though he claimed it was extremely painful. He dutifully always practiced walking in proper form so that his shame would never be discovered. Our family never spoke about this disability or ever revealed this fact to anyone for any reason. Both Chang-hee and I had made up a story that explained why he would never swim with us kids or remove his shoes. We both claimed that he had nearly drowned one time and that he was simply terrified at the prospect of getting close to water. So far, this story had always worked for us, but we were all scared that our secret might someday be revealed.

I was always glad that Chang-hee had been born before me to help ease all the pain of losing our older brother before I arrived. But I also knew that being a girl was not such a good thing and that my father barely tolerated me. He was not shy about showing that he would have liked it much better if it had been me who had died and not my oldest brother. He would then have had two sons to be proud of and to carry on his legacy, instead of a girl that he was obligated to feed and who would only cost him money. This is the way our Chinese culture in North Korea has always believed, and it is a burden that every girl in North Korea knows and feels daily. I did carry a small secret in my heart though, and that was that I knew my mother loved me without conditions or any reservations at all, and for that, I was eternally grateful. It was this knowledge about her love that would sustain me through the coming years of hardship. You can imagine the pain I felt when I learned and understood that, by giving Chang-hee and me half of her food so often during those desperate years, she had weakened her immune system so much that it caused her death. I know now that when she said she could not eat more, she was making sure that my brother and I survived at her own expense. Sure, deaths from diseases were common in North Korea, and every family experienced it, but maybe if she had been stronger…

❀

Even though they had an arranged marriage, I do believe that my parents were happily married. It had been the cultural norm and was not so difficult to accept. After the Korean War, my mother's father and my father's father worked together when they served in Kim Il-sung's, "The Great Leader" army. They had been good friends, or at least knew and respected each other enough to pledge that they would marry their children to each other if they had children. And that is exactly what happened. My parents personified the values of North Korea, with the woman being considered inferior but still responsible for all household duties. We lived in the capital city, Pyongyang, and later moved to Hyangsan, where my father, like his father, was in the military while my mother worked at the food distribution center not far from our house. Our home was a small, modest house that looked just like everyone else's. Chang-hee and I took turns dusting the portraits of Kim Il-sung and later his son, Kim Jong-il, which were hung so that they were the first and most important thing you saw when you entered our home. I loved my older brother, who always seemed to have a special place in his heart for me, and together we would trot off to school. I thought in my small child's mind that we had a rather good life.

❀

It was not until I was about nine or ten years old, in about 1996, that I noticed that food was in desperately short supply. Before that, we had never had food to spare, but after the hailstorms, flooding, and the extremely cold winter of 1995, we had even less. Mother went every day to the place where the government gave out daily food rations. The Public Distribution System (PDS) was the system by which every person received a certain amount of food as payment for working on government farms or in some other government capacity. I did not understand it well at the time, but "The Great Leader," Kim Il-sung, originally envisioned North Korea as being self-sufficient, requiring no outside help from any nation. This policy had worked without major problems until the Sino-Soviet split in the 1960s when the Soviets favored China over North Korea. After the breakup, they gradually reduced the amount of oil, fertilizers, and equipment they supplied to North Korea. Without enough oil, our debt gradually increased. These shortages were coupled with several natural disasters, and the outcome was a widespread and severe famine. My brother would go out hunting for scraps of paper or wood to burn to keep us warm, and Mother did all sorts of things to keep us well-fed. At the time, I did not think about it, but little treasures of Mother's began to be "put away," or so she said. I now wonder if Mother was starting to engage in "jangmadang." Jangmadang was a form of black market or bartering that was becoming more common because workers (even the military) were not receiving money or food as they had in the past from the state's Public Distribution System. And the wages that they did receive were becoming worthless, forcing people to trade on the black market. "Frog markets" could sometimes be seen down some side streets. Frog markets were what they called black market traders who would leap up and then disappear like a frog only to reappear behind you. How else could Mother have provided us with food sometimes?

✻

One day, when Chang-hee was sixteen years old, he did not return from his daily forage into the streets looking for fuel. That day, we had walked most of the way home together when Chang-hee sent me on without him, telling me that he had seen a pile of trash in the block behind us and that he would be home with some fuel shortly. When it grew dark and near dinner time and Chang-hee had not returned, Mother and I went in one direction, and Father went in the other direction, searching and calling for Chang-hee. We did not eat dinner that night but spent the whole time looking for him and knocking on doors. Father blamed both Mother and me, and we were both crying, sick with worry and so tired. In the morning, after a whole night of frantically searching for Chang-hee, Mother and I returned home and fell into bed exhausted. Father continued his search and went to the police station. No one had seen or heard of Chang-hee, and we never saw him again or learned what could have happened to him.

CHAPTER 3

❉

At the time of Chang-hee's disappearance, I was in total despair. But my anguish was nothing compared to Father's or Mother's. Father raged for weeks at Mother for "losing his second son." During this period, I noticed Mother seemed to have little interest in anything other than trying to get some news or information about her son's whereabouts. She learned what I had always known, which was Chang-hee loved to slip away to swim alone in the nearby river and that he did this away several times a week. When he was alone, no one would see his deformed foot, and he could swim at his own pace, enjoying the cold clear water. Mother began asking the same questions repeatedly about Chang-hee. This behavior was an attempt to figure out where he could conceivably be. She asked everyone she knew—all our extended family members, friends, neighbors, and even people who might have only remotely seen or known him. Of course, government officials came as well, but after a time, they could see that none of us had any idea what had happened or where Chang-hee was. And because they had no evidence or information, they gradually stopped questioning us, as I think they started to believe he had drowned. As the days, then weeks, and months went by, Mother began to eat even less food. Her eyes became dull, and her energy began to wane. It seemed there was nothing that I could say or do to make her life better and of course, Father was inconsolable and continued raging at her. Still, we knew nothing…

Years later, I began to suspect that Chang-hee, who had always been more worldly and smarter than me, had been so hungry and worn down and that he could not see a good future here in North Korea for himself. Had he defected to China or Russia and not told me or anyone in our family about his plans, simply because he knew that we all would have tried to stop him? By this time, Chang-hee was very adept at hiding the fact that he had a club foot, but he also knew that if anyone found out about it, he could be taken away to a "special camp." And while none of our family members, especially Chang-hee, ever spoke about it, I knew that Chang-hee lived in constant fear of this happening. At sixteen, Chang-hee was also old enough to know about the North Korean policy of killing or severely torturing anyone perceived to be disloyal to "Our Dear Leader" or to the North Korean government. By leaving, Chang-hee was showing extreme disloyalty and putting us all in danger. No doubt, he understood the government would also punish our family, and I think Chang-hee would have chosen death before he revealed who his family was. On my good days, when I am more optimistic, I like to dream that Chang-hee escaped and is living a good life somewhere. I doubt that I will ever know the truth for sure, though.

❉

As Mother's energy began to diminish, she began to do less and less around the house. She no longer took care of herself and looked dreadful—unwashed, unkempt, and oh, so very thin. She continued to rise every morning and go to the factory for the mandatory work that all people were required to do for our "great and wonderful" country, but really, she walked and acted like a zombie just going through life's motions. I tried to take over both Mother's and Chang-hee's jobs and stopped going to school entirely. Instead, I foraged for root vegetables in the morning and searched for long hours for anything I could find to use as fuel in the afternoon. Then I would try to tidy up our house and prepare whatever I found for us for dinner. Father continued his uncontrolled rage at both Mother and me while he stomped around the house in absolute fury and anger. I knew that in his heart, he knew we did not know where or why Chang-hee had gone, but he did not know how to calm himself. Some days, he would grab Mother by the hair and throw her across the room. By this time, she had no strength and even less desire to stop him or try to protect herself in any way. Her small, thin body would hit the wall with a dull, sickening thud, and she would crumble to the floor in tears. When I tried to stop Father, he lashed out at me with his fist, hitting me in the face. He would scream that I was such a disappointment and that it should have been me who died. I had no answers for him, and I did not know how long this could go on.

❁

I found that wild root vegetables were more abundant once fall arrived, but it was harder to find anything to use as fuel. Other people were out scrounging around as well. Our home grew colder, and one morning when I took some hot water (my sorry substitute for tea, which we did not have) to Mother, I discovered she had died in her sleep. My dear mother— the only person in the whole world who loved me unconditionally—was gone! That night, I cried so much that I thought I would never be able to cry again. First Chang-hee was gone, and now Mother! I felt overwhelmed with grief and sorrow. I wondered what I would do or how I would survive now.

CHAPTER 4

❈

Having lost his last beloved son and then his wife a mere seven months later, my father was beside himself. He began spending long hours away from home when he wasn't working on the government farms or doing whatever he did for the military. I did not know where he was spending his time or with whom, but when he did come home late at night, he would eat whatever I had prepared and then tumble into bed. He was grumpy and simply grunted at me when he had to. He was so sad and was not good company, but at least he was not beating me. He no longer could blame Mother (at least to her face), and by this time, I thought he was beginning to recognize how much work I was doing around the house, or so I hoped. I knew without a doubt that he did not love me, at least not in the same way that Mother and, to a large degree, Chang-hee had. I was extremely lonely and had no one to talk to. I missed Chang-hee as much as I did Mother and constantly thought and worried about where I would go and what I could do to make life better for Father and myself. Food had become an obsession ever since the famines started, but now I continually thought about getting enough food and how to stretch what we did have so that Father and I would not starve. Life was downright hard, and I knew that not everyone would survive. I had heard stories about neighbors and other kids that I had gone to school with who had died of diseases or starvation. I would have sold my soul for food and for my twin obsession, which was a kind nod or grunt from my father. Still, we were beginning to make a life together, such as it was.

Father and I existed this way for over six months. I knew that it would not be long before the officials would come and assign me to do factory work of some sort. No one was being paid money for this work, but just like Mother, I would occasionally be given corn or rice for my labor. I was not looking forward to that day at all. On the other hand, Father had not mentioned anything about arranging a marriage for me. I was nearly fifteen years old, and many girls were married at that age or at least had some sort of pre-arrangement in place by then. Father was dragging his feet on this matter, or so I thought, perhaps because I was so very lonely. I began to think he wanted me around to not only collect food and fuel but also, in his strange way, he too was lonely and needed me as his companion and to make his life easier. I was really confused.

One day in early spring, Father came home from work, walking briskly, and was all excited. He was happier than I had seen him since Chang-hee had disappeared, and he even called out to me to share some tea before we ate our meager supper. I wondered if he had somehow gotten a message from Chang-hee or if he knew where he was. When he did not blurt out this news, I began to fear that he had arranged a marriage for me and that I would be sold off to some old man who would be willing to pay him more than what he could get if I were to marry a man closer to my age. With trembling hands, I brought the small pot of weak tea to the table and sat down next to Father. He instantly grabbed the pot and started to pour each of us a small cup of tea. I did not understand what was happening. Father never poured tea or did any "domestic" duties, for that matter. He considered all this kind of work to be women's work and very much beneath him. Why was Father so excited? By this time, I was really worried about what lay in store for me.

"What is it, Father? What is the good news?" I tried to look as excited as I could, all the time dreading his next words.

"We're leaving!" he bluntly stated.

"Leaving—you mean moving to another house or another city? Did you get promoted?"

"Babo!" He said, "Babo! Babo!" He was calling me stupid but not in a harsh way, perhaps because he was so excited and in such a good mood.

"Then where are we going and when," I asked. I certainly had no idea what he was referring to.

Father lowered his voice and drew closer to me, indicating that we must whisper. "We are going to go to China, Daughter," he said with a quiet air of finality. "There is nothing here for me—for us— and things are getting worse. I have some connections, and we will leave in a couple of days. We must leave before the Yalu River thaws."

My stomach did a flip-flop. He had never said anything to me like this before. We had lived in this house for years, and what if Chang-hee came back and we were gone? How would my dear brother know where to look for us? What about Father's job in the military? What connections could Father possibly have? Where could we go, and wasn't it a betrayal to "Our Dear Leader" and the government as well? Weren't we doing OK, and what could be better? I looked again at Father, but he was staring off into space with a look of almost ecstasy but with total conviction. He had made up his mind that we should leave North Korea, and I knew he would be full of rage if I pressed him further. I could not believe what was happening, and I knew of nothing that I could say or do to change Father's mind. I felt sick.

"After dinner, you must start preparing," he ordered in a calm, quiet voice. "We won't need much besides our clothes and some food. It can be very cold in the mountains at night. Do not tell anyone. Tomorrow, go forage for as many vegetables as you can find. We will leave tomorrow night or the night after, depending on how much food you can find tomorrow." I could only nod and numbly took a sip of my lukewarm, weak tea. I had no idea where we would go or what would become of us. I felt so frightened.

CHAPTER 5

�֍

Just as Father had ordered, I went to the mountains close to us the following day, looking for any food that I could find. I saw a couple of girls that I had gone to school with just a few months before. They too were no longer attending school, but perhaps they had made marriage preparations and or were planning to begin working for the government. After all, we were not little children anymore, and every family needed all the members to work to make our great country even stronger and to collect the food rations that would be distributed. They waved at me and acted like they would like to chat, but I turned away quickly and began digging for what I hoped would be a small, sweet potato and not just a rock. What was the point of talking to them? I was already feeling extremely sad at the prospect of leaving these beautiful mountains and the only life that I had ever known. I would be gone by tonight or tomorrow, and I did not want to have them ask me too many sticky questions.

I was in luck that day. I got a small bag of vegetables for our upcoming journey and even caught a small ground squirrel for supper that night.

I waited until almost dark so no one would see me or beg for some of my food before I walked down the mountain and into our house that night. Father was waiting for me when I arrived and had an agitated look on his face. He merely grunted when he saw the squirrel (our only meat in weeks), but I could tell he was pleased.

Because I had had good luck finding food that day, Father decided we should leave that night. I was so tired and was still sucking on some squirrel bones while I washed and packed a bowl for each of us along with a frying pan, a knife, and chopsticks. I slipped the remaining bones into my pocket for later enjoyment as we put on our darkest and heaviest clothes and slipped out of our house to begin our difficult journey. Not wanting to be seen, we stayed in the shadows and quickly hurried down the backstreets toward the road leading to the mountains. At one point, we thought we heard footsteps and pressed tight against a building, not moving. As we waited there, I glanced one last time back at our house. It looked like everyone else's house, small and needing paint and so many other repairs, but it was ours, and I felt miserable at the thought that I might never see it again. What were we ever going to do in China? What had Father heard about China? I wish I knew, because then maybe I could be excited about what lay in store for us.

That night we made it into the mountains and just kept walking for hours. The half-moon was bright, as there were not too many clouds in the sky, and although it was cold, we could see quite well. Once we got further beyond where townspeople foraged for vegetables and herbs, there were fewer and fewer trails and we made our way by the stars. I had so many questions that I desperately wanted to ask Father. Instinctively, I knew that he was in no mood to talk about anything, especially pesky questions about where we were going and for what reason, *and* from a girl at that. I was bone-tired but knew that Father had to be even more tired than I was. He had to be, didn't he? After all, he too had worked all day, and he was not so young anymore. So, we walked along silently, each deep within our own private thoughts. We finally collapsed around three or four o'clock in the morning, and huddling close together for warmth, both of us fell into a deep sleep.

❉

I awoke with a start when I felt both the sunlight warm on my face and something moving close to me. It was Father, and he grunted then said, "Come, Daughter. Tea." I quickly realized where I was and that he was telling me to prepare some hot tea for him. I watched him stumble further into the mountains to do his personal daily business as I started a small fire to boil the water. Boy, was I stiff! But I soon forgot my pain when I discovered a small patch of wild baby carrots close to where we had spent the night. We would not have to use any of the vegetables that I had brought with us and could save the stash of food for another time when times were even leaner. What luck!

We walked all that first day, covering a good distance, stopping only when we were so tired that we could not go on and needed to rest. We did not see or hear anyone that day, and I believed it would be very unlikely to see other people this high in the mountains. We knew by now they would miss Father at his government job, and someone might even have been dispatched to our house to check on his whereabouts. We were both also very aware that we were legally not supposed to travel just anywhere in the country without permission. So, while we marched on, we were always listening and watching for anybody who might see us and figure out that we were where we should not be.

It took us about three days to climb up and over the Kangnam Mountain range. Each morning would start the same, with my father waking me, wanting his morning tea, and me grudgingly getting up to start another long, hard day. After drinking our pathetically weak tea and eating what few vegetables I could find in the immediate area, we would begin our hike. Father led us as we used what trails we could find, and where there were no visible trails, we worked our way through the mountains, always towards the western border between North Korea and China. We did not talk, and we were always listening for animals or other people. So, both of us, deep in our private thoughts, trudged forward until Father would indicate that he was tired, and we would stop for a short rest and a few mouthfuls of food. Then we would start again until it was nearly dark before stopping somewhere for the night. I was not alone, but I can tell you I was very lonely, exhausted, and very frightened about what lay in store for us in China. I believed that Father was having these same thoughts. It could not be easy for him either.

CHAPTER 6

Finally, late on the third day in the mountains, Father grunted something and pointed towards the border. We were able to view the Chinese border off in the distance. I noticed that he seemed extremely tired and was shaking slightly. He appeared as if he had been defeated, yet he was agitated by something at the same time. I wondered who he knew would be there to help us. What had he arranged for us? But I was tired too and did not argue as he indicated that we should rest there safely in the mountains until nightfall. It was already beginning to get cold again, and I was thankful for a couple of swallows of water and the handfuls of raw vegetables that we ate.

Once darkness fell, and we had more cover from North Korean soldiers, Father and I crept towards the Yalu River separating China and North Korea. Father had calculated the river was still frozen enough to support foot traffic. He must have known that North Koreans who lived close to the border used the river, especially in the winter, to cross into China and back again with forbidden products to sell on the black market.

Being in the military, he also knew some border guards who patrolled the river, and when he thought I was not watching, I saw him slip one of Mother's most expensive and prized pieces of jewelry into a guard's outstretched hands. It was a brooch that Grandmother had given to Mother just before she died. It had been in the family for generations and would be mine one day.

A huge lump formed in my throat at the thought of Mother's precious possessions being used by Father in such a way. But I gulped and fought back the tears as I realized I had believed that Mother had long ago parted with the brooch in exchange for food for our family.

Now Father was simply paying the guard to look the other way so we could quickly and safely scurry across the river in the dark. What was the difference anyway? The brooch was gone either way, and I sure did not want us to be shot trying to escape. I pulled my coat tighter around me and clutched the bag of vegetables closer as I hurried to catch up with Father as he raced across the narrow river. All the time, I waited for shots to hit me or for a guard from somewhere to yell at us to stop. I ran as fast as I could, finally reaching the other side of the river and stumbling onto the frozen bank of our new country. I lay there panting, not thinking of anything but how cold I was and that we had made it. Yes, we had made it to China, but now what? I hoped that Father had things arranged as well here as he had in getting us out of North Korea. I certainly knew nothing and was totally dependent on my father. I looked over at Father, who was lying there on the cold ground in a crumpled heap. He looked so small, and he suddenly looked so old and tired. This realization turned my stomach into a knot. After catching my breath, I went over to Father and helped him up, which was no easy feat—he was almost dead weight. But once on his feet, Father sniffed and wiped his nose on his sleeve, then straightened his shoulders and looked down at me with almost a look of contempt. I did not understand it at all. Shouldn't we both be rejoicing about our escape?

As he gathered himself together, all he said was, "Come Daughter." And he began a slow walk, leading me away from the river. It was clear that he was in no mood to talk or share any information with me. I followed a respectful distance behind him.

We had only gone a few meters when we saw a few Chinese men and women dispersed here and there as they spoke to the few people who had just crossed over the river. A middle-aged man approached Father and said a few words to him. Father snorted and seemed to dismiss the man, then continued to walk on. I was doing my best to keep up with Father when I noticed an old, weathered, stooped woman walk up to him. I could not hear what they were saying, but I did see that my father suddenly pushed his shoulders back and glanced at me. I wondered if this meeting with the woman had been prearranged and if this was part of my father's escape plan. Little did I know that while Father had not planned *this* meeting with *this* woman, he did indeed have a strategy and that I was his biggest and most valuable asset in that plan.

CHAPTER 7

The woman and Father stood talking, or rather, they were gesturing, as my father did not know how to speak Chinese, for what seemed like a long time. I was growing colder all the time and hoped that they would conclude their business quickly. I did believe that Father had more of Mother's jewelry or possibly even some North Korean won or some Chinese yuan, although I did not know how or where he would have gotten it. My father was proving to be even more deceptive and quiet as time moved on, so I did not know what to think. I just wanted to go someplace warm and safe, if only for a short time.

After a few minutes, my father glanced over at me, and they both walked toward me with the woman moving vigorously and Father close behind her. She did not touch me but stopped right in front of me and peered straight at me with her face only a couple of inches from mine. I instinctively drew back, and she stepped even closer and slowly walked around me, looking at my entire body. I looked over at my father, who was staring off in the distance, not wanting to meet my gaze. The woman gave one curt nod, and Father stepped forward with his hand stretched out. She gave him a handful of bills, which Father promptly put in his pocket, turned on his heels without a word, and started walking away from us.

"Father, wait!" I screamed as I hurried to catch up with him. The woman grabbed my arm and held on as I tried to brush her off. She was surprisingly strong for such a small woman.

"Father! Father, wait for me; I NEED YOU!" I screamed, again and again, hoping and believing that he would turn back. In a weak, trembling voice, I finally called out, "I love you!" It was a final desperate attempt to get him to stop. He kept on walking without looking back. With a terrible sick feeling in my stomach, I realized my very own father had sold me! At that moment, I hated him more than anyone or anything I had ever known in my life. It was the beginning of my understanding that my father did not love me in even the smallest way, and that he had seen me as a burden he could no longer bear. He had found his escape and had taken it. At that tender age, standing there in the cold that night, I recognized that I felt intolerable rage and anger for my father and that no matter what, he was no longer there for me. Had he ever been there for me? Had Father ever loved me? Would I ever see him again? I had never felt so alone or so betrayed in my entire life. Where was I supposed to go? Who could help me? What could I do?

✿

The woman interrupted my thoughts with a loud "Come!" At the same time, she gave my arm a hard yank. Of course, I did not know what she was saying, but she kept pulling me. It was not hard to figure out that she was telling me to follow her. I was so cold, and I looked toward my father again. He was still walking in a slow, determined walk over the hill, almost out of sight by now. It was clear he was not coming back.

The woman repeated the Chinese word for what I thought was "Come," and snatching my bag away from me, she began to walk in the opposite direction. I knew the bag only held one small, sweet potato and a knife in it, so I let her have it without a fight. Father still had our bowls, the frying pan, and other utensils, so she was not getting much. Because I felt so alienated and with no other options, I forced myself to follow the old woman, but to what, who, or where, I did not know. In my dejected and sad state, I only hoped it would be warm and that I could have some vegetables or possibly even a bowl of rice.

CHAPTER 8

✿

I cannot honestly tell you how many days the old woman and I journeyed together over the mountains and across the valleys, and to where? I had no idea where we were going, in which direction we were going, or for what purpose. The only thing I knew for certain was that Father had abandoned me. He had not just abandoned me—he had SOLD me! I had been given over to this strange woman almost like I was one of Mother's pieces of jewelry—valuable only for as much as he could get for me. I knew in my heart then that I might never see Father again, and I wondered if it mattered at all. And yet, it is funny how I was unable to just accept this fact and move on. As we walked on, I kept going over and over in my mind the little details of our lives.

Looking back on those days, I now realize I was searching for an instance or two that I could grasp onto —something, *anything* that would tell me that Father did love me a tiny bit even though I was a girl. Then I moved on to Chang-hee. I ruminated over and over about Chang-hee and our relationship, how we had played together, searched for food and fuel together, and how much we had shared. He had always been kind to me, had shared his secrets with me, and had protected me when necessary. And hadn't I always kept his dark secret and covered for him, making excuses for him when his foot was hurting? I knew Chang-hee loved me. I sure hoped he was safe somewhere. But it was thinking of Mother that gave me the most pain and always brought tears to my eyes. With Mother, I knew without a doubt that she loved me and that she held a special place in her heart for me. She was just not always allowed to show how much she cared, and for that, I wanted to shout out to her, "Mother, I knew you LOVED me as much as I loved you!! I will never forget you!" Many times, on that long journey, I would sob inwardly (and sometimes outwardly) as I trudged forward.

The days and nights just seemed to blend into each other and go on forever. Each day started just like the day before, beginning before sunrise and only ending when it was unsafe to continue in the dark. I was to learn that the old woman's name was Yun Ting and that she liked her tea strong and black, and served right away each morning. It seemed to give her life each day, and after drinking her tea, she turned into a raging tornado of energy and determination. Yun was generous with her tea, and after having only hot water or extremely weak tea for so many years, this was a real treat to me. Still, you could not say that we grew close or anything remotely like that. I did not know a word of Chinese, so we could not converse. Even if I had wanted to talk, the old woman's body language told me loud and clear that I was her ward and SHE was in charge. No nonsense or explanations were allowed, let alone a comforting word or two.

After her last swallow in the morning, Yun would jump up and yell, what I later learned was, "Come!" and would grab her bundles and start marching. She knew I did not know where I was or which way to go. She knew I would follow her closely so as not to become lost.

❀

One day, we emerged out of the mountains and looked down toward a deeply rutted path that functioned as a road. We could see far off in the distance a man riding on a slow-moving oxcart filled with something. Yun squinted at the man for a while, then snorted, "Come!" She quickly moved down toward the road. Then, running into the road, she stopped the ox and spoke to the man. Suddenly, she excitedly gestured for me to hurry and come down with her. I caught up with Yun as she hopped up into the back part of the cart bed and was wildly motioning for me to do the same. What a gift this short lift would be for the two of us. I wondered: did Yun know this man? Were we close to the end of our journey? Yun and the man chatted on and on. I listened very intently to the tone of their voices as I tried to pick out words that I had heard Yun say before. I did not know where we were going or what my part in all of this would be, but no matter what, I instinctively knew that I must learn the language and how to communicate. I had also learned on my journey so far that it did not do any good for me to continue to be angry at Father. I knew I simply needed to accept the fact that Mother and Chang-hee were both gone and that it was up to me, and me alone, to make a new life for myself in this new land. On the cart that day, with the sun shining on my face and rambling forward, I was still lonely, but for a short while at least, I was comfortable and thought life might not be as bleak as I had thought initially. I was determined to survive.

CHAPTER 9

�֍

A couple of mornings after our fortuitous ride on the oxcart, we woke up to a cold, heavy rain pounding down on us. I did not want to shove the plastic tarp back and get up, but "Ting the Tornado" was already up heating water for the tea, and she began poking me with a stick. She hopped around and sang a tune as she prepared her bundles, getting ready to start soon. What was this all about? Couldn't this woman rest even for a few hours? What was her darn rush today? Grudgingly, I got up, knowing that I wouldn't get any hot tea if I didn't make haste and that she would start walking without me.

What I did not know was that we would reach her farm that afternoon—that we would "arrive." That afternoon, Yun picked up her (and by necessity, my) pace and raced towards a small mud-brick cottage with a sloped roof close to the narrow path that we were on. It was a small house and needed a lot of work done on it, but Yun bound up to the door, gave a quick knock, and scurried in, leaving the door ajar. I glanced around, noting that the closest house was about a mile away, and wondered what I should do. Before I even reached the house, Yun appeared on the doorstep, frantically waving me on. Would this woman ever slow down? What lay in store for me behind that door?

As I walked to that door, a knot was beginning to form in the pit of my stomach. I did not know what it was all about, but somehow, I was not so excited to find out. As it turned out, I did not have to wait long to find out about the huge and life-changing plan that awaited me.

As I stepped through the door, I was instantly aware of the stale, cool, almost dank air and how very dark the small one-room house was after being outside. I first noticed a small square table sitting in the middle of the room where an old man sat drinking tea. I assumed he was Yun's husband, but no one introduced me. He looked up at me with mild interest and said something in Chinese to Yun, who just grunted, shrugged, and put her bundles beside him on the table. As my eyes adjusted to the light, I could see a small cot in one corner of the room with a dingy sheet separating it from another cot where a man of about forty was sitting. The man looked up immediately, smiled, and came toward me. His clothes were threadbare, dirty, and rumpled, and his hair was wild-looking, going in all directions. I could see that he had lost nearly half of his teeth, and those that were not missing were dark and stained yellow. He walked right up to me and stuck his face so close to mine that I could smell his awful breath. Before I could react, he began speaking Chinese, half-excitedly spewing out a string of words that I had no idea what they meant. I turned away, and he caught my arm and forced me to sit in a chair next to the table. I remember thinking, "Some introduction, some invitation."

Yun gave me a cup of tea and some corn, and they all sat together at the table, chatting at about a mile a minute, or so it seemed. It appeared that the old man and the ugly younger man were Ting's family members (maybe her husband and son?) and that this was her home. So, I thought, this is where we were headed—to this small, dark, dingy house with a small field behind it. Now what? Was I to be their prisoner and slave? Is this why Father sold me? Not one of them spoke a word of Korean, and I had learned only Yun's name and hardly any other Chinese since being in China, so I did not know what was being said or what was planned. Finally, I spoke up. Pointing to myself, I said in Korean, "I'm Ha-na. Ha-na." There was no recognition or change of expression at first. So, I repeated "Ha-na" several more times, all the time pointing at myself until Yun nodded and after glancing at the other two, pointed at me and repeated "Ha-na." Then she pointed at herself and said, "Yun." Pointing at the old man, she said, "Fong Ting." To the younger man, she pointed and said, "Mo Ting," and then she moved her hand from pointing to Mo Ting back and forth several times between him and me!

It was at that time that it all hit me like a ton of bricks! I could not get my breath as the realization knocked the wind out of me. Father had sold me to this woman to be her son's wife! But he was so old! So ugly! So poor! Oh, the shame and the dread! Tears welled up in my eyes; I could not swallow or breathe. For the first time in my life, I was not hungry. How could Father have hated me so much? I just wanted to die.

But of course, I had to breathe, and no matter how much one wants to die, their physical needs do continue. I felt sick to my stomach, and my mind was racing as I began to memorize the whole house and look for a way out. I wondered how I could escape from this place. After the family had eaten and the bowls and other utensils had been put away, Yun again said "Come" and gestured for me to follow her outside. I thought we were going to sleep outside or perhaps go somewhere else, but no, she simply led me to a small, boarded-up outhouse with a hole in the ground. I knew what that was for and hurried to go inside, attempting to shut the door behind me. Yun was quick though, and swiftly stuck her foot in the doorway, stopping me from being alone. I was not going to have a moment of privacy or was it that she thought I would attempt an escape? I did not know, but what I did know was that this was not going to be a good situation.

Both men had taken turns going out to the outhouse before turning in for the night, and Fong locked the door with a key that he put in his pocket. It was clear that they were locking me in. Fong brought in a piece of cardboard from outside and tossed it on the floor at me as Yun threw me a small, threadbare blanket. I grabbed them both greedily, as it was plain there was not a cot for me, and this was better than being outside on the ground. Fong spoke something in Chinese, and they all laughed as I curled up on the floor as far away from the three of them as I could get.

That first night, I could not sleep. Yun and I had walked a good portion of the day, and I was physically and emotionally spent, but I still could not sleep. It was not long before I heard all three of them snoring. Yun's snoring was essentially just loud breathing, but both men certainly whooped it up. But in truth, this was not what kept me awake. My mind would simply not shut off, as I now knew that Father had sold me to Yun as a bride for her son. How soon would it be before I was forced into the marriage? How could I escape and where could I go? These same thoughts went over and over in my mind as I played out various possible solutions. Towards the morning, when I was beyond exhaustion, I felt miserable as I realized that nothing was going to work. I simply had to learn the Chinese language, the locality, and local customs as quickly as possible before I could attempt any type of escape from these people. I was heartbroken, and I hate to admit it, but I was filled with rage, anger, and hatred for my father. If only he had cared for me even a little, we surely could have worked out a plan to survive together in North Korea. I fell asleep in the wee hours of the morning feeling lonely and helpless, not knowing exactly where I was or having any kind of plan on how to escape. The only thing I knew for sure was that I had a tremendous determination to survive and leave this awful place.

❋

It felt like I had barely fallen asleep, and in truth, it had probably been under an hour when I was rudely awakened by 'Tornado Ting' as I had taken to thinking of her. She was poking me, none too gently, with a stick and yelling, "Ha-na! Ha-na! Get up. Get up now!" At least, that is what I thought she meant. Did this woman keep a stick by her side, whether inside or outside, just to poke me? Did she ever act at a normal speed? I did not like Yun much at this point, but I dragged myself up off the floor.

She already had a cup of tea waiting for me at the table and was wildly gesturing for me to hurry up and drink it along with a bowl of thin, watery rice gruel that Chinese people commonly eat for breakfast. Rice had become such a luxury in North Korea that I savored every drop as I glanced around to see both men still asleep on their cots. I drank my breakfast and hurriedly made for the outhouse. Before I could even reach the front door, Yun scurried over and unlocked it. Again, she escorted me out to the outhouse, where she stood with the door ajar as I did my business. She was taking no chances of letting me escape, but in truth, where could I go once I was in the toilet? There were no windows or doors. Did she expect that I would dive into the nasty hole? This whole place and the whole family were disgusting. But I smiled sweetly and pointed to the outhouse and said in Korean, "Toilet?" I repeated it a couple of times before Yun nodded and said "Toilet" in Chinese. "Toilet. Toilet." I repeated it several times, letting the Chinese word roll off my tongue. My learning of Chinese had begun in earnest, as I was resolute in my desire to learn enough of the language so that once I got away from these people and this place, I could take care of myself and live.

As I assumed she would do, Yun led me to the field behind their home, and I officially became her slave as we planted and seeded corn all that day. The men joined us shortly after we had started, and we all toiled together on the family farm. I tried to keep my thoughts together as I pointed to objects and would say their names in Korean, waiting for one of the three to say the word in Chinese. Neither Yun nor her husband had much patience for any of this "chatter," but how else was I to learn to communicate? Meanwhile, Mo seemed to be off somewhere in his private little world, and I noticed he did not work as hard as the rest of us. His parents did not seem to mind at all, or had they just become used to his behavior? One time, he ducked behind some plants and went to the bathroom. Bringing back his excrement, he proudly placed it around the new little corn seeds. Both of his parents smiled and laughed as they continued to work. I secretly wondered if something was wrong with Mo or if he acted funny just because he was not around many others much. I was beginning to suspect that this might be why he had not married.

We did stop for a short break at lunchtime, and Yun served us tea and rice balls. Then it was right back to work again. I was tired from not having slept much the night before and, at one point, must not have been working as fast or as well as Yun wanted. She started yelling and hitting me over my head and back with her ever-present stick. I worked more diligently after that, doing what I had to do, as I continued to say the new Chinese words over and over in my mind so that I would remember them and occasionally ask the name of another object. I was beginning to understand the sounds, the tones, and how to say the words correctly.

It was turning dusk when we all headed back to the house, where we each ate a small bowl of vegetables and some corn, and then prepared to tumble into bed. Yun snorted at me and indicated that it was time for us to go to the outhouse. I followed willingly as I had to go to the bathroom, but really, I felt annoyed that I was not allowed to go alone and with a measure of privacy. Was this the way it was always going to be? I wondered. Both men made a trip to the outhouse, with Fong coming in last, locking the door, and then, as he had done the night before, slipping the key into his pocket. Not having slept much the night before, I was dead tired as I grabbed my precious piece of cardboard and the blanket and moved once again to the far corner of the room. I noticed Mo looking intently at me, and a certain dread came over me, but I was far too tired to make a fuss about it, so I simply rolled over and quickly went to sleep.

CHAPTER 10

✳

Early the following morning, "Tornado Ting" was again up and had pre-pared hot tea before she did her most favorite thing in the world, which was to poke me with her darn stick. No one can ignore being poked here, there, and all over repeatedly with a stick. So grudgingly, I got up and then drank my tea before my ever-present guard allowed me to go to the outhouse before ushering me to the field behind the house. The men joined us shortly after we got to the field, and we all began working the land. I had the sinking feeling that this was going to be my life for the foreseeable future, and I had better get used to it.

That day, we worked extra hard as we completed the planting. Again, Mo disappeared several times for fairly long periods. I had no idea where he was going or what he was doing, but his parents did not seem to mind or even notice his absences. As for me, I worked hard enough so Yun would not beat me. I also worked on learning the Chinese language as much as I could. I felt desperate to learn Chinese and knew that any escape plan would depend on this knowledge. For now, I had to learn the family's routines and how to fit in. I was hopeful that if I did this and appeared complacent, they would let their guard down and that life would be easier for me. I still did not know exactly where I was in China or where I could run, so staying put seemed to be my best strategy for the time being.

I realized that I knew hardly anything about the country of China. In North Korea, my family lived first in Pyongyang and later moved to Hyangsan, where we lived in the same house for many years. Because no one could travel without permission, we had not traveled much in North Korea. We had not lived close to the Chinese border, so we had not gotten any information or items on the black market from China. Of course, we learned nothing in school about any other country besides North Korea, and we were taught to worship "The Great Leader," Kim Il-sung, and "Our Dear Leader," Kim Jong-il. We knew we were living in the best country in the world and that the "American Bastards" were evil and our most hated enemy. Consequently, I had not learned much about Chinese culture or known much about the cities or even the country in general. Now I was a prisoner there and had much to learn.

❋

On the third night, the family all seemed to be in an extra-special mood. We ate a bigger, better dinner than we had on the previous nights, and they all chattered a great deal amongst themselves, glancing and smiling repeatedly at me. I thought they must be celebrating because the planting had been completed, but I really could not make out what they were so happy about. Finally, the door was locked, and Fong and Yun went to their cots. I was bone-tired again and grabbed my piece of cardboard and the blanket, thinking I could get away from them by going to "my" corner.

I had just laid down when Mo jumped up and grabbed my arm, jerking me to my feet and pulling me to his cot. He threw me down and pounced on me, pulling at my clothes. I had been startled and screamed out, but Mo was much stronger than he appeared and quickly overpowered me as he half-laid on me, holding me down with his body and one arm while ripping my clothes off with his other hand. I was not dumb, and I knew what he was going to do. I frantically called out to Fong to help me, but I could only hear Fong and Yun snicker behind the dirty sheet that separated the cots. They were all in this together! This was the reason they had a big meal tonight and why they had been so happy! They were celebrating Mo and my "de facto marriage"!

Mo was not at all gentle, nor did he seem to care that I might be a person with any feelings at all. He grunted and made loud noises as if he wanted his parents to know exactly what was going on as he proceeded to do what he wanted to with my body. Even as young, naïve, and inexperienced as I was, I could tell right away that Mo had never been with a woman before. He forced my legs apart and shoved his sex part into my anus! Didn't he know where it was supposed to go? I felt my tissues tear as the most horrific pain shot through my body, and I screamed. Still, he continued to rut, grunt, push, and shove. At one point, he pulled back and gave a mighty shove as his sex part went into my vagina. I screamed as a different pain seared my whole area down there. I could feel something wet and sticky trickle down my legs, but I did not know if it was blood, urine, or what. I just wanted this to be over.

In what seemed like forever but really was only a short bit of time, Mo grew tired of all of this, and with a final grunt, he rolled off of me and turned toward the wall, quickly falling asleep. I heard his parents clap and cheer as I somehow stumbled off the cot and managed to crawl to my blanket and cardboard bed in the corner. I was shaking uncontrollably, bleeding, and in terrible pain. Such shame! Such humiliation! I remember thinking, "Oh Father, how could you have done this to me? Could anything be worse?" I longed for my mother's warm touch and Chang-hee's companionship. I just wanted to die right there and then.

The next morning, Tornado Ting was up early, making tea and *singing!* I was mortified as she came over and inspected my poor bloody and broken body. She smiled as she gave me a wet rag and some clean clothes, taking my soiled things outside where she washed them and proudly hung them on a line. This was the most kindness that I had ever seen from this woman, but make no mistake, I still wanted out of there and away from all these ugly, mean people.

CHAPTER 11

✤

In time, my life in China began to fall into a pattern. I was expected to get up every morning ready to work in the family fields and to do work around the house. Yun remained the center of the household and kept things organized and moving along in an orderly manner. Her words and decisions were the law, and everyone followed what she wanted without objection or complaint. I never once felt that she cared for me or that she even wanted me there in her home—I was simply a work unit, and as such, I was treated like the work animal that I had become. I was given just enough food to survive and a place in my corner to sleep. Every night, and sometimes more than once during the night, Mo would grab me by the hair or by my arm and drag me to his cot to satisfy his pleasure. Now that I look back at those times, I am not so sure even Mo enjoyed these forays. They were pure hell for me, and I truly believe he did not enjoy them so much as he was attempting to satisfy his mother's wishes while producing a male heir.

Meanwhile, I was attempting to "save face" as best I could by appearing to engage and fit in with the family as much as possible. I was also busy learning Chinese as fast and as much as I could. And all the while, I was always watching and learning whatever I could that might help me in my escape down the road. This proved to be extremely hard when I was assigned the worst chores, such as emptying and cleaning the human excrement from the outhouse and then spreading it on the small field behind the house. I always felt so dirty, and yet Mo did not let up on his almost nightly assaults on me. Yun always had her stick at hand and did not hesitate to use it on me when she felt I was not working up to speed or not doing something correctly. I was a quick learner and always worked to please her as much as possible, and in time I received fewer beatings. Yun had a new form of torture that she used on me, though, and that was to run up to me and grasp one of my breasts in her hand and give it a hard squeeze. I wondered why she did that and did not have a clue until I heard her give out a loud wail one morning. She had been outside behind some bushes when she came across the two towels that I had been using as sanitary napkins. I had not been given sanitary napkins or *anything* to use for when I got my monthly period, so I had fashioned a couple of napkins out of a cotton towel that I had found somewhere. I washed them out at night and hung them behind the bushes to dry, with the plan to reuse them the next day. When Yun found the towels, it was proof that I had not yet conceived a child, and she desperately wanted an heir, preferably a male if I had guessed right. Every few weeks, she would look for the towels, find them, and wail. I knew I would be beaten that day and would need to work extra hard as well as look forward to Mo's renewed vigor when he assaulted me that night. I now believe Yun thought she could tell if I was pregnant or not by feeling my breasts for any engorgement. All I knew for sure was that she squeezed them terribly and that it hurt dreadfully. I wanted her to stop it.

❀

The days ran into weeks, and one day, after a few months, Yun announced that it was time to go to the mountains to gather wild vegetables and fuel for the upcoming winter. "Work is work; what does it matter?" I thought as I trudged up the mountain after her that first day. Tornado Ting was not climbing as fast as she usually did, or so I thought. Perhaps it was because it had been a few months since we had come down out of the mountains and stayed at her home, which was in the valley, and now climbing was hard for her. I then remembered that she had had a cough for the past few days, and I wondered if all this was affecting Yun. Still, she was her feisty self, and I pushed it all to the back of my mind. We had work to do, and that was that.

When we reached the part of the mountain that Yun wanted, I observed other women doing what we had come to do: collecting wood, the occasional wild vegetable, and some special herbs. People—I had not seen or talked to anyone for weeks! I was immediately drawn to two girls who appeared to be a little older than me and were chatting as they collected firewood. One of them waved a shy wave to me, and when I got closer to them, I heard them speaking Korean. This was exciting. I knew I had to be careful, though, and I glanced back at Yun. Partially bent over, Yun was having a severe coughing spell. She had not seen me so close to the girls. I ran to her, offering her some water, and urged her to sit or lie down, saying that I would collect the firewood. This all seemed like I was genuinely concerned about Yun, but I truly wanted to have her lie down so she would not notice me as I attempted to talk to the other two women.

Yun was not feeling well and did take my advice and lay down, dozing off for nearly an hour. I quickly ran up to the girls and introduced myself. I was so hungry for companionship, *and* I wanted to learn where

I was and what they were doing here in China. We moved away from the others and pretended to be getting some larger firewood logs as we talked and talked. I learned that the girl who had waved to me was named Mi-ran Sook and that she was nineteen. Mi-ran was only about five feet tall and very thin. She had a few fading bruises on her face and arms but had a beautiful smile. The other girl's name was Su-lin Sam, and she was about five foot, two inches tall, and had a bit more meat on her bones. Su-lin was only seventeen and had been in China for four years already, so she spoke exceptionally good Chinese and knew where we were and the history of China very well. Su-lin seemed so kind and knowledgeable, and we would become good friends later. But for now, the main thing on my mind was that I wanted to learn what I could about the area and get my bearings so that I could come up with a plan to escape my own private hell as soon as possible.

❋

That day I would learn that there were many North Korean nationals there, in the three provinces closest to North Korea but also throughout China, and that we were in Liaoning Province. The only thing I knew up to that point for sure was that if North Koreans were turned in either by Chinese people or by North Koreans living in China, or if the Chinese police caught them, they would be sent back to North Korea to be killed or sent to prison to be tortured and imprisoned for life. This is the reason I had been so surprised that Father wanted us to leave North Korea. I had assumed that he had some well-laid plans for the two of us. Now it appeared that after he had sold me, I was stuck with no resources and nowhere to go, with danger all around. Su-lin had heard of the "North Korean Autonomous Prefecture," which was a place where North Korean nationals congregate and where they can find work. I also learned that day that all three of us girls were in "de facto" marriages, which is why so many North Korean girls were in the same boat as we were.

For the first time in my life, I learned that China instituted the "one-child-only" policy in 1980 to curb the then-surging population and limit the demands for water and other resources. The Chinese people were just like the North Koreans in that they preferred sons over daughters, which led them to kill or abort millions of girls. Now those little boys were of marriageable age, and there were not enough Chinese girls to marry. North Korean girls were of Chinese descent ethnically and had become a good substitute. There was only one problem, and that was that the Chinese government did not recognize North Koreans as refugees or as people of worth in any form. They saw North Koreans as "economic migrants" and, as such, did not give them or their children the same rights as Chinese nationals. That meant that I and any children that I might have would never have the correct documents to be proper Chinese citizens with any rights at all. My children would never be eligible to go to school or move around the country, enjoying the freedoms that other Chinese people enjoyed. I felt so depressed learning this information.

However, I did not have much time to dwell on this new information as I kept a close eye on Yun, who was beginning to move around a bit more. I instinctively knew that she would not like it if she thought I had been talking to these women. I told them I hoped we could speak again in the next few days, and I hurried off to make sure Yun did not get suspicious and to help her. My goal was to get Yun to trust me more and let her guard down so that my escape would be easier someday.

That night, I could hardly sleep as all kinds of thoughts ran through my mind. I was processing this new information and trying to make sense of it all. I realized that with so few Chinese girls available and with Mo being a poor farmer AND being "odd" if not totally "wacko," he could not attract a nice Chinese girl for a wife. His parents, especially Yun, had wanted and needed a daughter-in-law to produce an heir and to take care of them in their old age. Father must have sold me to this family thinking that since all marriages are arranged anyway, what's the difference and that I would have enough food at least. Oh, Father! I was truly conflicted.

When Mo grabbed me by the arm and forced me into his bed that night, my mind was entirely elsewhere and entirely outside of my body. I was learning to endure his assaults while escaping, if only in my mind.

❋

The next day, Yun's cough was worse, but she was not one to give up; she was ready to march to the mountains. She had a terrible time making the climb, and I supported her as much as I could. The idea that I would see Mi-ran and Su-lin made me happy, though, and I quickened my step. By the time we got to the area that Yun liked, she was out of breath and breathing heavily. I persuaded her to lie down, assuring her that I would collect the wood and do the work. Yun did not protest, and I even saw a hint of a look that could be considered appreciation, I thought. I noticed the two young women right away and hurried over to them. When the girls heard that Yun was sick, Mi-ran gave me some herbs and told me to mix them in Yun's tea. She told me it would both help her to breathe and sedate her for a bit. I took the herbs and hurried over to Yun, who eagerly took the herbs and nestled down on a bed of leaves under a tree, quickly falling asleep.

When I returned, I noticed that Mi-ran's face and body were badly bruised, and I knew my surprise must have shown on my face. Mi-ran simply smiled, flipped her hair out of her eyes, and walked a short distance away to pick up some small branches. Su-lin filled me in on what had happened to our friend Mi-ran. It seems that Mi-ran escaped North Korea three years earlier with her mother and sister. The broker they had hired had probably realized he could make more money if he sold each of the women individually in China instead of delivering them all to one location. Mi-ran had ended up here in Liaoning Province as the "wife" of a farmer. Mi-ran, being so small, thin, and malnourished, had been unable to get pregnant, so her father-in-law had taken to sleeping with her as well. Su-lin told me that she thought the father-in-law had become frustrated when he too was unable to get Mi-ran pregnant, especially after paying so much money for her. He frequently beat her and worked her terribly hard. Mi-ran did not know what to do or where to go, as she had no idea where her mother or sisters were by now. Mi-ran's story was not unusual, and I would hear slight variations of her story over and over during the time I was in China. I was appalled when I heard this, but I was also very worried that this just might become my own fate. The very thought of sleeping with Fong, my "father-in-law," was nothing short of revolting. Mo's assaults were bad enough, and didn't I already know how much Yun's stick hurt? I shuddered and quickly worked to dig up some sweet potatoes that I saw growing there on the ground, trying to put the thought out of my mind.

We must have gone to the mountains for firewood and vegetables for about ten or twelve days in a row, during which time Yun's cold did not improve. Each morning, I would give her some herbs in her tea, and she would lie down to sleep, leaving me to work and talk to Mi-ran and Su-lin. We all became friends as we talked and shared our individual stories while collecting wood and food. I was surprised to learn that Su-lin had no siblings but loved her parents very much, and when she was almost thirteen, they made an escape plan together. Su-lin told me the plan was that her parents, believing it would be easier if the two of them left together, would escape North Korea into China and eventually make their way to South Korea, where they would settle in and save some money. Su-lin was to be left behind in North Korea with an aunt, and the aunt would send her later. Since they lived close to the Chinese border, they thought it would be much easier for a child to slip across the border alone, where they planned to have a broker pick her up and unite her with them either in China or in South Korea. Su-lin hated staying with the aunt. The aunt was nice enough and had kept her relationship with her brother (Su-lin's father) a secret for many years. The police had not even questioned her aunt when her parents went missing because they had no idea that she was related to the couple or their daughter. The aunt had carefully kept Su-lin hidden all the time so neighbors and the police would not suspect that she was harboring a child. Su-lin had not been allowed to go to school or even talk to any other person. The days had turned into weeks and then into months, and still, they had not heard from her parents. Su-lin missed her parents terribly and was anxious to be out with other children her age, but the aunt was extremely strict and kept her locked in a back bedroom—she was taking no chances. Then one balmy day, the aunt had been at the market when a woman jumped up and instructed her to buy a specific CD. Not understanding this, the aunt started to walk away, but the middle-aged woman had been insistent: "You must buy this CD!"

Thinking this could be a trap and knowing it was against the law to buy black-market items, the aunt tried several times to move away, but the woman persisted. Finally, to shut up the woman, Su-lin's aunt took the chance and bought the designated CD, quickly stuffing it in her pocket. Once home and out of sight of any prying eyes, the aunt opened the CD. In it was a note from her brother telling her to send Su-lin across the river as soon as possible, preferably that night. The message went on to say they had hired a man to pick up Su-lin on the Chinese side and escort her to where they were staying. There was no money in the package, but to the aunt, it sounded like Su-lin's parents had arranged everything.

That night, Su-lin's aunt gave her a small bag of vegetables, said goodbye, and sent Su-lin to the river. Her aunt instructed Su-lin to look for a man who would then pick her up and take her to her parents. Su-lin was, of course, scared out of her wits but was also so very lonely for her parents and, oh, so very tired of being kept shut up in that small back room. How Su-lin longed for her parents! Su-lin had observed many North Korean kids crossing the river and bringing back forbidden Chinese goods to sell to the North Koreans. If they could cross that cold, swift river, she felt she could do it as well.

So, after reaching the Yalu riverbank, Su-lin hid out, waiting for just the right moment when the guards were not watching so closely. She noticed a group of other kids doing the same thing, and when suddenly, she saw them all run for the river, she quickly caught up and blended right in. She half expected to hear shouts or guns firing at them, but nothing happened! When she reached the other side of the river, Su-lin breathed a huge sigh of relief—she had made it! Su-lin thought it would be easy from then on. "Little did I know what truly lay in store for me," she had lamented to me.

Once thirteen-year-old Su-lin caught her breath and had gathered her wits about her, she began looking for the broker who was supposed to be there waiting for her. She saw a man looking directly at her and then beginning to walk towards her. "Are you my broker? I am Su-lin."

Su-lin told me that the man had looked at her very critically, but that she had just assumed he was making sure she was the right girl. He had finally nodded and said, "Come with me." He turned and walked away, and she followed.

Su-lin sniffed as she said in a quiet voice, "I picked the wrong man. He was not the broker my parents had hired, and when he had looked at me for so long, he probably thought that I was a bit young, but he could still sell me." She continued, "That's how I ended up here, and I have been here for nearly four years. I don't know if I will ever see my parents again, but I do have a little boy." Su-lin looked so sad, but a hint of bittersweet joy played in her eyes. "And now they trust me more since I have my son and allow me to come to the mountains on my own. I guess they think I would never leave him. I just try to live day by day," she added.

The herbs had worn off by now, and Yun noticed that I had all the fuel we could carry, so she was ready to go home.

"Come," she said as she got her bony butt up to go. I hurried to her side, determined to come up with a plan before I was trapped like Su-lin or Mi-ran were.

On the ninth morning of trekking up the mountain for fuel and winter vegetables, Yun and I got there as usual. I settled Yun down while I glanced around for my new friends. I saw Su-lin all alone but did not see Mi-ran at all. Once I reached Su-lin, I asked, "Where is Mi-ran today? Is she sick?"

Su-lin replied, "I don't know. I am kind of worried. Her father-in-law is a beast and does not treat her well. I hope she is just late."

The mountains were where women and sometimes little children gathered as they came from the various little villages and farms to collect firewood and food for the winter. It was a great time to gossip and share the news, but rarely did any of these people take the time to venture over to another person's farm just to visit. Su-lin was not even sure which village Mi-ran came from, and we had no way to contact her, even if our husbands would allow such a thing. We both hoped she was OK.

Mi-ran did not come to the mountain that day or even the following day, and we both knew something terrible had happened. We were also painfully aware that China thought of all North Korean men and women as "economic migrants" and, as such, would treat Mi-ran and ourselves as if we did not exist. They did not count Korean nationals in their populations; we and any children we would have would not be allowed to go to school or have documents that allowed us to participate in any of the usual citizen rights and privileges. We knew we would spend our lives in the back shadows of China and that we were vulnerable to being used and abused by all walks of life there. When Mi-ran was unable to conceive, her new family could have killed and buried her somewhere, and no authorities would ever check or know about her disappearance. Or perhaps her father-in-law had turned her in to the police, and she had been deported back to North Korea. Neither of these options was good. Both Su-lin and I were greatly saddened about Mi-ran, and I became quite concerned as to why I had not yet become pregnant myself. What would happen to me if I did not have a baby soon? I was very frightened about the prospect of becoming a mother, but I was also very scared about not having a baby as well.

✻

Meanwhile, back on the tiny farm, our stack of wood and branches was growing. After a couple more days of hard work in the mountains, Yun announced that we had enough and that it was time to weed the crops back on the farm. I was sad not to be seeing Su-lin anymore, and we vowed to meet again next summer in the mountains if possible. I had grown to like her a tremendous amount, and she had taught me so much, including some Chinese customs that would help me, some language, and as much as she knew about the lay of the land and a bit about commonly used wild herbs. Su-lin was my best friend in this inhospitable land. Fighting back tears, I said an emotional goodbye as I clutched a small handful of herbs that she said would help Yun with her cough that had persisted all the time we were in the mountains.

Once done with our trips to the mountain, we all settled back into the grind that had become my life in China. Yun's health improved, and she once more became the real ambition behind the farm activities. Unfortunately, she also resumed her private torture of me as she continued to grab my breasts at least once a week for an extra hard squeeze. I did not like this little ritual and tried to avoid any close contact with her as much as possible so she would be unable to do this. Still, I was kind to all the family members, hoping that they would continue to tolerate and feed me until I managed to escape. I did not want to be beaten or worse, like what most likely had happened to Mi-ran.

✻

One day in late December, Yun did her customary squeeze, and I caught my breath hard. Gosh, did that ever hurt! What had she done differently to make it hurt so much? That night, I gingerly caressed my breast where she had squeezed. It hurt as much as when Yun touched me! I touched my other breast and was surprised that it hurt like heck too. What was going on? A couple of weeks later, I missed my cycle, and for whatever reason, I felt nauseated. I knew what that meant. I did not know if I should be happy about the turn of events or if I was actually sad.

I know Yun searched for my towels drying out behind the bushes, and after a few weeks of not finding them, I heard her singing. She came into the house one afternoon and placed her hand on my stomach as if to tell me she knew. I guessed that that was my official diagnosis. The whole family treated me nicer after they realized I would be having a child. I was numb. I did not know what or how to feel.

CHAPTER 12

While they eagerly awaited the birth of their son, the three family members treated me better. Mo did not drag me to his bed during this time, and that certainly was a relief, although he never offered to let me sleep on his cot, and I remained on my piece of cardboard. I honestly did not mind as I was becoming used to it. As time went on, I began to hope for a boy, as this pregnancy thing was hard and I did not want to go through it again. I was expected to carry on with my usual amount of work, of course. Yun told me, "Once our son is born, I will give you an egg." I hate to admit it, but I began to fantasize about that darn egg. Eggs were such rare items to eat in North Korea, and it seems they were far and few between here in China as well.

Time went on, and finally, one day, I was out in the field, big as a barrel, when my water broke. Yun was ecstatic and became very animated as she guided me into a small little building not far from the house. She laid me down on some straw, gave me some water to sip, and disappeared! I was truly frightened as I lay there wondering if she was going to come back or if I was expected to do all of this myself. The pains were hurting, although not as bad as they would become, and I did not know what to expect. I had never seen an animal, much less a woman, give birth before and doubted if I could do this birthing thing. Women died giving birth, didn't they? I was terrified, and for the very first time, I wanted my mother-in-law.

Within an hour, Yun reappeared at the door. I was so relieved! She had gone for the midwife, it seems. Isn't that what husbands do? I wondered: Where was Mo? I labored for what seemed like days but was only for about twelve extremely long hours. Yun was flittering all around the room, yelling out advice to me, while the other woman seemed only half interested in what was going on, or so it seemed. Finally, the pains came closer together, and it became time to push. Naturally, Yun did not think I was pushing hard enough and pounced on my stomach, which only made matters worse. "Please! Please!" I remember saying over and over, and in truth, I don't know whom I was asking for help from. I just wanted this boy out of me and for Yun to leave me alone. Finally, I heard a tiny baby cough, or so I thought, and yet I could feel that the baby was still inside of me. I was confused when the midwife told me to push again. With a final push, the baby was out, and I remember hearing Yun's long, mournful wail.

❋

It was Yun's sorrowful cry that told me that I must have given birth to a girl. Otherwise, Yun would not wail like that, I surmised. Just then, the midwife shoved some herbs or something into my vaginal area. A searing pain instantly shot through the lower part of my body, and everything went black. I really do not know how long I was out, but when I regained consciousness, both women were gone, and I was lying there in my sweat and blood all alone. They took my baby, I thought! I managed to raise myself on one elbow and look around the small room. In the far corner lay a small, discarded bundle that was not moving at all. "There!" I cried as I somehow managed to reach it. A baby was lying face down in the dirt with no blankets or anything on it. I lifted the baby and turned it over. It was a girl! She was awfully cold and kind of blue and not breathing much at all. I instinctively pushed my finger into her mouth and scooped out some blood, mucus, and a bit of dirt as I tried to get her to take a deep breath. I put her small body next to my skin and wrapped her up the best I could. They left us here to die, I thought, and tears were forming in my eyes.

"Breathe Baby! Breathe!" I kept repeating over and over as I jostled the little bundle. "I want you to live! Breathe!" Finally, she kind of squirmed a little and made a choking sound. There was hope! I renewed my attempt to revive her and rubbing her vigorously all over, I tried to warm her up. I cannot explain it, but at that very moment, I loved this tiny baby more than anything or anybody I had ever known in my life. Right then. It did not matter that I did not love her father or that I was essentially in prison. All that mattered to me was that this little girl needed to live and needed love—my love.

CHAPTER 13

✿

Of course, the entire family was extremely disappointed that I had not given them the long-awaited son that they all wanted. I had grown up knowing that girls were inferior and that all families wanted a son who would bring home a wife who would then work hard and even take care of the parents. I knew this. And I knew that a girl was expected to go off to join her husband's family one day. I understood this concept and had lived it my entire life, and yet every time I looked down at my daughter, my heart would swell with love for her. She was NOT inferior! Once I wiped the blood and mucus away, I saw that she had a small tuft of dark hair and a bright pink face. She was beautiful! Her small eyes looked up at me but, of course, did not focus much. I had such love for this child! I swore to her that I would love and protect her all my life. This family would not defeat us.

I remember that I stayed a long time in that small building, making sure she was warm, and breathing properly, and then I tried to feed my daughter her first taste of milk. I frantically tried to think of a girl's name, but all this time, we had all been so sure the baby would be a boy! I finally decided to call her Yoon-ha. Yoon-ha—I let the name roll off my tongue several times. Yoon-ha, Yoon-ha, I sang. I was happier than I had been in months, perhaps even years.

In time, I cleaned myself the best I could, and, taking Yoon-ha, I went into the house to face the family. Fong and Mo were sitting at the table when I entered the house, but no one even looked up. So, I boldly walked over to where Mo was and bent down to show him our new daughter. "Yoon-ha," I said. "Yoon-ha," I repeated as I stroked her sweet little face. I really felt that Mo would at least acknowledge the baby, but he simply gave my arm a strong shove and turned his face away in total disgust. Yun snorted and said something in Chinese that I did not understand, and all three of them laughed. Not to be deterred, I went and sat on my piece of cardboard and cradled Yoon-ha. It was then that I noticed a small cardboard box sitting on the floor next to my bed. Why that must have been intended to be a cradle for the baby, I thought. I got up and reached for the box, but Yun was quick to kick it out of my reach.

That is when I had it, and I said, "Boy or not, this baby needs a cradle!" I looked straight at Yun, who was eating the last of an egg—my egg! She simply shrugged and let me take the box and put the baby in it.

✻

This continued to be the general attitude there at the farm all that winter and into the following summer. The three of them treated Yoon-ha as if she did not exist, and I was expected to not only care for my baby but to do my full measure of work. If my baby cried, they complained loudly, and I did my best to make sure that she did not make noise and that she was well cared for. I admit that I was certainly happy being a mother to my precious little Yoon-ha, but I did not care one bit for any one of the Tings. It had been over a year since Father and I had left North Korea, and my Chinese was improving every day. In my mind, I was always practicing the pronunciation of the words, and I began to imagine just what I would need to take when I left—not that I had a date or even a general time frame of when that would be. I managed to steal a small bag and a knife, and I found a place in the back of the small building where I buried them. They were the beginning of what I would need, or so I thought.

Yun told me I would be responsible for either sharing my food or finding food for Yoon-ha when she started to eat whole food but for now, she was only being breastfed. When she cried, and I thought she was hungry, my milk would "come down" and a small stain would appear on my loose shirt. This totally disgusted Mo, and he would turn away every time. This made me feel pleased, especially since he did not yank me up to go to his cot as much anymore. I deliberately left the milk stains on my shirt so that I would smell more, which repulsed him. I also figured out that Mo did not like touching me when I had my cycle, so I wet the towels and hung them on the bushes out behind for more days than was necessary. I knew old Yun would see them and report this news to her son.

It was hot that summer, and I longed for it to be time to go to the mountains to collect wood and winter vegetables. I also wanted to talk with Su-lin and Mi-ran if they were still there. I was afraid Mo would want me pregnant again so that I could provide them with the coveted boy they all wanted. I knew having two children would make it even harder for me to leave. All in all, I was biding my time and hoping to escape as soon as possible.

Finally, the day arrived when Yun announced that it was time to collect the yearly supply of firewood and winter vegetables. I was ecstatic and had to hide my pleasure at the mere thought of going to the mountains! I had hoped that by now, she would trust me enough to let me take Yoon-ha and go without her, but she squashed those hopes, saying that I would be unable to carry both the wood and the baby back down the mountain. I knew she was right. The next option was to have her stay at the house with Yoon-ha and let me go alone. Tornado Ting showed me how to express enough milk from my breasts to feed Yoon-ha while I would be gone. She was not gentle at all, and the whole process hurt like heck. Besides, we only got a small amount of milk. When I suggested that we mix a small amount of rice milk with my milk, she almost hit me. Not wanting to provoke her, I left my precious baby and went to the mountain alone that first day. I tell you; I worried all day about what she might do to my baby girl and decided that I would not leave Yoon-ha at home with her the next day.

But when I was not thinking and worrying about my daughter, I had a great time. I immediately spotted Su-lin and ran up to her giving her a big hug. I did not see Mi-ran and asked Su-lin about her. Sadly, Su-lin had not heard about and knew nothing about Mi-ran, and indeed, we would never hear about or see Mi-ran again. This was both frightening and provoking. That, of course, propelled me to ask some very direct questions about an escape plan. How much did Su-lin know about the Yanbian Korean Autonomous Prefecture? How far was it from here? Could we walk there? Were there jobs there? Was it safe? Wouldn't it be best to go now before winter sets in and it turns dreadfully cold in the mountains? And finally, would she go with me? I privately wondered if she wanted to find her parents enough to escape her life there on the rural Chinese farm. She knew her son was loved and safe on the farm, but it was next to impossible to find or even inquire about her parents if she stayed here in this region.

Su-lin answered my questions as best she could, considering that everything she knew was hearsay. Su-lin was very perceptive as well as a smart girl, and she made it a point to learn as much as she could about her new country. And yes, she felt that the Yanbian Korean Autonomous Prefecture was the best and safest place for a North Korean woman to hide and blend in. She also finally acknowledged that it would be the most likely place her parents would be if they were still in China. She had heard that approximately 750,000 North Koreans were living there and thought that one could find some sort of job and blend in easily once there. The hard part, she acknowledged, would be traveling there. We needed clothes that would make us look as if we were native Chinese and, of course, be able to speak the language without much of a North Korean accent so that the police would not detain and deport us back to North Korea.

The Chinese clothes would be a problem for me, as I would need to persuade Yun to allow me some new or at least different things to wear. I did not know just how successful I would be in this, as she controlled all the family finances closely and did not think much of my needs. On the other hand, Mo had been complaining bitterly about how dirty and stained my clothes were and how badly I smelled of sour milk. I thought it turned his desire for me off. (I could not get rid of the milk smell easily, although I had not been trying hard to do this.) And I knew that they all wanted a boy so badly. Mo would have to muster some sort of interest in me if I were to produce a baby boy. My conflict was that I did not want a second child, as I knew it would make things harder for my escape. I was also aware that the family would never let me take a son with me, and if the baby were a girl, Yun would kill her immediately this time. And of course, this did not even consider the fact that I hated having Mo touch me. He had learned where to put his sex piece, but one thing he had never learned, perhaps because he did not want to, was how to be gentle with me. Mo was a brute, not at all unlike his mother, and I always thought he was not only odd but dumb as well. I was still a nonperson in his mind. So being forced to have sex with him and to go through a long, hard pregnancy and birth for a second time was almost more than I could bear. The trick would be to get the clothes without exciting Mo *and* without becoming pregnant. I longed to speak with Mi-ran because she knew so much about Chinese herbs, and she would have known what I could secretly take to prevent a second pregnancy.

Su-lin surprised me when I mentioned that I needed some herbs to prevent a pregnancy. She had heard about an herb called Queen Anne's Lace or wild carrot seed that girls sometimes chewed. She had also heard that Ginger Root, which was very plentiful around these parts of the country, would often make a girl menstruate more. She warned me, though, that I could not use these herbs for long or Mo might suspect something was going on. I knew this well, but I did need something to buy me a bit of time before my escape. Su-lin described what these herbs looked like, and we started searching immediately for them. I knew that I needed to find some Queen Anne's Lace today if possible because I could not be sure that Yun would stay home again tomorrow, and even if she did, I wondered and worried that she might not be treating Yoon-ha well. That day, Su-lin and I went around the mountain practicing our Chinese, trying to get rid of our accents while looking more for herbs than for any vegetables or wood.

I was disappointed when I realized that Su-lin had not answered the final question that I had asked her, which was, "Would she come with me?" I noticed that she had sort of danced around that one. I felt we would be safer and be able to cover each other's backs more if we left together, and I knew that even though she was only a year or so older than me, she had been in China for four years now and was very knowledgeable on Chinese ways. I had never traveled much in my life, and I was, frankly, very scared. I decided not to pressure her on that issue anymore that day but intended to bring it up the next day or so after she had weighed her decision a bit more. I was hopeful but incredibly resolute that I would go with or without Su-lin.

※

That night, when I returned from the mountain, my breasts were heavy, and I had missed my little girl so much. Yun met me outside the door and almost immediately started to berate me for not bringing back more firewood. I tried to explain to her that it was harder to find today, but she screamed at me and hit me with her stick. I was black and blue before I even made it into the house. Once in the house, I could hear Yoon-ha crying, probably because I had not been able to leave her very much milk for the day and I knew she would be hungry. I scooped her up and immediately sat down on my cardboard bed and began feeding her.

This infuriated both Yun and Mo, and they both stood over me screaming at the top of their lungs. I tried to ignore them both and concentrate on my beautiful baby when I noticed a huge, big, long bruise on Yoon-ha's tiny arm. "Oh, NO!" I screamed as I fingered her arms and began searching for other signs of injury.

All the while, Yun was beating me with her stick all over my head, back, and arms. I knew right then that I needed to leave within the next day or so and take my baby with me. Both Yoon-ha and I were in immediate danger. This had NOT been my plan. While I recognized that Mo had not paid any attention to Yoon-ha, I believed this would all change as soon as she was old enough to interact with him. How could a father not love his daughter enough to make sure she was cared for, especially in a country where there was at least enough food? Not once had I ever thought they would hurt little Yoon-ha this much! I had planned to leave after Yoon-ha was old enough to be weaned and could stay with the Tings, surviving on whole food but before she would remember me. With all my heart, I did not want Yoon-ha to cry for me with a terrible longing and the belief that I had abandoned her. I thought that Yun would then be able to care for my child until one day in the future when I would have enough money, I would come back and buy her freedom. Surely Yun or even Mo would love and care for Yoon-ha enough to get her through this difficult period. Seeing that horrible bruise on Yoon-ha's arm changed everything! I knew I could not leave my child with these monsters.

What a gamble! What terrible, horrible stakes! Where would I go? What could I do to make money? What choice did I have? To stay here meant that both Yoon-ha and I would be beaten and possibly starve as we slaved on the small family farm. And all the time, Mo would be raping me until I was able to produce a son. Or they might even kill little Yoon-ha. My heart was so heavy, and I felt sick—my poor baby…

❀

That night, Mo came to my cardboard bed, shoved Yoon-ha over and out of my arms, and took me right there on the floor. He raped me with his usual roughness and toughness, but if he wasn't hurting Yoon-ha, I could stand it, as my mind was on our escape the entire time. I just hoped that the Queen Anne's lace that I had chewed earlier that day had had time to work.

Tornado Ting was up before dawn, shoved some tea in my hands, and indicated that she was going with me that day and that we needed to make haste up the mountain as "I had not done my duty yesterday." I was so bruised and stiff that I had a hard time getting up from my bed that morning. But I had to know if Su-lin was coming with me, and I had to tell her we needed to go as soon as possible. I immediately started feeding Yoon-ha and was still nursing her as we began our climb up the mountain while neither Yun nor I said a word to each other.

When we got to a new place on the mountain where more vegetables grew and where there were more branches and logs to gather, the sun was just rising, and I could see Su-lin working on a big log in the distance. I settled Yoon-ha and Yun on the ground under a shade tree. I was so reluctant to leave my baby with the woman, who I was sure had hurt her the day before, but what choice did I have? I wanted to be close enough to keep an eye on the two of them but far enough away so I could talk to Su-lin. I had never understood why Fong and Mo couldn't have come up to help here in the mountains with this heavy work. What did they do all day? If they had come, I could have taken care of Yoon-ha myself. But all this did not matter much now, did it? Yoon-ha and I would be leaving in a day or so.

I maneuvered it so that I got close to Su-lin, as I appeared to be working hard in case Yun looked my way. Su-lin was shocked when she saw how battered and bruised, I was. "What happened?" she blurted out, staring at my bruises. "Did you resist your husband?"

"No," I replied. "It was my mother-in-law. She rules the roost with an iron fist, and she was unhappy with how little wood I brought home yesterday. She was probably tired from caring for Yoon-ha all day too. But it doesn't matter now. I cannot risk staying any longer. She hurt Yoon-ha too." I hurried on, "I am leaving tomorrow. Are you coming with me?"

Su-lin looked a little surprised and turned away. I heard her give out a long, tortuous sigh, and it was a long time before she responded. "Yes, we should leave tomorrow. Bring what you can to the mountain," she managed to whisper and she started to walk away.

A great sense of relief washed over me. My plans were coming to fruition, finally! We were going to be free! I wanted to hoot and holler but instead worked even harder on a stubborn log. I felt like an enormous burden had been lifted off my shoulders knowing the decision had been made and the date set, even though I knew a long, hard journey lay ahead. Meanwhile, Su-lin moved far away from me, and we did not speak for the rest of the day until close to quitting time, when she came over, behaving as if she wanted to see my baby. She smiled at the baby and briefly touched Yoon-ha but did not linger long as Yun had gotten up, gathered her bundles, and was preparing herself for the trek down the mountain.

❄

I did not discover the small bundle of herbs that Su-lin had hidden next to Yoon-ha inside her blanket until I started to nurse her halfway down the mountain. I knew immediately that the special herbs were intended to sedate Yun heavily so that we could slip away tomorrow. "Hum," I murmured and cuddled Yoon-ha closer. I felt my world brighten a bit, and I felt like I could take on the universe at that moment.

That night, I could not sleep as I played out our escape over and over in my mind. I knew so many things could go wrong, but I was so determined to leave this house. I had been here nearly two years and had done everything in my power to fit in with the family, and still, none of the three Tings could stand me. I now understood that they would always think of me as subhuman, no matter how long I stayed here or what I did.

It was clear that these very poor people with a poorly functioning son wanted a pure Chinese girl for a daughter-in-law, but I suspected that even a pure Chinese girl would not have been considered good enough. The truth was, I despised these people. They seemed mean-spirited to me, and I genuinely believed my fate would not be changing, and now I had Yoon-ha to think about. I did not want my precious little daughter to be a slave all her life. There had to be something better out there awaiting the two of us. I was eager to begin this next phase of my life, and I was pleased that my friend Su-lin would be coming with Yoon-ha and me.

CHAPTER 14

❃

Towards morning, pure exhaustion overtook my body, and I fell into a deep sleep. Yun jolted me awake by poking me ridiculously hard with her stick here, there, and everywhere on my poor body. I had been sleeping so hard that I was temporarily disoriented. It took a moment for me to remember where I was and to recognize that my misery was coming from Yun conducting her favorite pastime of inflicting pain at my expense.

"Get up, you lazy girl!" Yun shouted repeatedly as she continued poking me, with every jab becoming more painful. At that moment, I craved sleep and did not want to get up, but I sure was not going to lie there taking this abuse!

"OK, OK, I'm up!" I shouted as I grabbed Yoon-ha and rose off the piece of cardboard. My mind snapped to attention as I remembered that today was the day we were leaving. For a moment I felt utter panic as I realized that no matter how much I hated it here, I was not truly prepared to leave this farm. I knew that I did not have everything that Su-lin and I needed for our journey, and I also knew that Yun would be in an absolute rage when she learned that I had attempted an escape. I knew without a doubt that there could be no "attempt"—that I must be successful in Yoon-ha's and my escape. Yun would not only be angry about the money she "wasted" on me but also that I would be taking her "slave to be," my precious little daughter. I knew she did not love either Yoon-ha or myself and thought only of us as economic units to be used to enrich her and her family's well-being. I knew without a doubt that the Tings would all be searching for us and that I could make NO mistakes.

I grabbed a cup of tea and took a couple of swallows as I yelled, "OK, OK, I need to get my rags." I knew that would put Yun off a bit, but I needed an excuse to go fetch the small bag of vegetables and the knife that I had buried out back in preparation for this day. I also grabbed the three small rice balls that she had laid out for our lunch, as I knew I would need everything I could find. I rushed out of the hut carrying Yoon-ha, looking at every little thing that I passed as a possible item that I could smuggle that just might be of use to Su-lin and me on our journey. Unfortunately, there was not much that was just lying around, as Tornado Ting kept such a close accounting of all their possessions and they were snuggly stored in their places. I could not risk looking for or going for these items at this time. I was truly leaving the farm with nothing to my name and only my precious baby. I hoped that Su-lin would be more successful in collecting items of possible use for our journey to who knows where.

My mind was racing as I nursed Yoon-ha while we trudged up the mountain that last morning. We were going for herbs and firewood that day, but my new plan was to settle Yoon-ha and Yun down under a shade tree not far from where I would be secretly collecting vegetables. I would give Yun a cup of fresh tea heavily laced with the sedative herbs that Su-lin had given me the day before. I would pretend to be gathering firewood but would collect more of the needed vegetables for our journey instead. As soon as I knew Yun was asleep, I planned to sneak up and take Yoon-ha so that Su-lin and I could climb down the other side of the mountain and be long gone before she awoke from her sleep and discovered us missing. Thankfully, everything went as planned, and Yun quickly fell asleep. I came over immediately and observed that Tornado Ting was no tornado—she was out cold and *really* sleeping deeply. It was then that I got the idea to steal her Chinese clothes. I knew that her clothes would help me blend into my surroundings, even if they were a bit on the small side for me. I had not gotten the chance to even bring up the subject of newer Chinese clothes for me as I had initially planned, so now taking Yun's clothes would simply have to do—that is, if I could get them off her without Yun waking up.

❄

A few minutes later, the three of us were hustling down the other side of the mountain. Yoon-ha had not even stirred while I had undressed Yun. I had not bothered to redress her in my Korean clothes as I thought that might wake her, so I had simply thrown them over her and taken off. We practically ran the first couple of miles before we slowed for a bit of a rest. Su-lin had noticed the change in my clothes and asked me about them. I explained the situation to her and how Yun was so knocked out and barely breathing. At first, Su-lin was alarmed that Yun had been so "out of it" and that she had not woken up while I was undressing her. But we both agreed that it did not really matter as we were on our way and what was the difference if she woke up hours later and had to make her way down the mountain alone in the dark? Yun had done worse things to me, and now Su-lin and I were both wearing Chinese clothes. We laughed at how "Chinese" we looked but knew that people would know we were

Korean runaways as soon as we opened our mouths. We knew we needed to cover as much distance that first night as we could and remain hidden in the mountains and out of sight as much as possible. Our journey had truly begun.

The clouds partially covered the moon that first night, which made visibility somewhat difficult, but we trudged on. We could hear birds calling and small wild animals rustling around in the area, and one time, a small pack of about five or six wild pigs ran right in front of me. It was scary, but we knew we had to keep moving. When we were far enough away from people, we started talking to keep us awake and alert. Su-lin took over the lead as she claimed she could tell directions by the stars. Her uncle had taught her when she was just a child, telling her one never knew when such knowledge might help her. Su-lin was a smart and very alert girl. Since her four years in China, she had learned as much as she could about the country, its people, and its language. Su-lin explained more about the Yanbian Korean Autonomous Prefecture, which some fellow escaped Korean girl had told her about. She said that the Prefecture had seemed like a distant dream at the time, but now we both agreed it should be the place for us to go. We knew we needed a safe place where we could blend in as well as get jobs. Where better to go than to an area where Chinese Korean people lived and worked? Heck, it had even been reported that they spoke Korean there.

As the night wore on, Yoon-ha grew heavy. We stopped for a short rest, and I fed my baby while Su-lin and I munched on raw vegetables. Later, Su-lin carried Yoon-ha, saying she was not heavy at all. And we talked and talked. We practiced speaking Chinese without a Korean accent. I was amazed at how well Su-lin spoke the language and how much information she had absorbed during her short stay in China. It was a way to keep us awake as we moved through the forest and mountain area.

We knew that we could sleep in the morning when more people might be out and about and when we did not want to be seen. I learned that night that Su-lin had come from a wonderful North Korean family and that she had always been loved, even though she was a girl and the only child her parents were able to have. Her father must have been a high-ranking military man, and she had not suffered a great deal. She had hated being locked up in her aunt and uncle's house, waiting for the funds and proper time for her to join her parents in China. She blamed herself for picking the wrong broker that night, four years ago, and now wondered if she would ever find her parents in huge China. Su-lin was incredibly sad about this and cried as we walked along.

❋

As we continued our journey, I learned even more about Su-lin. Once "married" off to her husband, she conceived a boy within the first year. Neither her husband nor his family was abusive to Su-lin, and they were so happy that she had produced the desired son. She had earned their trust and even a measure of affection as well and was now allowed to go to the mountains on her own. I could hardly believe that she was not beaten regularly. Still, Su-lin was unhappy and so sad because she believed she wanted to be with her parents and feared she would never see them again. She seriously doubted that they would still be in China after all this time, and if they were here, how would she find them? She thought that they must surely be in South Korea by now. She felt helpless and hopeless in finding them, yet had an overpowering need to go try to find them. That ever-present need, plus the fact that she knew her son was loved, protected, and needed by both her husband and his parents, is why she had agreed to come with me. I was humbled by this simple, kind girl.

CHAPTER 15

✳

The days turned into weeks, and still, Su-lin and I trudged onward toward the Yanbian Korean Autonomous Prefecture in Jilin Province, the next province over from Liaoning Province where we had started. The trip was much longer than the trip I had made with Yun from the North Korean border to her farm over two years before, and so much had happened since that time. But somehow, the trip did not seem nearly as hard, even though I was carrying and nursing a nearly ten-month-old infant. Su-lin and I stayed in the mountains and followed riverbanks as much as possible. We did not have the money to pay for railroad tickets or any other means of transportation, and with two women and a child traveling alone, we knew we stood out from the general Chinese population. We did what we could to stay warm and healthy as we foraged for vegetables and managed to kill the occasional small animal to eat.

It was during our long journey that Su-lin and I became close friends, and I began to love her as I imagined I would have loved a sister, had I had one. She taught me as much as she knew about the various herbs and their medicinal purposes, as well as about different plants, berries, and wild foods. We rejoiced together when we happened upon an old torn tarp that could be used as a tent against rain. Such a small thing, but oh, so valuable to us! We both laughed at the things little Yoon-ha did and marveled at how much she was growing and changing every day. Su-lin became Yoon-ha's second mother, as she loved and tended to Yoon-ha's needs almost as much as I did. I know she was deeply missing her young son back in her husband's village. Yet she just bit her lip and played extra hard with Yoon-ha. Su-lin even rinsed out the rags I had brought that served as Yoon-ha's diapers. The one thing she could not do was nurse Yoon-ha, but she was the first to discover the small pearly white tooth just peeping out of Yoon-ha's lower gums. She giggled when I asked her what was so funny and said, "Oh, dear Ma-Ma, you will find out soon enough!" And find out, I did! Later that day, when giving Yoon-ha her evening meal, she did a vigorous sucking motion, and WOW! I thought old Yun once again had my breast in her hand! I instinctively jerked back, and poor Yoon-ha looked at me with a startled expression like, "What happened, Ma-Ma?"

❀

Su-lin and I continued walking and talking. We talked about everything—our hopes, plans, fears, and inadequacies—well, just about everything! I truly felt Su-lin's deep sorrow and emptiness at losing the love of her parents. We brainstormed for hours on possible ways to locate them. I must admit, it all seemed like an impossible feat and we both doubted that Su-lin would ever see or even know where her parents had gone. We knew we were on our own, with no help in the entire world. I knew that Su-lin was continually thinking about her little boy and how much she missed him. She sometimes talked and reminisced aloud about her life on the farm, but mostly about her adorable little boy. About how his black hair was so shiny and healthy and how much he loved a little red ball his father had given him. She never once mentioned that either her husband or his parents were mean to her, but rather how happy they were and how much they cared for her little boy. Su-lin cried with me as I told her of Chang-hee's disappearance and then Mother's death. She could hardly believe it when I described how Father had sold me to Mo's malicious mother and how the whole Ting family treated Yoon-ha and me. She was aghast when she heard how Mo had raped me repeatedly and how I had been left alone after giving birth to Yoon-ha while my newborn baby had been thrown in a corner to die. Su-lin had never known such despicable treatment. Her husband had at least treated her with respect, and her life on his family's farm had been quite pleasant, although hugely different from her previous life. She could not fathom how I had withstood it for all those months. We assured each other that our lives would be better now that we were "free" and on our own in China.

I was extremely grateful that Su-lin's husband had recognized the importance of Su-lin learning to read and speak Chinese, and now she was teaching me. We sang and practiced speaking without the dreaded Korean accent even though we knew we would be living in a region of China where ethnic Koreans lived and worked. I was determined that I would someday teach my daughter both languages and would try my best so she would not remain in the lower subclass of citizens prevented from participating fully in day-to-day life. I wanted her to go to school and someday marry for love. Another subject that we spent a great deal of time chatting about was what to expect in the Prefecture part of China once we got there. Neither of us knew much about the area other than that a huge majority of Koreans who had made their escape from North Korea congregated in that region and had done so for many decades. We knew Koreans had immigrated there first for political reasons and later for economic reasons. After the Chinese Civil War, the new Chinese government rewarded the Koreans by upgrading the area to an ethnically autonomous prefecture in 1955. Su-lin's family had lived close to the Chinese border and had participated in the black-market trading between North Korea and China that had gone on, especially once the famine and hard times had hit North Korea. Her father had spoken frequently about the family moving to that region, particularly after the North Korean government cracked down on the underground trading that he was conducting in his off-hours. Her father and mother had lived in constant fear of her father being caught, and yet they depended on the money he made on the black market just to get by. Her father had spent months researching an escape for the family but had always added that there was a lot more opportunity in South Korea. So, while China would be a good refugee place, he ultimately thought they would all have better lives in South Korea. He had explained to the family that China viewed North Koreans not so much as refugees but more like economic migrants. This fact meant that they would be ripe to be taken advantage of or even turned in to the police, who would repatriate them back to North Korea, where they would be tortured and starved if not killed outright. This was the reason Su-lin believed her parents would eventually leave China and go to South Korea. Su-lin explained that since we had no money or a trusted broker (hadn't her choice of a broker landed her in hot water before?), our best bet would be to first go to Yanji, the capital and largest city in the province. After discussing it further, Su-lin and I believed we would be able to locate Su-lin's parents there if they were still in China. We thought we could obtain jobs as cleaning ladies or as waitresses in one of the pubs there and blend in quite well. At all costs, we swore to stay together because it was safer, and at this point, we were "family."

❋

And so, we proceeded closer to our destination, excited and enthused but also more than a little scared. One day late in the afternoon, when we were getting close to Yanji and had let our guard down a bit, a middle-aged woman observed us and got close enough to hear us speaking. By the time we noticed her, we knew she had heard us, so we immediately began acting as if we were two young Chinese girls out hunting for herbs, enjoying the sunshine and each other's company. She quickly saw through our ruse and walked over to us stopping to chuckle little Yoon-ha under her chin. She slowly smiled at us and, in a calm, non-threatening voice said:

"Girls, you are Korean, aren't you? From the looks of it, you have been here a while, haven't you? But I think I can help you. I know you must be tired of traveling and are or will be looking for jobs, right?"

She had spoken slowly, had looked us directly in the eyes, and was friendly enough—not at all threatening or with an air of contempt. When she touched my arm, she was gentle and reminded me of my own dear mother. "I have a friend who owns a pub in Yanji and is always looking for waitresses. It is a nice, clean pub where many Chinese Korean people go, and since you speak both languages, you would be a real asset to him," she said, then cocked her head a little and waited as if to let this all sink in.

"Really," I thought, "could this be the break that Su-lin and I needed and were looking for?" I glanced over at Su-lin, who was smiling and had a little twinkle in her eye. I knew she was thinking the same thing as I was.

CHAPTER 16

The woman explained that we would be provided with a place to stay, food, and a small wage, and she was sure that Little Yoon-ha would be safe and happy there. We would work as waitresses, but since it was also a karaoke bar, we would sometimes be expected to sing along with the Korean and Chinese patrons. She did not think that learning Chinese songs would be difficult for us. She assured us that we could make a very pleasant life for ourselves there in Yanji and that the three of us could stay together. The lady did not pressure us but told us to think about it and to go speak with her friend, the owner if we were interested. After leaving us his name and the directions to his establishment, the woman told us to be sure to tell him that Meilee Yang had sent us to him. She was very specific that we remember and use her name, as if doing so was our ticket to the job. Then she was on her way.

Su-lin and I did not have to discuss the decision much at all—we both knew what we would do. That night, as I prepared our meal of vegetables, I added the leftover meat from the small squirrel Su-lin had caught the day before. We were having a feast to celebrate our good fortune. And such good luck it was! We had a lead on a job, and our journey was close to being over. Su-lin sang the only Chinese song she knew over and over as she worked around our campsite, and I was sure that little Yoon-ha somehow knew that we were happy and that life was good. We all slept well that night, content with our private thoughts.

❋

The next morning, we were all up bright and early as Su-lin and I prepared for the final day of our long journey. We were sure we could reach Yanji and find the bar before nightfall. As we packed up, we even hesitated when we began to fold up the tarp. Should we take it with us? Nay, we decided—we would not need a tarp where we were going. We were so excited about our new life!

We walked all day until about 5 o'clock that afternoon when we entered the outskirts of the city. We had laughed and talked as we walked that day and were teaching Yoon-ha how to say "Ma-Ma" in Chinese. We wanted her to blend in as much as possible, and speaking fluent Chinese was paramount for all of us. We had to ask for more directions to the restaurant/bar a couple of times, as we did get lost in the big foreign city. The streets all looked the same! And there were few signs, so I was completely lost. Su-lin gave me a slight push the first time we approached an old man who looked safe enough to ask for directions. She was making it perfectly clear that I must speak and speak clearly if I were to survive in China. Now was as good a chance as any to practice my Chinese.

About an hour later, we all stood outside of the restaurant/bar listening to the music as the smell of food drifted out towards us. It made me realize how hungry and tired I was. Quickly entering the dark restaurant, we noticed that there were a good number of customers (mostly young Chinese men and a few Koreans) drinking and eating. Several young girls, not unlike us and about our ages, were waiting on them. They conversed and occasionally laughed with the customers as they moved quickly and purposefully around the room. Su-lin took the lead, pushed her way up to the bar, and forcefully said to the bartender, "We need to speak to the owner, Mr. Wong." She then bowed her head respectfully while we all waited.

The bartender looked at us all in a very deliberate manner as we stood there for what seemed like an eternity before he wiped his wet hands on his not-so-clean pants and gestured for us to follow him. Su-lin and I anxiously followed the man to a small room where he knocked, hesitated briefly, then entered, leaving us standing in the hallway. In a short time, he very quickly reopened the door and motioned for us to enter. Sitting at a desk piled high with stacks of loose papers was a small, tired-looking Chinese man in rumpled clothes and with dark, squinting eyes. The room was quite dimly lit, and he looked annoyed at being disturbed, but he seemed to perk up and become more interested once he saw us. He began immediately to stare at Su-lin and me as if he were sizing us up. And he was, I guess. He was sizing us up to see if we were up to the job he had in mind.

Without waiting for him to speak, Su-lin spoke up, "My name is Su-lin, and this is Ha-na Song and her baby. We have come because we met Meilee Yang, who said that you are hiring waitresses, and we would like to apply for jobs here at your restaurant. Meilee Yang said to tell you that she sent us." She then lowered her eyes in respect and waited. Mr. Wong did not say anything for what seemed like a long time, all the time staring at first one and then the other of us. Yoon-ha squirmed in my arms, and I shifted her to my other hip, half expecting him to dismiss us right then and there. I had no idea where we would go or what we would do if he did not want to give us the jobs. I was quite hungry and could tell by Yoon-ha's squirming that she was ready to nurse.

Finally, Mr. Wong touched his chin and said, "Why yes, I could use some new waitresses, especially ones that Meilee Yang recommends." He took a deep breath and hurried on, "You will be given your room and board plus a small salary for those days you work. My girls live in the rooms above the bar and down the hallway. You must always keep your baby out of the bar and restaurant, and she cannot be a noisy child. You will not get bigger accommodations or any extra money because you have a child. You can use the money you receive to buy her food. One thing I can do for you though is to schedule you in such a way that one of you is always with the child." With that said, he reached over, picked up a small bell, and rang it twice. A small Chinese woman scurried in, and he told her to take us to our rooms. "Let them eat and rest tonight," he instructed. "But one should work tomorrow, and the other tomorrow night." I was ecstatic and had a hard time containing myself! We found jobs on the very first day. And Yoon-ha was not going to be a burden. What more could we ask for?

The woman, Mr. Wong's assistant, then led us up a small, narrow wooden staircase to the second floor, which opened to a long hallway with several closed doors along it. We could hear women talking and the occasional giggle or laugh but kept going until the women stopped at an open door leading into a larger room that we assumed to be a community room because multiple voices were coming from it. The room was filled with chairs, a couch, and a couple of tables, and there were six or seven other young women about our age lounging there. Everyone looked up when we entered the room and openly stared at us, especially at Yoon-ha and me. The Chinese woman gestured at the girls and said, "These women all work here. You will get to know them later." She did not stop, but a couple of the girls smiled at us while a couple looked away as if we were nothing. We continued to follow her out of the room and down the hallway. Finally, at the end of the hall, she took out a key and opened one of the rooms. "This is where the two of you and the baby will stay," she said. "Are these the only clothes you have?" We both nodded at the same time. "OK," she said, "I will deliver two uniforms each to your room later tonight. We will deduct the cost of the clothes from your first paycheck, and you will be responsible for your own laundry. You eat in the kitchen part of the restaurant, and there is no charge for food. As Mr. Wong mentioned, we have no special baby food, so you will be responsible for that. Which one of you will take tomorrow's day shift?"

I promptly spoke up, "I will… I want to be home to put Yoon-ha to bed at night at first, anyway." Su-lin simply nodded and smiled.

"Fine," the woman responded. "You are technically off for the night, so go down and look at the restaurant, get some food, and settle in. Be downstairs and ready to work a little before 10:00 a.m.," she said, looking at me. With that, she was gone, leaving Su-lin and me standing in the tiny room.

I immediately sat down on one of the beds and began to nurse Yoon-ha as I slowly took in the extremely small room. It had two single cots, not true beds at all, but certainly better than sleeping under a tarp on the ground outside or sleeping on a piece of cardboard like I had been doing at the Ting's home. I noted that if we made some space, we could, in time, make a small bed on the floor for Yoon-ha to sleep on once she and I were unable to share the cot. There was also a small spot in the other corner where the few items that we had could be stored, but there were no windows, and the room was not clean and had an odd smell to it.

"While you are working tomorrow, I will clean the place," Su-lin said.

I nodded and said, "I hope the women accept us and are a little nice to us."

"They will," she immediately said, "if only because they will love little Yoon-ha." Then, touching Yoon-ha's cheek, she said gently, "Hurry up, Little One, we are hungry too!"

❧

While eating our simple meal of dumplings and a kind of thin, watery soup, we gazed around the kitchen and looked out at the restaurant a bit. Then we went upstairs, where we hoped to learn more about our new jobs. I walked up to the girl who had seemed friendly and who had been the first to smile at us. "My name is Ha-na Song, and we just got hired here," I said to her in my best Chinese.

She smiled again at me, looked at Yoon-ha, and answered in Korean: "I am Sun-hee Guan." She said, "I hope it works out so you can keep your baby here."

Sun-hee introduced us to her friend, Ah-lee Zhang, and the two of them began talking with Su-lin and me about working and living here at Mr. Wong's restaurant and bar. We learned that the hours were extremely long, especially the night shifts, which frequently lasted well into the night. We stay until the patrons are tired and either pass out or go home, they explained. The food was "OK"—certainly better than starving and the rooms were tolerable. They assured us that we would get used to that "different" smell. The one thing they both warned us about was that "thugs" would occasionally raid the place looking for ethnic Koreans. They explained that those caught were expected to pay them a ransom, or the thugs would turn them over to the police. In turn, the police would be rewarded for catching these "economic migrants," who would be repatriated back to North Korea. We knew that meant we would be beaten, tortured, and starved for being disloyal to "Our Dear Leader," Kim Jong-il. Not only would we be disgraced, but we knew many people did not make it out of these "re-education camps." They went on to explain that all the girls carried a piece of blue cloth in their pockets, and should they hear or suspect that there was going to be a raid by the thugs or by the police, they would take the blue cloth and hang it in a certain spot by the bar. If they were unable to get to the bar spot, they would place the cloth somewhere around their neck area. It was up to us girls to keep glancing at the spot and to never wear blue so as not to give a false warning to the others. Su-lin and I were each given a piece of blue cloth and told that if we saw someone with blue close to their neck or a blue cloth at the bar spot, we should drop everything and run out the closest door and hide. No one wanted to see blue in the establishment. This information horrified both Su-lin and me. I privately wondered how I could reach Yoon-ha should this happen. I made a mental note to discuss this with Su-lin and to come up with a workable plan.

But what they said next frightened us even further! It was true; we were to be waitresses and sing along with the patrons, who were primarily Chinese men who had not yet found wives, but also to be their sex companions! And that was the true nature of the work expected of us. I heard a small gasp from Su-lin when she heard this.

I meekly asked, "What, what do you mean—be a sex companion?"

Ah-lee replied rather dismissively, "Oh, sometimes they want you to do more than just sing along with them. Our job is to do whatever they wish. But that's how we make extra money." She went on playing with Yoon-ha without blinking an eye.

When we went to bed that night, neither Su-lin nor I knew just what we had gotten ourselves into or what to make of our new situation. The only thing I knew for certain was that we had food and a roof over our heads. Tomorrow was a new day, and I was determined to make the most of it. But sometime in the middle of the night, I thought I heard Su-lin softly crying on her cot against the wall. I wanted to believe she was just missing her little boy, and I hugged Yoon-ha closer to me and went to sleep.

CHAPTER 17

✿

At first, working at Mr. Wong's restaurant and karaoke bar was not bad at all. Of course, I had never worked with the general public before, nor had I ever been a waitress, but the work proved not to be all that difficult, especially compared to working on the Tings' farm and putting up with their abuse. It took me no time at all to catch on to the Chinese yuan, how to charge the customers, and how to make change. It was a bit more difficult learning how to get the tables and orders straight and how not to get them mixed up. But the other women were very accepting and helpful to me and showed me little tips and tricks to keep myself straight. I found that many of the patrons spoke Korean or at least understood it enough to order correctly, but I forced myself to speak Chinese after the first two days. I knew that if I were to survive and navigate around China, I must know the language and be able to pass for Chinese as quickly as possible. It was the perfect place to practice Chinese and learn as much as possible. I learned to frequently look at the bar spot to check for the dreaded blue cloth, but thankfully, it never appeared.

One of the best parts was that, on occasion, I could escape upstairs to "go to the bathroom," but really to check on Yoon-ha and Su-lin. Su-lin would need to sleep during the day because, on many evenings, her shifts often lasted well into the night. But the other women loved little Yoon-ha, as she was a novelty, and they helped to look after her, especially when Su-lin was sleeping. They introduced her to her first solid food, congee, which is a thin, watery rice porridge. Rice was so expensive and so difficult to get in North Korea that it and real tea, or any tea made to normal strength, were still treats for me. I'm not sure what I would have been able to provide for Yoon-ha had we been in North Korea, but all the women here loved feeding and playing with her. They sang to her and were teaching her both Chinese and Korean—not that she spoke much at this time. They told me that it would not be long before she would be taking her first steps. I knew I would probably not be there when this happened, but I knew she was in good hands.

Su-lin and I had vowed that we would stay together no matter what. We agreed that I would take the day shift for the first month and get Yoon-ha settled into her new environment. Then we would switch, and Su-lin would take the day shift and I would take the night shift for the next month. I was not looking forward to that as I knew that it would be much harder and longer work. Su-lin and I did not talk much about our work, and because we were working opposite shifts, we rarely had time to be together. When we passed in the halls, we were always in a hurry, but I did note that she seemed a bit thinner and did not smile as much as she once did, or so I thought. I heard her crying many times in the early morning when she finally got off work. I knew she was missing her little boy terribly and thought that was why she was crying. But one morning she cried especially hard, and I asked her about it. "They make you do horrible, nasty things! It is disgusting!" I knew she really hated the work, but how could it possibly be worse than what Mo had done to me nearly every night? I stuffed any thoughts like these down, as I knew Su-lin was desperate to find her parents. I also recognized that it was far better for me than being on the Tings' farm and being abused by my mother-in-law during the day and sexually assaulted by Mo at night. They would have wanted me pregnant with the preferred son by now, and I suspected that they would have found a way to kill little Yoon-ha or any future daughters that I might have until a son was produced. After all, this was the Chinese way, and the wishes and desires of economic migrants like me and our children were not given any status as "people," let alone as citizens. According to the law and without the proper documents, Yoon-ha would not be allowed to go to school, and neither she nor I would be allowed to do so many of the things that Chinese natives could do. These thoughts were always on my mind. I shuttered and vowed to work hard so little Yoon-ha could go to school and have a good life in China. So, I put on a smile, at least outwardly, as I waited on the patrons, and as I got more proficient with the language, I began asking nearly everyone I encountered about Su-lin's parents. Our goal was to locate them if that was possible. As the first month went by and no one had seen or heard of her parents, I began to wonder if her parents had given up trying to locate Su-lin and had made their way to South Korea according to their master plan. This made me more than a little sad for Su-lin. I was also learning a little about the country of South Korea. We had always been taught that we lived in the absolute best country in the world and that Kim Il-sung and then Kim Jong-il were Gods! We were so extremely lucky to have them as our leaders. We also learned that South Korea was the puppet of the evil and horrible United States. I had never heard much about what went on in these countries, much less ever dreamed of going there. Now I occasionally overheard some patrons speak of going to South Korea.

Su-lin had been the first person to speak to me about South Korea or what it was rumored to be like there. She had filled me in on how her parents wanted to get through China and into South Korea, where they felt they could live more comfortably, not have to fight for food, and perhaps even have more economic opportunities. I was beginning to understand that perhaps China was not all that my father had thought it was when he had chosen for us to leave North Korea. I was also becoming aware of the reality of China's limitations. I now listened more intently whenever I heard anyone speak of South Korea and what it offered. I was truly listening and learning all I could. I was beginning to realize that because I loved Su-lin so much, I not only wanted her to find her parents, but I also secretly hoped that she and her family might be able to help me and Yoon-ha as well. I began fantasizing about going to South Korea and sharing their lives there. I understood they would not be able to help me financially, but they would know what to do and the best way to do it, and this would help me work toward my goal of making a better life for my daughter and myself.

❉

And so, the first few months went by. I learned how to do my job effectively and efficiently. I was getting by. Sure, sometimes the patrons were a bit on the wild side, but I was learning how to interact and avoid much of the rowdiness. For me, when a patron wanted "more than just a bit of karaoke," we would do what was expected and go up to a private little room upstairs for a few minutes and take care of "business." Then the patron would go on his way, and I would go back to work downstairs in the bar. I always kept it short and to the point, and truthfully, these little sessions were always so much easier and less painful than any encounter with Mo had been. And I was earning a bit of money for a better life for both my daughter and myself, somewhere, somehow, someday.

On the plus side, the girls there adored little Yoon-ha. Yoon-ha had learned to walk and got around all over the upstairs. She thought of both Su-lin and me as being her mothers. She called both of us "Ma-Ma." But the women had taught her to make a slight difference in how she called us so that when she wanted me, she put in an extra syllable, making it sound more like "Maa Maa" and when she wanted Su-lin, it sounded like "Ma-Ma." We all thought it was very cute. She was growing up happy and healthy with plenty of adults who cared for her and were there to teach her things, answer her questions, and generally make sure she was safe. Life was at least manageable if only we could find Su-lin's parents.

❋

Su-lin and I must have been working at Mr. Wong's bar/restaurant for well over a year when I had my first terrible experience with a patron. While neither Su-lin nor I had heard even one clue about her parents, we both kept asking nearly every new patron who came into the establishment about them. And this is what happened that night. I was working the night shift, and in the early part of the evening, things had gone along pretty much as usual, but when I put forth my inquiry about Su-lin's parents to a new patron, he thought for a bit, then said he thought he knew of "such a fellow." I was all over this new information and, in retrospect, may have given him the wrong signal. We should have quietly gone upstairs and "done the business" in the relative safety of the establishment and continued the discussion about her parents slowly over several visits. But instead, when he suggested that we take a short walk, I did not think of the immediate danger and agreed, thinking I could get more information out of him that evening.

We had not walked more than a couple of blocks when he shoved me into a dark alley, where he began to grope me and tear at my clothes. I was not immediately frightened because, after all, this was the nature of my work. "Hey, Hey!" I said, "Slow down! I will do what you want! Just take it easy!"

But he did not listen to me at all, and he flew into a rage that I could not reason with. He slapped me so hard a couple of times, I saw stars, and my lips were cut. Then, after tearing off my clothes, he raped me in such a vicious manner that I knew I would be sore for a week. He was every bit as brutal and savage as my husband had been. He was done eventually and shoved me aside, and without even throwing me a few yuan, he stomped off. I lay there in the alley in terrible pain, but mostly angry at myself for being so naïve. I was grateful that I would be on the day shift in a day or so where the patrons were much more civil, but I still vowed to not let something like this happen to me ever again. After all, wasn't this part of the reason I left the Tings?

❀

The following week, a dreadful thing happened to one of the young girls working at Mr. Wong's establishment that shook both Su-lin and me to our knees. Ah-lee was one of our first friends there, who had immediately befriended Su-lin and me and who genuinely loved and cared for Yoon-ha. We liked and respected Ah-lee a lot. She had been working the evening shift when a middle-aged patron had come in under disguise, eaten, and then sang a bit with her. He eventually asked her to go upstairs with him for "a bit of business." Once he got Ah-lee alone and away from other waitresses, patrons, and Mr. Wong being able to hear, he told her his real identity and propositioned her. He was the owner of a competing business down the street and told Ah-lee that he would not only pay her more but also claimed he gave his girls better accommodations at his establishment. He wanted her to come work for him and asked her if she had any friends who would be willing to "upgrade themselves" and work for him. She, of course, did not say yes right away but said she would think about his proposition and come look at his place of business the next day. No one knew who it was that saw Ah-lee go into the competing establishment when she went in to check things out, but this news must have gotten back to Mr. Wong. That next evening, Mr. Wong called her into his small office and interrogated her. We could hear Mr. Wong screaming at her. "You cannot just go shopping around for another place to work! Who do you think you are?" We could hear him hitting Ah-lee. All the time, he continued screaming, "You came to China for economic opportunity, and I gave you that opportunity! You belong here and have no right to leave! If you want to leave so much, maybe I should just call the police! They will make sure you leave all right. They will take you back to North Korea, where you will have a cell for accommodations IF they don't kill you first! I am the one who says where you can go and where you work!" He hit her again and again as he continued his rage. "Remember, you are a NOTHING! And I am your boss!" We could hear Ah-lee sobbing and begging for him to stop, but we felt like we were powerless to stop him.

Finally, he stopped hitting her, swung the door open, and stomped out, still screaming. "Now, she will never forget who her boss is." We knew he was using the incident as an excuse to teach us all that we were not free to go or work just anywhere here in China. We all knew without question that he thought of us as his property. And while we had food to eat and a place to stay, we were his private slaves. We rushed in to find Ah-lee unconscious, lying in a pool of blood. Mr. Wong had been careful not to leave marks on her face but had been unmerciful when he hit her stomach, chest, arms, and legs. A couple of the women and I carried her poor, broken body up the stairs and to her room. We washed her wounds with a cool cloth, and in time she regained consciousness. I knew she would never again even think about leaving Mr. Wong's establishment. Su-lin and I got his message loud and clear, and after secretly discussing it, we decided we must take Yoon-ha and leave immediately.

Looking back, I think I was still hurting from my bad encounter with the patron the previous week. And poor Su-lin was so lonely for her little boy (and, in truth, for her husband) that she was not thinking clearly. She had never been treated badly sexually, even though she had been sold into marriage, and this line of work thoroughly disgusted her. She was only here to help me and in the hope that she would soon find her parents.

❀

Four days later, without telling a single person, we separately slipped out of Mr. Wong's restaurant/bar and ran to the establishment down the street, where we were promptly hired. We were *extremely* careful to never again be seen on the street where Mr. Wong's establishment was located or to speak in public to the girls that we had known there. We knew he would be looking for us, so we were extra careful whenever we went out for anything.

We did pretty much the same type of work and worked the same long hours seven days a week, but at least we would not be beaten up by our boss, or so we hoped. As I suspected what might happen, my daughter, Yoon-ha, quickly won over the girls at the new establishment as well. She became something of a little mascot, and they all pampered her to extremes. She loved it. Su-lin continued to be more withdrawn and lost even more weight. I knew she was depressed about not seeing her little boy, but we did not speak about it. Instead, we continued our endless inquiry into the whereabouts of her parents. We had no clues, and Su-lin began to lose hope.

Life moved on until one day some new girls convinced me that Yoon-ha would potty train easier if she were permitted to wear "grown-up" girl's panties instead of diapers. Yoon-ha was old enough to use the toilet, but she needed some new panties to help her make the transition. I knew that if Yoon-ha would use the toilet, it would make life easier for me, so I agreed to give it a try. I would buy the panties as soon as I could.

A couple of days later, Su-lin was down working the day shift, and I slipped out to a store nearby and purchased the panties before I started my evening shift. It was a beautiful day, and I left Yoon-ha with the girls in the community room while I left on the short errand. Su-lin was due up shortly, and I would not be gone long. It was in that store that I first learned the joy of shopping for a little girl. Just touching the items made me feel so good. I hated my life, but I was in an entirely different world when shopping for my little girl. I did not like "doing a little business" with patrons very much and avoided it as much as I could. I did only as much "business" as I needed to do to keep the owner, Mr. Tan, happy and satisfied that I was doing my share. He took eighty percent of all the money we made doing that kind of "business," which was better than the ninety percent that Mr. Wong took, but still, this left precious little for me to buy Yoon-ha's food and a few nice little things for her. Outside of being with Yoon-ha, shopping for her was my favorite thing in the whole world to do, and I went as often as I could.

Su-lin and I worked for Mr. Tan at this second restaurant/bar for over two years. It was not fun doing what we were forced to do, and by now, Su-lin had accepted the fact that her parents were no longer in China. While no one had told her that for certain, she just knew it and withdrew more and more into her private little world. I tried to share with her the trick that I had learned when I had been with my husband, which was how to let my mind wander everywhere and not pay any attention to what the men did to my body. I was there, but I was not there. But for whatever reason, Su-lin never learned how to let her mind escape when doing this humiliating work. I knew she missed her parents, her little boy, and perhaps even her husband and his farm. It was extremely hard for her.

I had accumulated a bit of money and wanted to buy Yoon-ha a new pair of shoes, so of course, I wanted to go to my favorite little store for them. As usual, the best time for me to leave the bar was late in the afternoon before starting my scheduled evening shift. Su-lin and I still worked opposite shifts, and she would be off work and up to the community room to watch over Yoon-ha for me shortly. Some of the women were playing with Yoon-ha in the lounge, so they agreed to watch over her while I dashed over to the store. I would be right back, I assured them. Almost as soon as I left, a fire broke out in the bar/restaurant and quickly spread throughout the building. They thought it started in the kitchen, but no one knew exactly what happened. Su-lin, a few waitresses, and most of the patrons were able to escape because they were on the bottom floor. However, Su-lin was unable to get upstairs to rescue my precious Yoon-ha. The entire staircase had been engulfed in smoke and fire in just minutes.

I saw the fire and smelled the smoke almost immediately after I left the store. My stomach did a complete flip-flop, and I knew I had run the total distance to the bar screaming at the top of my lungs. I was absolutely panicked and wanted only to know that my little girl was safe! It was the most horrible feeling! When I reached the bar, I was running full speed inside when Su-lin, all blackened and wet with tears, tackled me and held me down. She was crying almost uncontrollably as she hugged me, gasped, and spat out the very words I did not want to hear. Yoon-ha was on the second floor, and no one had survived the fire that had been on the second floor! My baby was gone! We sat there on the street for the longest time, oblivious to anyone else, and just rocked and cried huge sobs and wails at the loss of our baby! I suppose we were persuaded to move away from the building in due time, but I honestly do not know when or where we were taken. I just knew I could hardly get my breath, and the deep sense of loss was overwhelming. I just wanted to die.

That extreme sense of deep loss and grief was still with me the next morning, and I do not know how I got through those early morning hours that next day. Su-lin was still in her blackened clothes and in the same state of grief and mourning as I was, but I know she also felt another layer of feelings, and that was guilt. We had pledged that we would always be there for little Yoon-ha and always save her, and now Su-lin felt she had let down both Yoon-ha and me. We were both inconsolable.

CHAPTER 18

Time made no sense to Su-lin or me, and we walked and walked, but where or for what reason, I do not know. We just knew that our world was gone. Finally, exhausted, we collapsed in the shade of some stairs leading up to a building on a street not far from the restaurant/bar that was still smoldering. I have no idea how long we were there, but I must have finally fallen into a completely drained and fatigued sleep.

The next thing I knew, I heard the voice of my little daughter excitedly cry out, "Maa Maa!" And then, "Ma-Ma!" I inhaled deeply, smelling that ever-present odor of the burning building, which oriented me to the present and to the painful fact that my little daughter had died in a terrible fire. I know I groaned. Then I heard her again, "Maa Maa!" which was followed by "Ma-Ma!" I thought I was dreaming, but I wanted to continue the dream. At least I was seeing and hearing Yoon-ha, which was better than facing my reality. I was in so much pain!

The next thing, I felt something thunder into my body and try to crawl into my lap. It was not easy because I was curled in the fetal position, but the thing just kept coming. Reluctantly, I shifted from my position and slowly accepted the fact that I could not continue my dream any longer. I took another breath, really a kind of snort of resignation, I guess, when I sniffed what I thought was my daughter's special smell! This immediately woke me up and brought me to my senses when I saw Yoon-ha in my lap! I let out such a hoot and an ecstatic holler that they must have heard me several blocks away! I could not believe my eyes! I grabbed her little body and crushed her to me, rocking back and forth in pure, unadulterated joy. This noise, of course, woke Su-lin up, and soon she had joined Yoon-ha and me in a group hug with unabashed shouts of sheer happiness.

In due time, Sun-hee caught up to us, and we all again did a group hug complete with hoops of joy and more than a few tears. We had believed that she, too, had perished in the fire. "How?" I finally managed to ask her. "How did you get out?"

Sun-hee sat down beside us and told us the magical story of how little Yoon-ha had wanted to go outside to play. She had begged and begged Sun-hee until Sun-hee thought, "Well, why not? It is a beautiful day, and we do not have to stay long. Maybe she will sleep better tonight if we go outside for a little while in the sunshine." So, they quietly crept down the staircase and disappeared outside. They had been gone when the fire erupted. The old building had been made almost entirely of wood, and the fire had spread very quickly, trapping all those upstairs.

Later, Sun-hee explained that she did not know where I had disappeared to, or even where she should go or what to do with Yoon-ha. She has no family and no support in China, she said. She could not believe Yoon-ha and her good fortune in not dying in the fire. It was a miracle, she exclaimed. They had spent the night looking for either Su-lin or myself. They had no plans, and she was so glad to find us both alive and well. We spent the rest of the early evening just basking in our good fortune and the miracle that had been given to those of us sitting there. I still cannot believe how I went from the depths of all that agony to the heights of the joy I felt in such a short time. I am still so grateful to the universe for the miracle that day.

None of the women who worked for either Mr. Wong or Mr. Tan kept what little money they managed to save in their rooms or on themselves. To do so was simply too risky, so like them, I had hidden what few yuan I had managed to save in a small sock buried under a rock down by the river wall. At least it, too, had not gone up in smoke. Su-lin had proven to be awful at saving any yuan at all. We had often joked about this, but since she was not having to pay for a child and all her other expenses were paid, what was it hurting? Only now could we have used it big time! Sun-hee proudly gave me her small stash of yuan.

This is all the money we had as a group, and no one had a job. Taking some money I had on me, we bought a little rice to settle our rumbling stomachs, then we huddled together under a nearby tree for the night. It was cold, and we needed to get some rest before deciding what to do and where to go tomorrow. Little did any of us know just how rough this next stretch of time would be for us all.

CHAPTER 19

❀

The next morning, when the sunlight shone through the trees and began to warm us up, we all felt better by a large measure. We sat there looking at each other, talking about how fortunate we all were, how sad we were, and how much we missed our friends, the girls who were trapped upstairs yesterday. But the big question hung over us, and that was just what we should do and where we should go. We all agreed that it would be useless to go back to find Mr. Tan, as he had no jobs to offer us and we were certain he would not help us in any way even if he could.

"Let's just walk for a little, and something will come to us," I suggested. So, the small group gathered our meager possessions, and we all walked. "Now walk like we are Chinese, look like we have a purpose, and observe everything," I advised. "Perhaps that way, an idea will come to one of us." Looking back, though, I do not know how much we each were searching for the solution as much as we were watching for the police or anybody who might guess what we were really doing and who might turn us over to the authorities. It was harrowing.

And walk we did for nearly a week. We were not going in any specific direction other than staying away from Mr. Wong's old street. At night, we would huddle together for warmth under a tree or in the shadow and protection of some stairs. We would put little Yoon-ha in the middle of us, trying to keep her warm. It was cold and miserable, and we ate very little. I knew we could not continue this way for long and that we needed to come up with a better plan.

All this walking and observing gave me a chance to think a lot about my situation. I walked along, thinking that it had now been over five and a half long years since Father had taken me from our home in North Korea. I was now over twenty years old and a grown woman. I surmised that I would have been married by now and perhaps had a child or even two if we stayed in North Korea. That is if I had not starved to death like Mother or left like I was sure Chang-hee had done. That would have been a real possibility. As for Father, I could not even think of where he would have been or what he would have done. In truth, I do not think I cared enough to even think about Father anymore. When he sold me to Yun Ting all those years ago, I knew by the way he never looked back at me when I called him that he was glad that I was gone.

My mind jumped to Yun and her son Mo. Oh, what despicable people they were! I hoped never to see or hear from either of them or even from Fong, who, in my mind, never actually beat me but who had been clear that he did not think much of me either. I had been their slave! Even though I was now essentially a prostitute, I was glad I had gotten away from them and that I had my precious daughter with me. I was certain Yun would have killed Yoon-ha sooner or later, and she might have even killed me as well. No, as bad as all this was, I was happy to be free of "married life."

At night, we would talk. I should say that Sun-hee and I talked because Su-lin was mostly quiet and just stared off into space. Of course, we discussed the idea that we could try finding jobs as waitresses at another bar/restaurant there in the Yanbian Korean Autonomous Prefecture, even if it were not here in the capital city. Sun-hee was leaning towards this option. She pointed out that none of us had skills in any other area, and even if we did, none of us had the necessary documents to get jobs. She stated, "These last nights are an example of what we can look forward to in our future without jobs. I, for one, was darn cold last night and not at all comfortable. We can live and hide on the streets, but our money will run out soon, and then what will we do for food? People are mean here, and someone will turn us in to thugs or the police. Do any of you think life would be easier in a North Korean camp?" She then looked directly at me and asked, "And what about little Yoon-ha? How long do you think they will keep her alive there?"

I avoided her eyes and looked over at Su-lin, who not only had shrunk back against the tree but looked like she did not know whether to vomit or cry. It was then that I realized how small, how thin, and just how sick my friend had become. She began rocking back and forth while curled up in a fetal position. She looked totally defeated and was visibly upset by the mere thought of going back to work in a bar. But it was the thought of something happening to Yoon-ha that tore me apart the most. How well I remembered the pain I was in just a few days ago when I thought she had died in the fire. There was no way I would ever let such a thing happen to her again, and to think of soldiers starving, raping, and torturing her was just more than I could bear. We just had to think of a better option.

It was then that I remembered how happy Su-lin, Yoon-ha, and I had been when we had lived and traveled in the mountains. "Why couldn't we just all go live in the mountains? We always found plenty of food." I asked. Both Sun-hee and Su-lin gave me a look that showed their total loathing for the idea. We did not even need to discuss that idea further.

"Well then," I continued, "let's brainstorm every single person any one of us knows who might be in a position to help us. If we don't come up with anyone, perhaps we should just begin knocking on doors and asking for help."

"Going around like that and asking for jobs or help is extremely dangerous!" Sun-Hee replied, "Someone will turn us in for sure. I don't want to risk it."

All this time, Su-lin had not said a word. She just kept staring down at the ground and rocking back and forth. I knew she was close to the breaking point. What could we do? I briefly thought about Father and wondered at that point if he could ever have envisioned what I would be going through when he sold me a little over five and a half years ago. Would he have cared? I admit that at that moment, I felt nothing but pure hatred for him.

Then Sun-hee came up with a brilliant suggestion. She started timidly, "I do have an uncle who lives not too far from here on the outskirts of Yanji who owns a medium-sized hotel. Maybe we could go there and ask him for jobs as cleaning ladies. He is always looking for help, I guess."

"Of course, that is a great idea!" I was nearly shouting, "Why didn't you suggest this before?"

"Because he is not really my uncle," she replied, lowering her gaze at me. "You know how all Chinese and Koreans call people aunt and uncle? And he is kind of creepy."

I heard Su-lin give out a groan, but she did not look up or stop rocking.

CHAPTER 20

❁

"That's it! Let's go, Su-lin!" I jumped up and started gathering Yoon-ha and our possessions together. I could not help it, but suddenly I had a new enthusiasm for life itself. "Can we get there by nightfall?" I asked Sun-hee.

"I suppose," she said tentatively. She rose slowly and put her hand out to nudge and help Su-lin to her feet.

"Great! Which direction is it?" I was ready to be on my way, and somehow I just felt that this was not only an excellent option for us but was the *only* option we had. This small group was becoming worn down, and I hoped that this new direction in life would get us on not only a better path but also a happier path. I wanted to get Su-lin there and settled in before she completely fell apart. I really did not know what else to do.

Sun-hee took the lead and started walking in the new direction. I followed, grasping Yoon-ha's little hand, and started singing a Chinese song that I learned in the bar and that I knew Yoon-ha would know. Yoon-ha grabbed Su-lin's hand, and together we skipped along on the sidewalk singing. Pretty soon, both Su-lin and Sun-hee were actively singing with us. This seemed to lighten the mood, and we began to cover the distance to the hotel.

Our tired, small, ragtag group reached the hotel by late afternoon. Sun-hee seemed to walk slower the closer we got to the hotel. Finally, we saw several hotels grouped together in the distance, but I had no idea which hotel Sun-hee's uncle owned. She abruptly stopped, and we stopped with her, waiting for her to speak. She gestured to the largest of the hotels and said in a small voice, "This is his hotel, but I don't want to go in. I don't want to work for him or clean rooms."

"What?" I said incredulously, "We walked all this way!"

"I know, I know." She continued, "I brought you here because this is what you wanted, but I want to go back into town and work somewhere as a waitress." She slowly looked at each of us, waiting for our response. "I don't like cleaning."

No one moved or spoke a word. I did not know what to think or say. Sun-hee's behavior was unbelievable and completely unexpected. "Ah well…." I was searching for what to say. "Well, maybe you could introduce us and perhaps… perhaps put in a good word for us," I finally managed. I looked at her in my most pleading way.

"Ah, sure," she hesitated and let the words hang in the air. "Sure—of course." She concluded. She continued to hesitate for just a few seconds more, and then she straightened her dress and ran a small hand through her hair. Sun-hee straightened her back and stepped up to open the door. She walked up to the front desk, followed by the three of us.

"Are you looking for a room?" the Chinese man at the desk asked, looking at our group. "I only have a single room left."

"Ah no," Sun-hee said, "we have come to ask my uncle for jobs as cleaning ladies." She smiled, then lowered her eyes in a most respectful manner and waited.

In time, an ugly, short, pudgy Chinese man came out to greet the four of us. He glanced at Su-lin and me but made a face at Yoon-ha. I could tell he was not too fond of children. But it was Sun-hee that he looked at the longest and hardest. He smiled at her, but in a way that was almost like he was smacking his lips and rubbing his hands together at the same time. He looked like he could not wait to ravish her in bed. I wondered if he had ever abused poor Sun-hee and if that was why she did not want to work for him. Sun-hee did not miss any of this, and I thought she even shuddered a bit before she quickly introduced us. She told us his name was Mr. Un and told him that we were looking for jobs as cleaning ladies. He never took his eyes off her and even looked as if he were undressing her in his mind. Having made the introduction, Sun-hee then moved towards the door, saying she had to get back to her job, and without even saying goodbye to any of us, she was gone. Of course, she had lied—she had no job, but clearly, she needed to escape this man. I could not blame her. Maybe I would have done the same thing. Without saying anything aloud, I wished Sun-hee well.

I moved closer to Mr. Un and asked him if he had any jobs available. He did not answer right away but continued to look at the door through which Sun-hee had disappeared. Finally, he nodded.

The work at the hotel did not prove to be hard at all. Certainly, it was much easier than any of the farm work I had done at the Tings. And I liked it much better than working in bars or restaurants. While we did not make much money, I did not have to please the patrons constantly or go upstairs for "a little business." What a relief that was! I decided that this "sex thing" was totally overrated, and I did not care if I was ever with another man "that way." All three of us shared one of the guest rooms and ate our meals in the small restaurant connected to the hotel. While the food was only passable, we knew we were safe and believed we would not get beaten. We did not actually see Mr. Un much. He always seemed to be busy, and he did not pay much attention to us or even to Yoon-ha. He simply wanted us to make sure all the rooms were cleaned on schedule and that Yoon-ha did not disturb the guests. We did suspect that he drank a lot in the evenings and spent a great deal of time gambling, but given that he did not bother us, we did not care.

My baby was no longer a baby. Yoon-ha was now over four years old, and I did not have to constantly watch her as I did when she was an infant. I knew she missed Sun-hee and several of the other women, especially as I watched her play with the doll Su-lin had made her out of rags. I missed all the girls too and was deeply saddened at how so many of them perished, but at least Yoon-ha still had both her "Maa Maa" and her "Ma-Ma." She had plenty of room to play outside and in the hallways while both Su-lin and I cleaned the guest rooms. Su-lin and I both had blue cloths, and we hung them outside of whichever room we were cleaning at the moment. We taught Yoon-ha that seeing a blue cloth meant we were in that room and that she could quietly enter the room if she needed us for anything. It was our secret way of messaging where we were always at. She seemed to get a big kick out of our secret.

Su-lin seemed to perk up a bit and even began to gain some weight back. She had a better color in her cheeks and played with Yoon-ha a lot. I never grew tired of Su-lin telling me the storylines of some of her favorite books. Under the leadership of the Kims, North Korea always censored the books people were permitted to read. However, stories that took place in dictatorships or communist countries were sometimes allowed. Su-lin had been raised in a wealthier family than mine and had access to books I had never heard of, including stories about the Russian czars. Her favorite story was about Sophia Alekseyevna and her half-brother, "Peter the Great." Sophia was a powerful and strong woman who, in effect, ran Russia after her father died in 1682 until 1689, when her younger brother, Peter the Great, grew up and took over. Su-lin confided that if she ever had a daughter, she would call her Sophia, even if it were only her nickname. Su-lin no longer mentioned her parents, her son, or her previous life on the farm. Outwardly, she seemed to have begun to accept her life as it was now in China. I knew I was much happier than I had been in many years. It was a joy to watch Yoon-ha grow and develop, and I somehow achieved some peace knowing we had a home and plenty to eat. I sometimes thought about Mother and Chang-hee and our life back in North Korea, but then I recognized that was all in the past and that I now had a new life. I thought we would all remain like this for many years.

CHAPTER 21

✤

And so, the months passed. We had been at the hotel for about six months when there was a soft rap on our door one night. At first, we did not pay much attention. We were playing cards—it was a simple game and one that even little Yoon-ha could play and understand. Then the rapping became more insistent. I glanced at Su-lin and she was looking at me. We never had visitors! Who could it be?

"Hide!" I whispered to Yoon-ha, "Go hide in the bathroom! Now, Yoon-ha!" She looked at me, her eyes as big as saucers, but she immediately ran into the bathroom and softly closed the door. Rising out of her chair, Su-lin scattered the cards across the table so no one would know how many people were in the room playing, and she grabbed a broom that was standing in the corner. She nodded at me, and I slowly moved to open the door. We were both scared, and she stayed a few steps behind me, half hiding the broom. I slowly cracked the door and saw a small bloody hand on the door jamb. Almost instantly, the door was pushed open, and a woman's body fell inside the room. I heard Su-lin gasp, and

I quickly looked outside to see if there was anyone else out there. Seeing no one, we quickly moved the little body completely into the room, and I closed the door.

The woman moaned and tried to move as we turned her over to look at her. Then both Su-lin and I both screamed as we recognized the battered body of our friend Sun-hee Guan. She was covered in blood, and the left side of her face was smashed. Her jaw was hanging at an odd angle, and her eye was pushed back into her skull. Her right arm was broken, and I suspected that she had several broken ribs as well. A huge gash on her leg was bleeding profusely. She was gasping for breath. How she got to the hotel or found our room, we did not know. Su-lin ran to the bathroom and retrieved some cold, wet towels. I heard her tell Yoon-ha to stay in the bathroom.

I pushed Sun-hee's hair back off her forehead and saw that she had a deep wound on her scalp as well. We gave her a sip of water and helped her sit up a bit, so she could breathe easier. We thought she was dying. We did not know, but we had never seen anyone so severely injured. We really did not know what to do.

"Did your uncle, Mr. Un, do this to you?" I blurted out. I could feel the rage welling up inside me. But it was more than just rage. I was frightened for the three of us if it was her uncle. We just might all be in real danger if it was.

"No," she managed to get out. "It was my pimp."

"Your pimp?" I asked. I looked at Su-lin and repeated the word pimp. I had never heard the word. Neither of us knew who or what a pimp was.

"The bar owner." Sun-hee spit out. It was so extremely hard for her to talk that we told her not to say anything more and encouraged her to do nothing but rest. She closed her good eye and slumped back onto the pillows. We took advantage of Sun-hee being unconscious and cleaned her wounds the best we could. Su-lin took the bloody towels and disposed of them, bringing back a heap of clean ones. We got her situated the best we could on the bed and stopped her wounds from bleeding by putting clean, wet towels on them and by applying as much pressure as we dared. We found two relatively straight sticks and straightened her arm, then bound it into a makeshift splint using torn strips of a sheet. We were amazed that she only groaned while doing all of this; we thought she would be fighting us. The fact that she remained out during this time worried us a great deal.

All the time we were doing this, Su-lin and I were trying to figure out if we knew anyone who could help us. We knew Sun-hee should go to a hospital, but we were afraid that the hospital personnel would then learn that she was Korean and report her to the police, who would then repatriate her back to North Korea. We all knew that meant she would die for sure, as the North Koreans would not medically treat anyone who would have disgraced the country, especially Kim Jong-il, by leaving that wonderful country. They would most likely starve and beat her to death. And, of course, they would link her to us and possibly report us as well. It was not a good situation, and I was sick with worry.

Su-lin and I could not think of anyone who could help us at all. The only thing we could think of was that as soon as it was light, Su-lin would slip out and go up into the mountains looking for some herbs for pain and healing. The plan was for her to leave before light and be back as quickly as possible for two reasons. The first was that Sun-hee would be in terrible pain by then, and secondly, Su-lin would need to be back at work, as I could not do both her work and mine, and Mr. Un would think she was lazy or gone. We wanted nothing to look suspicious, and we did not want to lose our jobs.

All this time, Yoon-ha sat quietly, not saying a word. She had this awful, sick, scared look on her little face, especially when she looked at the blood. When I noticed this, we tried to make light of it and worked her into our plan. "Maa Maa is going to need you to help me tomorrow," I told her. She looked up at me with her big brown eyes, which now looked even bigger and more scared. She even drew back slightly but continued to stare at me as she asked in a tiny little voice, "Doing what, Maa Maa?"

"Well, I need you to be Sun-hee's nurse and give her water or some congee that I will make and leave for you to give her. She might even need some help to go to the bathroom. I will also need you to keep a watch out for Mr. Un, and if he starts to get close to this room or the room where I am working, I need you to step outside and sing our Chinese song as loudly as you can. Do you think you can be a big girl and do those two things to help us all tomorrow?"

A big smile crossed her face, and she responded, "Yes, Maa Maa."

"Good," I said, "I will leave the blue cloth on the door handle of the room that I am cleaning each time as I usually do. I want you to come and tell me how Sun-hee is doing every so often. That will be a big help to Maa Maa." I smiled at her and knew we had sealed the deal. She was such a good little girl, and I had no doubt she would do her best tomorrow.

The next day went exactly as we planned. Su-lin left before dawn, and little Yoon-ha was a real trooper as she ran errands for me and tended to Sun-hee. I worked as fast as I could and, in truth, only cleaned half as well as I should have, but I was trying to go twice as fast as usual. The only bad part that morning was that Sun-hee was in so much pain that she was in and out of consciousness, which was good for her but scared Yoon-ha.

Yoon-ha would come calling for me every time Sun-hee did not answer her. I tried to explain that Sun-hee was simply sleeping, but Yoon-ha knew better and said, "But Maa Maa, she doesn't answer me when I touch her and rub her good arm."

"Well, she needs her sleep, so let her be," I said. I tried not to show my real worries and just hoped Su-lin would be able to find the right herbs and get back soon. Then I tried to distract Yoon-ha for a few minutes by having her do some small but helpful things for me. I sure hoped we would be successful in both keeping Sun-hee hidden and getting her through her recovery. The stakes were high.

❋

Really in no time at all, Su-lin was back. She first slipped into our shared room and gave Sun-hee something for pain, then unwrapped all her open wounds and sprinkled some herbs on them to fight infection. Su-lin then applied fresh bandages and towels to Sun-hee's wounds. When she left, Sun-hee was more comfortable and was sleeping quite soundly. She then made haste looking for the blue cloth and came in to give me a report.

"I've met someone," she whispered.

Great, I thought! Here I am, worried sick, hiding a girl who desperately needs medical help while working at twice my normal speed, trying to keep everything together, and she wants to tell me about someone she met who has swept her off her feet. This was crazy. "Well, tell me later, girl." I replied a bit curtly, "We are behind on our work, and I don't want Mr. Un getting angry or worse at us. You can tell me when we stop shortly for lunch. OK?"

"Yes, sure," she meekly replied, shot me a "what's wrong with you look," and left to clean the next room over.

When we finally took a short break for lunch, we gathered back in our room for a few minutes so Su-lin could check on Sun-hee. "So, who is the guy?" I asked, only half interested.

"Oh, it isn't a guy," Su-lin enthusiastically replied. She hurried on, "It was a lady working as a nurse or missionary or something, helping Korean women. She was in the mountains, gathering herbs because they don't always have enough pain meds for their patients. I told her that we are hiding a Korean girl who needs urgent medical help, but we are afraid to take her to the hospital. I talked to her for a while, and she is willing to help us!" She frantically looked over at Sun-hee, who was, in truth, going downhill. She was not conscious, and her breathing was quite shallow. We thought she had some broken ribs but, of course, did not know for sure.

"Why didn't you say so?" I screamed at her so loudly that it startled both Su-lin and Yoon-ha. "We need to get her now!"

"I know, I know! Su-lin answered. She promised she would come to our room as soon as possible this afternoon. She told me, in the meantime, to keep Sun-hee's wounds clean and make her as comfortable as possible. She gave me some stronger herbs that I didn't know about." She pulled them from her pocket and said, "She instructed me to give them to her as soon as she wakes up and complains of pain."

I breathed a huge sigh of relief. Just knowing help was coming took a big burden off my shoulders. I looked at poor Sun-hee and willed her to live. "Pull through, my dear friend, and get well," I kept repeating over and over in my mind. At this moment, we all had our doubts. Little Yoon-ha sat holding Sun-hee's hand with a worried look of not quite understanding what was going on written all over her tiny face.

It seemed like an eternity before the nurse or missionary (we did not know what she was really) arrived. She just represented the help we so desperately needed. Yoon-ha saw her first coming across the lot and squealed, "I think she is here!" At that point, Yoon-ha ran out of the room, looking for the blue cloth hanging on a room door. She found me, and I told her to go to the lady and ask her if she was the missionary and if she was to take her to our room. I told her I would be there shortly, and doubled my speed, trying to finish the last room for the day and put the cleaning supplies away.

By the time Su-lin and I arrived in the room, the woman had a genuine look of concern on her face and was bending over Sun-hee. I knew immediately that it was not good and that we might lose our friend. She indeed had several broken ribs, and with our help, the woman wrapped the torn sheet around Sun-hee's chest. She had a severe wound to her head and a broken arm. The lady checked the splint that we had put on Sun-hee's arm and announced that we had done a surprisingly good job. But that was not her main worry, she said. She explained that she would be concerned if some clear liquid should seep from Sun-hee's head wound or nose. If we saw the liquid, she thought for sure that Sun-hee would die. We were confused. I never knew people bled clear fluid; I always thought blood was red and knew it would be dangerous for a person to lose too much of the red fluid, but what was this clear stuff?

The lady said she did not have time to explain all of this to us at this moment, but she directed us to try to get Sun-hee to drink fluids and to get her up to go to the bathroom. She further instructed us to have her cough or laugh several times a day and gave us a powder to sprinkle on her wounds. She then gave Sun-hee a shot, but Sun-hee did not flinch, which worried Su-lin and me. We did not know at the time if this lady was a nurse or a missionary, but we took her instructions to heart and agreed to do everything she said. She then gave us a card and told us to come to a certain building in Yanji if we had questions about Sun-hee or if we were interested in learning about Jesus. Even with our limited reading skills in Chinese, we could tell the lady was a doctor whose main job was working at the university. We did not know why she was working outside of the university or if she was gathering herbs to help people like us. But were we ever grateful for her help! What we did not know was anything about this "Jesus."

The only thing we knew about Jesus was that he was associated with the hated Americans and that "talking Jesus" was not allowed in North Korea. We knew that we could go to prison for "talking Jesus" or talking to South Koreans or Americans. But this lady had helped us, and we were in China. Was it prohibited in China? Su-lin and I both hoped that we would not need her services anymore and that Sun-hee would recover. Boy, were we ever going to follow her instructions! Little Yoon-ha became Sun-hee's private nurse and worked hard to get her to laugh, and ran for everything Sun-hee wanted until she was able to retrieve a glass of water herself, and so on.

CHAPTER 22

❀

It took Sun-hee about two-and-a-half months to recover from her ghastly injuries. We made her wear her splint until we learned that she was secretly taking it off part of the time. She began to breathe easier and was able to move around on her own, and her pain was much less, but she continued to have awful headaches. Luckily, we never did see the dreaded clear fluid coming from her head wound or her nose. Every time we looked at her, we were always checking and watching for the clear fluid. Only once in all that time did we think we saw any trace of it. We all panicked, but it turned out that a washcloth had not been wrung out fully and dripped down her face. She was also able to dodge any trace of infection. What a relief!

All this time, we kept Sun-hee hidden in our room, and she slept on my bed while I slept on the floor with Yoon-ha. Yoon-ha grew up a great deal during this time. She was now over four and a half years old and was proving to be a great little nurse and mommy's helper. When Sun-hee was feeling well on her better days, she began teaching Yoon-ha how to speak and write Korean and even started teaching her numbers. Sun-hee and Yoon-ha spoke Korean to each other, but Yoon-ha knew she must always speak Chinese with everyone else. After all, we wanted her to blend in well with the Chinese and for no one to guess she was the child of an "economic migrant." Both Su-lin and I hoped that perhaps she could pass for a Chinese girl one day and be allowed the privileges that Chinese girls were given. We knew it might be that Yoon-ha would never be allowed to attend school, and these intermittent lessons were invaluable to her. In the meantime, she worked hard, and I loved her and was extremely proud of her.

Sun-hee knew we were not making much money working at the hotel and that we were paying for her meals. This bothered her a great deal, and she was anxious to leave. In truth, we did not know if it was because she felt she was a burden or if, down under, she always carried the fear that "her uncle" would find her there. At any rate, she stayed quietly in that small room. I understood how much she wanted to leave.

And so, one evening, she brought up the fact that she wanted to leave. "But where will you go? What will you do?" I blurted out.

She smiled slowly and said, "Why back to work in the city, of course! I have thought it all out, and I believe I am well enough to carry meals and drinks. I will not go back to work for my old boss. He probably thinks I died anyway. But I plan to go to the other side of town, and I will change my name." She flipped her hair a bit and, with her uninjured arm and hand, pulled a lock of hair over her injured eye and continued. "I have already changed my hair and the rest of my scars have healed nicely. I think I am ready to go. Besides, I need the money for a few things."

Yoon-ha began to cry, "But we won't see you anymore, Sun-hee! I don't want you to go!"

"Yes, but I have a plan." She said it matter-of-factly. We just stared at her, waiting for her to explain.

"I need to go thank the lady doctor who came to help me here—the one who helps to run a church or underground or whatever that helps Koreans here in China." She rushed to continue, "We all could meet and see each other there at the meeting place. I am sure we could learn a lot from them. I think we should all go."

Meanwhile, Yoon-ha continued to cry softly. There was a long pause where no one said anything as we let what she had just said sink in a little. Finally, Su-lin spoke up, "We could be punished for talking Jesus."

"No," Sun-hee replied emphatically, "we are in China and should use all the help we can find!" Again, she paused.

And so, it was that a few days later, Sun-hee left and went back to the work she knew best. No one had set a date to see each other, and Su-lin and I were left pondering this horrendous and risky new step.

CHAPTER 23

✺

I moved back to sleeping in my own bed, and Su-lin and I continued working at the hotel. Yoon-ha, of course, missed Sun-hee immensely, but no one spoke about going to see her in the city. Life gradually fell back into the pattern that it had been in before Sun-hee visited us. We still rarely saw Mr. Un who was nearly always gambling or drinking in his office. He always left our meager wages at the front desk and did not say much to us if we completed the required work. The truth was, we were nearly always exhausted at the end of the day, and heading back to our room was a pleasure. That is how most of the summer passed until one day in mid-September 2008, when something happened that changed our lives forever.

Two young, loud Chinese men had checked into the hotel a few doors down from our room. While taking their luggage into their room, they must have spotted Su-lin ducking into our room at the end of our long day. Later that night, after she had taken the garbage down the hall-way, the men came out from behind a pillar, clamped their hands over her mouth, and dragged her into their room. They ripped her clothes off and took turns raping her repeatedly. They beat her when she fought them, and thankfully, she was unconscious for most of her ordeal. When they grew bored with her and Yoon-ha and I had gone looking for her, their door suddenly opened, and they shoved her out into the hallway, throwing her torn clothes after her. When they saw us standing there, one of them shouted, "You should be happy it wasn't your daughter! If you tell anyone, we will turn you in to the police. You should not be in our country! Go home!"

Su-lin had landed in a heap, sobbing. Yoon-ha and I somehow managed to get her into our room. We were all shaking uncontrollably, but Su-lin was bleeding from "down there" and crying hysterically. It was not pretty. She had two black eyes, her lips were cut, and they had punched her all over her body. We cleaned her up, and she finally did stop bleeding, but she cried uncontrollably all night no matter what we said to comfort her. Yoon-ha crawled into bed with her and held her for hours as she cried and cried.

The next day she was sore and stiff all over and could hardly move, but that was not the worst of it. That incident had completely broken Su-lin. She stopped talking and would not eat, and I think she just wanted to die. With a lot of cajoling, Yoon-ha could get her to drink and then eat congee, a thin, watery porridge, but nothing else. She cried for hours on end. Her behavior went on day after day, during which time Yoon-ha and I were at our wit's end. I, of course, was out doing my own and her share of cleaning. We needed every bit of money just to get by. The first time poor Su-lin went to the bathroom, she gave out a long, painful mournful wail that I will remember for the rest of my days.

All this went on for a couple of weeks, when one morning, Su-lin stopped crying and announced that she could take it no more. "I am going back to the farm," she said. "They were kinder to me there. My husband did not beat me, and I miss my little boy."

"Oh, Su-lin!" I cried out in disbelief.

"It's just too hard here!" she moaned and started to cry again.

CHAPTER 24

I was able to calm Su-lin down, and she agreed to stay for a couple more weeks while she healed more and could prepare for the journey properly. I was heartbroken and scared at the thought of losing my best friend. How would I survive financially? I pushed those thoughts down when Su-lin confided in me one day, "I am going to the bathroom out of the wrong hole." It was clear she was embarrassed. I knew they had really messed her up down there. But what did this mean, and what could we do?

Then it hit me: we could go see the lady doctor who had helped us when Sun-hee had been hurt, and while we were at it, we could find and visit Sun-hee. The lady doctor could help Su-lin, AND she would surely know where Sun-hee was working! It lifted my spirits just thinking about it.

When I brought up the subject, Su-lin's face visibly brightened because she had not thought of it either. "I hurt down there all the time," she admitted. "And it smells too." I knew that this was a good decision, and I hoped there was a cure for Su-lin. Life was just not fair sometimes.

The next day, Yoon-ha and Su-lin helped as much as they could, but getting the rooms cleaned quickly was quite a push. Immediately after we completed the cleaning, we hustled downtown to search for the lady doctor. "Where is this place?" I asked Su-lin as she was trotting us along.

"I think it is in the back of a warehouse, not far from where we used to work. It is not a church building or anything but more like a meeting place where religious volunteers and people who want to help Koreans meet. The lady doctor volunteers there. It should have a tiny cross somewhere on the building."

"What is a cross?" I asked.

"It is a sign," she said as she made a T with her two fingers. "An old Chinese woman who was looking for herbs told me it is a sign of safety. That's about all I know." So, we all hurried on with a great deal of hope but not much knowledge of what we were getting into or what we would find. I just knew we needed some help for Su-lin.

Su-lin saw the building way before either Yoon-ha or I did and hurried ahead of us. She probably wanted to explain a few things in private, I thought. When Yoon-ha and I got there, there was no one in the room except Su-lin, who turned to us and told us, "She just left. But they thought they could catch her and that she might come back."

I breathed out a sigh of relief and just looked around while we waited. The place had a few chairs, a few blankets on the floor, and not a lot else in the room, but it did look reasonably clean. There were a couple of doors leading off this main room. One of the doors opened after a few minutes, and the doctor and a young girl entered. The doctor walked over to the other door and motioned for us to follow. The young girl stopped Yoon-ha and me and told us that the doctor should see the patient, meaning Su-lin, alone first. We could wait here.

It seemed like a long time before Su-lin and the doctor came out of the room. Su-lin looked very anxious—or was she in pain? I could not tell. The doctor walked over to the young girl and spoke with her for a couple of minutes, then came over to us. "She has been severely injured and now has an infection. She needs some gynecological surgery. I can do it tomorrow. Can you bring her back? If not, we will have to wait until I return in a month or so, and that would not be good for her."

Without even conferring with Su-lin, I nodded and said, "Yes, what time do you need her?"

"As early as possible." She continued, "She will need to stay here for a few days. Will that work for you?"

"Here?" I asked and gestured to the room. I clearly did not understand.

"She will have the surgery here but stay in a house not far from here—just for a few days. Then she will need some other place to stay for a while where she can rest." I nodded numbly. I did not know what to say. I had no idea it would be so involved. Somehow, I had thought she could just give Su-lin some pills or something, I guess.

"Yes, we will be here tomorrow," I said, turning and taking Yoon-ha's little hand in mine. The three of us silently walked out of the building.

Once outside the building, Su-lin burst into tears. "How can we manage this?" She cried.

"Look, you will come here tomorrow. We won't say anything to Mr. Un and Yoon-ha will help me do our usual work. If he asks, we will tell him that you are very sick but that we are doing your work for you. We need the money, and hopefully, he won't expect us to do double work all the time and pay us for only one." I did not know what else we could do.

This all was a shock, but I knew Su-lin needed help both physically and mentally. We had to do this!

The next day, the three of us went to town, and Su-lin had the surgery. She was moved to a house close by to recover. As planned, Yoon-ha and I worked together. What a little trooper Yoon-ha was! I was so proud of her, but still, the extra work wore me out. A couple of days later, we were able to trudge back into town to check on Su-lin. Mr. Un had never caught on to our scheme—at least not yet. We first went to the place behind the warehouse building, and after they told us where Su-lin was, we thanked them and left immediately.

When we got to the small home, I softly knocked three times, paused, then knocked once more. This was the code they had given me, but nothing happened at first, so I waited, then knocked three more times, followed by a pause, then the final single knock. This time I saw a curtain drop at one of the windows and heard footsteps before the door opened. You can imagine my surprise when there stood Sun-hee! She quickly grabbed my arm and pulled me and Yoon-ha into the house.

"Sun-hee!" I stammered, "What… What are *you* doing here?"

"Oh, Ha-na!" She grabbed me close and hugged me to her as she let out a little cry of joy. "I am so glad you found me!"

"Of course, Sun-hee, we were coming to look for you! We missed you! But what are you doing *here?* Are you all right?" I had so many questions to ask her once I got over my surprise. I was worried she was here to see the lady doctor. Had she been abused again?

"No," she assured me. "I am just fine, but don't you want to see Su-lin?" She gave Yoon-ha a good, tight hug and patted her on the head, saying, "I will explain everything in a minute when we are all together." She led us to Su-lin's room.

We all had a cheerful reunion before Su-lin grabbed my hand and cried, "Oh Ha-na! They took some of my parts. I will never have another baby!"

I was so surprised! We cried together for a long time, until Sun-hee said, "Well, at least you won't be chewing that nasty Queen Ann's Lace!" At that, we stopped crying, and we all laughed except Yoon-ha who was totally confused.

"Queen Ann's Lace, can I have some?" she asked innocently.

"No honey!" Sun-hee said, hugging Yoon-ha. "It is a bitter herb that women sometimes must take. I hope you don't ever have to take it."

The conversation naturally drifted over to why Sun-hee was here. What a story she had to tell us! It seems that she had gone back to the little building behind the warehouse to thank the lady doctor but had learned some astonishing things while there. We had called the place a church, but churches were generally prohibited in China, so really, it was a warehouse of sorts and was used as a meeting place for Korean defectors. They did "talk Jesus" there and so much more! While not a top-notch hospital or even a particularly good care center, the doctor volunteered her services here. She did what she could to help the Koreans, primarily girls, and women, who showed up there asking for help. She also connected people with an "underground railroad" of sorts. In other words, she was helping North Korean women escape China and go to South Korea or the evil United States!

Sun-hee laughed and said, "When I heard this, I recognized how much I HATED Queen Ann's Lace and how much I wanted to go somewhere where I would have enough food and be safe. I don't ever want to do a "little business" again! I don't want to do sex, and I am ready to leave China! I want to go to South Korea, where I won't have to learn a new language."

It was taking a minute for all this to register in my mind when Sun-hee hurried on. "Some kind South Korean and United States people have raised enough money to smuggle me out of China and into South Korea. I am either going to leave later tonight or tomorrow night. I want Su-lin to come too!"

Su-lin was shaking her head and shrinking back into the pillows with a horrified look on her face. It was clear to me that they had been speaking about this and that Su-lin was not convinced that this was the best thing for her to do and did not want to leave China. Plus, she was in no shape to make such a journey at this time, even if they could take her.

Without thinking for a minute, I blurted out, "If I could take Yoon-ha, I would go in a heartbeat!"

"No-o-o!" screamed Su-lin, "Not my little Yoon-ha!"

❋

It was all too much, and Yoon-ha and I left shortly after that exchange. Sun-hee needed to be completely prepared for the journey whenever her smugglers appeared, but she promised she would speak to the group about Yoon-ha and me wanting to go to South Korea soon. We said a tearful goodbye to them both after we established the fact that we could get communications back and forth through this place. After that, I promised Su-lin that we would be back again to visit in two days. I remember walking out of that house extremely elated, confused, and sad all at the same time. Yoon-ha and I walked back to the hotel as quickly as we could. And it was a good thing we did. I had barely gotten Yoon-ha into bed when Mr. Un banged on the door.

It seems that a guest had gotten sick in his room, and it needed to be cleaned up. I said I would go immediately. I was so relieved that he had not found all of us out at night, and I could not have slept anyway as I was in such turmoil trying to process all this new information.

✿

Two days later, Yoon-ha and I again walked into town to the little house where Su-lin was recuperating. I knocked again with the coded rap, and a different girl let me in this time. Sun-hee had begun her journey, and this young woman was the next to leave. She showed me to Su-lin's room, where Su-lin was sitting up by the window with a smile on her face. I wondered why the change but thought it was because she felt so much better and because she was to be released the next day. She told me the doctor had agreed to drop her off a couple of blocks from the hotel the following day on her way home from work. Yoon-ha and I could walk with her the rest of the way back to the hotel, where Su-lin would finish her recovery. It was all set up.

Things went as planned the day Su-lin returned home. Yoon-ha and I cleaned and did all the expected work at the hotel. We were getting to be a great duo working together, even if the sheer volume of the work exhausted us both. We watched, and soon, after the doctor dropped Su-lin off, we met her and walked back to the hotel. Yoon-ha was so happy to have her Ma-Ma back. They both loved each other so much.

The walk tired Su-lin out a lot that evening, and we all went to bed early. It was good to have my best friend back again. The next day, she insisted on at least helping a little as Yoon-ha and I cleaned. She said she wanted to get her strength back. I must admit it helped ease the strain a bit. I learned that the church charities were trying to raise money for Yoon-ha and me to leave China. I was elated but still thought Su-lin would change her mind about wanting to return to her husband's farm and her little boy and instead come with us. After all, her parents were most likely in South Korea. Didn't she want to find them? A couple more weeks passed without us talking about this subject. Su-lin was getting stronger every day when she announced that one of the girls we both had worked with at the first bar, Mr. Wong's bar, had dropped by with the news that she had done "a little business" with a man from the farm village where Su-lin's husband still lived and worked. They had spoken about her husband, who was reportedly still lonely and waiting for her to return!

"O-oh," I groaned. The idea of Su-lin returning to her farm churned at me all day and made me almost sick just thinking about her leaving. Could Su-lin still want to go back to her husband and her son and not go with Yoon-ha and me? This thought deeply saddened me, but we did not speak about it for the rest of the day.

I had thought about it all day, and that night, after Yoon-ha was finally asleep, I just had to ask Su-lin, "Do you still want to go back to the farm and not go with Yoon-ha and me to a better life in South Korea?" I had spoken in my most questioning voice, and now I was looking at her with what I knew was a pleading look—one of almost desperation. I truly could not believe she wanted to go back.

"Yes." She replied firmly, "Yes, I do want to go back to the farm, to my little boy, my husband, and his family. They were always kind to me, and it was not a bad life. Besides, I have no other family. I cannot go on living like this." That is when she dropped the real bombshell!

She came closer and sat right next to me, put her arm around me, and said in a soft voice, "Ha-na, I want to take Yoon-ha with me."

My head exploded at that moment, and I could not hear what she was saying! I felt like someone had just ripped my heart out of my chest.

This could not be happening! I jumped up and moved away from Su-lin and turned to look at her. I could not catch my breath as she was still talking, "… and she would be safe."

I looked at her, and she was staring right at me as she continued. "Ha-na, you know how much I love Yoon-ha! I can never have my own daughter, and even if I could, this government would not allow it since we already have a son. The truth is, I still think of her as mine. I have been with her and loved her since she was such a tiny baby. She calls me Ma-Ma, and my husband will accept her as our own child." Then she hit me with, "You know it would be much easier for you to travel alone and…"

"But she is MINE!" I screamed. "Yoon-ha is my only family now, and I promised her I would never leave her!" I was crying so hard and felt almost desperate: "Your husband will think you went off and had a child with some Korean or Chinese man! He will punish you AND Yoon-ha!"

Su-lin looked at me compassionately and in a calm voice replied, "NO, I know that man and his family. I now know that I love them. Besides, they will look at Yoon-ha and know she is not my child. Plus, she is over a year older than she could have been if I had her while I was gone. They will know. I will tell them she is the daughter of a dear friend who is no longer with us."

At that, I thought she meant that she would tell the family and Yoon-ha that I was dead! I could not stand that thought and just cried harder and began to rock back and forth. It was too much to bear.

"Just think about it, Ha-na," Su-lin said, giving me a strong, loving hug. "I am not going until the man from the village comes into the city again. He will be giving me a ride to the farm. I know that family. My husband will buy Yoon-ha and me the proper documents so we can pass for Chinese. She will have a good life."

I looked over at my beautiful daughter, who lay sleeping there so trustingly and with not a care in the world. Her dark hair had fallen over one eye, and her cheeks looked so rosy. How could I let my precious baby go? I just sat there rocking and moaning.

CHAPTER 25

The next day, Su-lin and Yoon-ha got up, ate some congee, and prepared for the day. I did not want to get out of bed; I had a splitting headache, and I felt nauseated. I had not slept a wink all night as my mind had played the various scenarios over and over. My heart was so heavy. I dragged myself through that day, and Yoon-ha noticed and said, "Maa Maa, are you sick? I will do your work for you."

My precious little girl! How could I let her go? And yet, it gradually dawned on me that this would be the best choice for Yoon-ha and Su-lin as well. What a choice! What a horrible, awful choice!

I somehow got through the day, and that night, after Yoon-ha had fallen asleep, I told Su-lin my decision. She was ecstatic and jumped up and hugged me hard while I felt as if a dagger had been thrust through my heart. I then asked Su-lin to help me get through the pain, and we planned when and how to tell Yoon-ha of our decision. I was determined to make the most of the few days we had left together before the man returned from Yanji and they drove off to the farm. I secretly wished that day would never arrive.

❀

But arrive it did. In just a bit over three weeks, the man came into the city, with his list of items that he needed as well as the desire to do "a little business" in the bar. At the hotel, Su-lin and I had told Yoon-ha all about this wonderful farm where there were pigs and chickens and where she could run free all day long with a new friend who was just a couple of years older than she was. I must admit that her eyes shone when she understood how nice it would be. She had no reason not to believe that both her Ma-Ma and her Maa Maa would be there with her. The truth was that neither I nor Su-lin could bring ourselves to tell her the whole story, and several times during those weeks, we had come close, but until the man arrived at the motel that day, we did not tell her about her future.

Yoon-ha was running around excitedly when I caught her. I knelt in front of her and tearfully told her, "Yoon-ha, you will love it there on the farm, but Maa Maa cannot come with you and Ma-Ma. I want to with all my heart, but I cannot come."

"No! Maa Maa," she cried, "come! Come with us!" She was crying now too, as she could tell I really meant it.

"I will always love you," I told her. "I will never forget you, and I will see you someday. I will see both you and Ma-Ma someday, so don't forget me." I hugged her tightly and did not want to let her go. We were both crying so hard.

It was only when the man and Su-lin pulled Yoon-ha from me that I let her go. Su-lin gave me a warm but quick hug. She was also crying at this point. It was hard for us all.

The man helped both Su-lin and Yoon-ha get into the car. I could see them hugging each other as they both cried. The man drove the battered old car swiftly out of the parking lot. I sunk to my knees, crying in total defeat, banging my head on the ground, and crying Yoon-ha's name over and over. Never had I felt so alone and or so shattered—not even when Father had sold me. Now I wondered if I could get my next breath, let alone go on living.

CHAPTER 26

✽

I was a zombie for the next few weeks, more like a dead woman than a 21-year-old woman. I was not hungry, and nothing appealed to me. Mr. Un now knew that if pushed, I could do twice the amount of work that one person usually did, and of course, he expected that of me every day. The mean bastard! He had not increased my pay, but still expected me to do both Su-lin's work and my own—and I didn't even have little Yoon-ha to help me! I was completely exhausted every day. Still, I waited and hoped the volunteers and the doctor would somehow be able to pay for and arrange for my escape to South Korea *soon*.

Out of necessity, I began to gloss over the cleaning of the rooms simply because I was so tired. One afternoon, Mr. Un cornered me outside one of the rooms I had just completed cleaning. He had gone in and inspected it, and it had not passed his inspection. With no warning, he began to beat me. I had no place to run, so I squatted down while covering my head with my arms. I tried to turn away from him, but he hit me repeatedly with a bamboo stick. Finally, he stopped, grabbed me by the front of my clothes, and pulled me to my feet. With his face about four or five inches away from my face, he screamed, "This is the last time you will do careless, sloppy work! Next time, I won't tell you! I will just call the police, and you can do your work back in North Korea!" He gave me a shove, and I fell back hard on my butt while he stomped off.

I sat there crying for the longest time, thinking I did not have any option but to continue to work there at the hotel. I really did not know anyone who could or would help me. I felt trapped, and I hurt both physically and mentally.

As the days slowly passed, my thoughts were always on little Yoon-ha and Su-lin. I wondered what Yoon-ha was doing and where she was going. Did she like the farm? Had her new father accepted her? And of course, did she miss me? Su-lin and I had agreed to get messages back and forth through Mr. Wong's bar. She promised she would keep me updated on how Yoon-ha was doing, and I was to let her know what was happening with my escape plans. But the truth was, I did not know how all this was progressing. I was simply too exhausted to travel into the city center to talk to the people there. I began counting the days until I thought the village man would again travel to the city to shop and do "a little business" at the bar.

Finally, one day, a young girl appeared at the hotel. It was clear that she was not a hotel guest, and I wondered if she could be looking for me. I knew that none of the women who had worked for Mr. Wong at the time Su-lin and I were there were probably still there. Too much time had passed. Some of them may have died or been killed; some would have married Chinese men; a lucky few would have escaped to South Korea or the United States; and some, well, I had no idea what would have become of them. I thought this girl looked like she was from the bar, and I ran out to her.

I was right! She had a note from Yoon-ha! It was not an actual letter, but a picture of some chickens and a pig. There was no writing, but she was still young, and there was a short note from Su-lin. I clutched the picture to my chest and looked at the note. It was in Korean, and it read:

"Darling Ha-na,

How are you? How is your escape plan coming along? My husband and his family are happy that I am back and have accepted my story about Yoon-ha. She won them over quickly, but she misses you. I hope they will start trying to get our proper documents soon. I miss you!

Love,
Su-lin"

I sat there crying for the longest time, reading, and rereading the note and staring at the picture. While I was happy for Yoon-ha and Su-lin, I missed them both SO MUCH! I felt so lonely and extremely left out. That night I did not eat again, and I cried myself to sleep.

❀

The next day, I felt hollow as I went about cleaning the darn hotel. I decided it was about time for me to go see the volunteers and learn about what I could do to hasten my escape. So, I did not clean so thoroughly that day and hurried into the city. I was, of course, welcomed, and I told them that Yoon-ha would no longer be coming with me. They were relieved! They said I could get out faster without her! That was bittersweet news. I know I just stood there, not saying anything. The volunteers assured me that they were raising money on my behalf and that they would be in touch as soon as they had all the arrangements in place. I trudged back to the hotel, bone-tired and dejected.

It was several months before I heard any real news from the volunteers. I checked in with them every few weeks, usually after not hearing from Yoon-ha and Su-lin when I was feeling low and needed to be cheered up. I even attended a few "church services." I did not know what to expect, but it was essentially a gathering of a few people in the back of the warehouse. They socialized and talked a lot together. It seemed to me that they were telling each other how to live, but they did "talk Jesus" part of the time. It was all strange to me. I thought this Jesus guy sounded a lot like our Great Leader, Kim Il-sung. They sang songs to him, and the people all seemed so warm and friendly. They asked me to join their group. I felt some pressure to come every week, but really, I was so tired these days. They all knew I was working extremely long hours. I was also kind of afraid to do this "Jesus thing" because in North Korea, people would be punished for even mentioning Jesus, and I thought that was the way it was in China and everywhere. The last thing I needed was to be locked up or punished for doing something I did not understand or want to do. So mostly I went to see them during the weekdays when there were not as many rooms to clean and when they didn't have their big gatherings.

❋

Time slowly passed. The reason it seemed like such a long time was that I not only missed my daughter and my best friend and all the things we did together, but I had no one to talk to! Mr. Un had not replaced Su-lin after she left, and there were no other employees or cleaning ladies. Mr. Un and his wife, who ran the front desk, kept to themselves, and quite frankly, I was afraid to interact with the guests because I thought they might turn me in to the authorities. The $5,000.00 reward for turning in a North Korean would be just too hard for many people to pass up. I was taking no chances.

I had just finished cleaning about half of the rooms one day and needed a bathroom break when I carelessly slipped in a small puddle of water and fell about three steps. I landed with a big thud against the wall outside of one of the guest rooms. I remember seeing the bucket of water come flying down the steps after me, but then I hit my head, and everything went black.

When I regained consciousness, I was lying on the bed in a guest's room, and a Chinese Korean man was standing over me, holding a wet cloth to the bump on my head. I knew immediately I had to get out of there, and I tried to get up, but I was so woozy. He gently pushed me back.

I recognized him as a regular customer there at the hotel and knew he was the man who came about every two weeks, staying for one night only. He always brought about six suitcases into his room and immediately locked the door. He would never leave his room until early the next morning when he again carried the six suitcases to his battered car, checked out of the hotel, and left. I never spoke to him or any of the guests, and I always thought this man was just passing through. Beyond that, I had never thought much about him or any of the guests.

"You are Korean, aren't you?"

"NO, NO! I am Chinese!" I blurted it out as forcefully as I could. I tried harder to get up this time.

"You are Korean, and you need help," he said in a calm, low voice as he held me firmly down on the bed. "I can help you."

"No! I don't need your help. I am fine!" I was determined to leave.

He let me get up and make my way to the door before he grabbed my hand and shoved a card into it. "You need help, and I can help you," he again repeated. I opened the door and ran.

I got to my room and sat down, shaking. I knew the man was right. I did need help. I could not stand it much longer here. I was sure Mr. Un was going to turn me in soon, but could I trust this man? What did he mean when he said, "He could help me?" I looked at his card, but all it had on it was his name, Cheol Hwang, and his telephone number. I did not have a strong feeling about just what I should do other than the knowledge that I HAD to do something, and soon! I was completely scared out of my wits and went to bed in a depressed and unsettled mood.

CHAPTER 27

❀

The next day, I cleaned the rooms with renewed vigor as I thought and thought. What should I do? It had been another month; the lady doctor who had helped us had moved from the University, so she no longer came to the back of the warehouse to help Koreans. I had no idea where she had gone, and it seemed that everyone had forgotten about me and my desire to leave China. I was extremely lonely, but I had begun to suspect something was just not right with Mr. Un and my work at the hotel. I was doing the work of two people for meager wages, and now I had a premonition that something bad was going to happen. I could not shake the nagging feeling that I had to leave the hotel as soon as possible. I knew I wanted to survive. But where should I go?

That night, after I thought Mr. Un would be in bed, I slipped out of my room and ran down the road to find a telephone. I called Cheol Hwang.

Mr. Hwang answered on the second ring, and I told him who I was. He was so cool, calm, and kind! "I am glad you called Ha-na. I was worried about you."

Mr. Hwang then proceeded to tell me NOT to go back to the hotel! He told me to go to a place a few blocks away and to wait in the shadow of a tree at a certain intersection. He would be there in a few hours to pick me up! This all scared me. I wanted to go back to the hotel for the letters and drawings from Yoon-ha and Su-lin. None of the rest of the stuff mattered to me, but there was something in Mr. Hwang's voice that frightened me! I also wanted to send Yoon-ha and Su-lin a message to let them know where I was going! The problem was, I did not know what I was getting into or where I was going! Putting everything together in my mind, I decided to take my chances with Mr. Hwang and follow his instructions. I was afraid to go, but even more afraid to stay!

It was hours before I finally spotted Mr. Hwang's battered car coming slowly down the street. He pulled over, and after I made sure it was him and not someone else, I ran out to him. He squeezed my arm lightly as he helped me into the back seat of his small car. He made me sit covered by his big suitcases, then he got back in the car and quickly drove away. I struggled to get comfortable under what seemed like a lot of weight.

"Ha-na," he said, "I am taking you to Shenyang. It is a place where smugglers meet and take people out of China to Thailand and then on to South Korea."

"Mr. Hwang, why are you helping me? I don't have any money to pay you."

"I know. I know. The reason I am helping you is that I couldn't live with myself if I didn't." He said no more and concentrated on his driving for a long time. With stops, it took nearly eighteen hours before we got to Shenyang. After we had driven for a short while, I was able to crawl out from under the suitcases and get in the front seat. I slept part of the way, and eventually, Mr. Hwang did pull over for a nap himself. While eating some mandarin oranges, Mr. Hwang told me he was in the smuggling business and that he knew some human smugglers where we were going. I asked him again why he was helping me, and that's when he told me the story that completely horrified me.

❈

I learned that Mr. Hwang had been smuggling merchandise between China and North Korea for a long time and that he had been coming to Mr. Un's hotel for many of those years. He had noticed all the maids were Korean nationals, but that they did not stay for many years. Mr. Un worked them so hard, and if they did not do as he said, he suspected that Mr. Un simply called the police and collected the reward money for turning in the "economic migrants."

"There were two young women who were suddenly gone right before you and your friend showed up. I know for sure he turned those girls in to the police." He turned his head away, but I saw how he was upset, knowing they would be tortured or killed. "I vowed I would not let that happen to another girl," he said resolutely. I felt so lucky to have left the hotel at what may have been just the right time. I was fortunate that I had not been the one turned in to the police or thugs. How would I ever repay this kind man?

❈

The next night, it was extremely late when we arrived in Shenyang, where Mr. Hwang turned up a narrow street and drove to a small house. He parked in the back and motioned for me to follow him as he knocked on the door. A Korean man answered the door, and the men exchanged smiles and handshakes and laughed as the man quickly drew Mr. Hwang and me inside. A middle-aged woman quickly escorted me into a small room in the back of the house while I could hear the men chatting in both Korean and Chinese.

The woman told me she would hide me until the next group left for the long journey to Thailand. She gave me some rice and a small blanket. I was stunned and did not know what to say to her. Shortly, I heard the men as they were saying their goodbyes. I ran out of the bedroom into the kitchen, where they had been eating, and ran up to Mr. Hwang. I know I had tears in my eyes as I thanked him profusely and bowed my head. I thought I saw Mr. Hwang brush away a tear as he turned and left that night. I realized he had felt so much guilt when he did not help the other two maids at Mr. Un's hotel, and that is why he helped me. I knew I would probably never see him again, and I will always be grateful for what he did for me. If it hadn't been for Mr. Hwang's generosity and his wonderful connections, I don't know if I would be alive today.

In under a week, a man, two other women, our smuggler, and I were ready to start the long, difficult journey through China, Laos, and finally Thailand. My heart was heavy, and I felt terrible that I had not gotten to say goodbye or even leave a message for Yoon-ha and Su-lin. The truth is, I was in complete survival mode at this point. We went by car, bus, motorbike, and by walking through the mountains and jungles. It was hot and tiring, with lots of scares along the way. I had to concentrate all the time and think of nothing but keeping moving and staying safe. We were always afraid of getting arrested, detained, and repatriated back to North Korea. The five of us traveled in three groups. We did not speak and always acted as though we did not know each other, especially when on the bus or in other public places. I was so thankful I was with a smuggler who knew the way and what to do. I hoped he also knew the bureaucracy and the best way around it. It was a very intense and frightening time!

We were traveling to Thailand because Thailand has a troubled relationship with North Korea but a good relationship with South Korea. They would help us by sending us to South Korea, which recognizes both North and South Koreans as citizens. This was the plan, at least. As soon as we crossed the border into Thailand, our smuggler pointed to the closest police station and instructed us to go turn ourselves in. He assured us that we were now safe. The two women began to cry with joy, but I knew I still had a long journey ahead and did not feel safe at all. How well I knew that things did not always go as planned!

❄

The Thai Police very quickly processed us by charging us with minor immigration violations and alerting the South Korean Embassy in Bangkok. They then put us in holding cells that held about two dozen others until they had a busload of people. We were there almost ten days before the bus was full. During this time, no one spoke their real name or their relatives' names out of fear of retribution by the Kim regime against their family members back in North Korea. It was crowded and lonely, but they did give us food and warm, dry clothes. I was still suspicious of everyone and did not feel completely safe yet. I kept to myself as much as possible.

Once there were enough people, we boarded a bus for the more than twelve-hour bus ride to Bangkok, where we were checked into an "Immigration Detention Center." They told us we would be there until the government completed the third-country resettlement process. None of us had any idea how long that would be. The Immigration Detention Center had extremely poor sanitation, and many people were getting sick. The food was not good. Most everyone in the detention center wanted to go to South Korea, where they would not have to learn a new language and would be free to look for work. There were so many people ahead of me, and I had not talked to any authorities or filled out my paperwork yet when I met a young girl my age named Ji-yeon. Ji-yeon said she was asking for asylum in the United States. I was stunned!

The United States? Why would anyone ever want to be around "American Bastards"? How could the United States be better than South Korea? It is so far, and you would need to learn a whole new language! Plus, in South Korea, they give you resettlement support, help with housing, the citizen process, education, transportation, etc.—basically, how to survive and fit in.

"I don't know Ji-yeon..."

"I know, but my cousin's friend went to South Korea, and she reported back that everything is so competitive and close-knit in South Korea. She said North Koreans could only find "3-D jobs"—jobs that are dirty, dangerous, and difficult. People struggle because they lack education and connections, and they don't know the rules of social behavior. They can't easily advance socially. It is better than here in China, but in South Korea, they discriminate against North Koreans! It would be hard, Ha-na!" She finally stopped and took a breath, then continued.

"Ha-na, come with me!" She suddenly pleaded, "The United States is a nation of immigrants. It will be easier for both of us to go together, don't you see? We can go and fit right in!"

This was all so confusing. I was numb, excited, and scared all at the same time. Most of all, I was thinking, I cannot leave Yoon-ha or Su-lin. She is talking about the hated United States! Hadn't we all learned how much better North Korea was than any other place in the world? I had been taught in school how to shoot "American Bastards." And now it was hard to think of going there to live with the American Bastards! I needed some time to process all of this. I just did not know...

CHAPTER 28

✻

As luck would have it, I did not get my chance to fill out my paperwork until later in the following week. And during this time, I kept thinking about what Ji-yeon had said. She did not pressure me but had made up her mind completely that things would be better in the United States. I kept comparing it to what I knew and what I had heard about South Korea during my years in China. The young women I had known had always spoken about how much the South Korean government helped North Koreans—how they would give us a three-month course on integrating into society, using public transportation, the money system, and so on. No one had spoken about how difficult it would be to live and survive in South Korea after the course was over. I thought about what our leaders, the Kims, had taught us about how we lived in the absolute best country in the world. My parents, my teachers, and everyone else believed them, but I had learned there was more food in China! They had lied about food and so many other things!

But China was not great either, and I thought about how very tired I was of struggling. The thought of struggling again in South Korea made me sick! When I thought about Yoon-ha and Su-lin, I had that same painful ache in my entire body. Where should I go? What should I do? I brooded for days on this question.

❁

When it came to my turn to request asylum, I wrote, "U.S."

And so, I began my long wait to be cleared to go to the United States. While I waited, many North Koreans had been sent out of the detention center and on to South Korea. Even Ji-yeon left for the United States! We would not be going together. I was sad but happy for her to finally be leaving this place. I was beginning to wonder if, for me, all of this had been a cruel hoax.

Months passed, and I wondered if I had made the wrong decision. Finally, the authorities came, and I was fingerprinted, photographed, and vaccinated. They required me to fill out more paperwork, and on one form, it asked me to pick a Western name, or at least the first name had to be Western. I did not hesitate. My name would be "Sophia Soon" in memory of the character my best and most loyal friend ever, Su-lin, had always admired. Oh, how I longed to hold both Yoon-ha and Su-lin in my arms!

But still, I waited. At last, it happened! They cleared me to come to the United States in October 2010. I was elated! They told me that the International Organization for Migration was now helping me and that I would be flying to Los Angeles and then on to Phoenix, Arizona, where a small number of Koreans lived. Where was that? I had no idea. Another North Korean man and I were each given a small white plastic bag inscribed with big blue letters "International Organization for Migration" written on it and driven to the airport. It was filled with a few toiletries and things we might need on the trip, and they informed us that the officials would recognize us when they saw the bag and help us. I clung to my bag the whole way to the United States. It was the first time either the man or I had ever seen an airplane up close, and it was all new and scary. I think we were both amazed and dumbfounded about how everything was progressing. We did not know what lay ahead for us, and I was excited but very frightened. Neither of us said anything. We simply went along as instructed in a state of wonderment.

Once in the air and settled down for the long flight, I stared out the window and let my mind wander. I left North Korea eight and a half years ago. I was now a young woman of twenty-three, and Yoon-ha was now a little girl of seven. What a struggle it had been! In a bit over nine years, I had lost my daughter, my brother, my mother, my father, and so many friends! I had traveled so many miles and been through so many tough times. Some people abused me, but I met some nice people as well. I will never forget the kindness Mr. Hwang showed me, and I will always be grateful for his help! Su-lin, my dearest best friend, and of course my beloved baby Yoon-ha…

Big, wet tears rolled down my cheeks as I thought of Yoon-ha and Su-lin. I blinked back the tears, and I swear I saw Yoon-ha's little face in the clouds floating by. Yoon-ha, the little girl I had sworn to love and protect forever. "Yoon-ha… Yoon-ha, I love you! Yoon-ha, don't forget your Maa Maa! Yoon-ha…."

PART III

Seng-il /Adam's Story

CHAPTER 29

I never wanted to come to the United States. I never even thought of it. After all, weren't we living in North Korea, the best and most beautiful country in the world? We were so lucky to have Kim Jong-il, "Our Dear Leader," and before him, Kim Il-sung, "The Great Leader" watch over us, provide us with everything, and be our father. But I was also hungry—very hungry!

Growing up in North Korea in the late 1980s and 1990s, I was *always* hungry. I do not remember when I did not want more food, or at least "just a bit" more to give me that full, satisfying feeling. It did not happen. My mother was too smart for that. Knowing she might not have any food tomorrow, she knew she had to ration what we had to save some for the next day. It was just never enough.

My mother was beautiful. Tall for a Korean, she was about five feet six inches tall with long, straight black hair that she wore clipped at the back of her neck. Her complexion was olive-toned and so clear that it seemed like you could look deeply into her face forever. She always stood bone straight with her shoulders thrown back in what I knew was both pride and a certain amount of defiance. Mother smiled often as she went about our home, doing the things all mothers do to keep their husbands and families fed and comfortable. She was light on her feet and very efficient in everything she did. My mother worked long hours at a food processing plant and was paid in either corn or rice but no money, which is how they often do it in North Korea. She washed clothes by hand when she came home and hung them out to dry nearly every day. I do not remember my father ever working much around the house or helping to bring in more money or food. People thought he was quite lazy. He smoked and drank too much. He was good-looking, with lots of dark, straight hair and a wide, toothy smile, and was charming to a fault, but he simply did not like to work. However, both of my parents worked the required number of hours per week mandated by the government to help farm the land owned by the government. This was compulsory, and Father could not avoid doing his "fair share." If you did not work for two or three days, the authorities would come to your home. The military police determined if your reason was "good enough." Like all other families, we could plant a garden and grow whatever we wanted on the land inside the fence that surrounded our house. We planted fast-growing vegetables and some corn, but it was not enough for the whole family. We were poor by anyone's account. And the pursuit of food was a continual activity while being hungry was a constant, unrelenting feeling.

My parents did not show much affection to us kids or each other, and I often wondered how my parents came to be married. It was only later that I learned that my grandmother (my mother's mother) had married my grandfather after he had lost his first wife. My mother had been born into that union but had always played a secondary role to her two older half-siblings. The truth was, she was flat-out discriminated against and longed to leave home. When she got the chance to marry my father, she jumped at the opportunity without thinking much about it. Father was not bad-looking, and it beat staying at home. She did not think about "Songbun" and its effects. I wonder if Mother even knew about "Songbun." Kim Il-sung devised the Songbun System. He had been appointed Premier by the Soviets and was later the first President of North Korea, right after they first formed the country. Kim formulated the Songbun System to protect the regime by isolating and controlling perceived internal political threats. He did this by categorizing every North Korean resident over seventeen according to how politically safe or risky they might be. Some key factors considered were your ancestors' socioeconomic background at the time of liberation (1945), their activities during the Korean War (1950-1953), and whether you had relatives outside of North Korea. North Korea keeps a file on every person over the age of seventeen. Your Songbun level affects nearly all aspects of North Korean life, including your occupation, education, family, where you live, food, and medical care. Mother might have had an easier life if she had waited to marry a man with connections. People whose families had good relationships with men of power received more opportunities, better jobs, and even more food. I believe she later had regrets about this.

❧

I was the oldest child with brothers who were two and five years younger. We played soccer and worked in our small family garden. Some days we fished in a nearby mountain lake. I found a piece of string, tied it to a bamboo pole, and used an old pin that I bent into the shape of a hook. I used some worms for bait that we found while digging for vegetables in the mountains. We never caught too many fish, but it was fun anyway.

One day my pin/hook got tangled up in some lake weeds, and I waded in to get it loose. I slipped and fell into the water. When I tried to stand up, I found that the water was over my head. I did not know how to swim. Panicking, I thrashed around, trying to get some solid footing and remembering what I could about swimming, all the while gulping mouthfuls of water and trying not to drown.

"Help! Help Me! I'm drowning!" I screamed frantically.

Na-mu saw that I was in big trouble and stretched his small arms out to me but could not reach me as he attempted to wade deeper into the water. Neither Na-mu nor Lil-ho knew how to swim, and they both were much smaller than I was. Na-mu inched closer but was afraid to go further into the water. Meanwhile, I thought I was going to die right there and then. One of them must have thought about extending the bamboo pole out to me. Finally, I was able to grab the pole, and both brothers held on to it as hard as they could without being pulled into the water over their heads. I somehow managed to pull myself closer to shore and into shallower water. I got to the shore and lay there vomiting water and coughing for a long time. We all knew it had been a close call, and we decided two things: First, we would NOT tell our mother, and second, we HAD to learn to swim.

So later that summer, I taught myself how to swim, and my brothers learned as much as they could. I loved being in the cool, clear water where everything seemed to float away, even the distant but always present nagging feeling of hunger. We would swim until we could hardly move, then crawl up onto the rocky beach and lie back in the sun, dreaming about food and life in general.

We lived in what seemed like a big house in a country located in central North Korea and farmed mostly fast-growing vegetables, including corn and potatoes. Our house had one big room where we all lived, slept, and ate. Just like in everybody else's home, there was a big picture of The Great Leader, Kim Il-sung, hung in a prominent place for everyone to see. It was our only picture in the house. Most days, we had electricity, even if only for a few hours. We had no running water, and our toilet was in a small building that sat behind our house. It had a hole in the ground, which we covered with a small board after using it each time. It was our responsibility as kids to empty the hole every ten days or so and spread the manure across the fields. This chore was not my favorite job. In the usual manner, the government of Kim Il-sung made the decision and told my parents they would become farmers. Their Songbun (or place in Korean society based on Kim's caste system) dictated that they would do manual labor, so the government provided the land along with the raw materials to build our house. Then a government organization came and built the house. It was a pretty basic house, like everyone else's. We accepted these realities.

I went to school just like other kids until I was in the sixth grade. Like other North Koreans, I was taught "Our Great Leader," Kim Il-sung, was the "Sun of the Nation" and could do no wrong. Later, this same thought extended to his son and successor, Kim Jong-il, whom we referred to as "Our Dear Leader." As children and students, we did not learn much history or anything about the outside world other than the fact that our Great Leader, Kim Il-sung, had become the first premier and president after the establishment of North Korea in 1948. They trained us on how to carry and fire AK-47 rifles so we would be prepared to fight and defend North Korea against the "American Bastards." As children, they taught us to bow down in front of Kim's statues each time we passed them as well as on other occasions. We learned in school and at home never to say or even think disparaging things about the royal family or our government. This was extremely important. If someone heard you say something unflattering or derogatory about the government or how it was run, the whole family plus the generation above and the one below could be taken away for punishment or put in a state collection station. No one left these camps, and no one ever wanted that for themselves or their families. While Kim Il-sung was in power in the early years, he built up his military and took most of the crops to support the troops. Ordinary families like ours received enough food to barely feed us. Later, after his death, his son and successor, Our Dear Leader, Kim Jong-il, continued this policy, and the government became even more centralized and autocratic. We had no concept of this. As a young child, it did not seem like a bad life except that I was always so hungry. We did not think of other countries—we had no radios, televisions, or internet. Our teachers and parents taught us that North Korea was the strongest and best country in the world. China was a distant second to North Korea, although, to be honest, we did see pictures of cars and other items and heard rumors about how nice it was there. No one in North Korea except for government officials and the military had cars, and we were lucky if our families owned one bicycle per family. America was our worst enemy, and no one thought of ever wanting to go to that evil country. Neither I nor any of my family or friends ever talked about "human rights" or "freedoms." We were all extremely busy with our daily lives.

❃

Mother woke us every morning and gave us each a small bowl of corn or, on rare occasions, some porridge for breakfast, then we walked to school. While we were in school, Mother went to work in the food processing factory or the state-owned fields, doing her mandatory work for the government. After school, my brothers and I collected some wild vegetables from the mountains whenever we could and gathered wood for cooking and heating. These vegetables would supplement the small garden we had in our yard. This was in good times. At other times, when we could not find enough wild things to eat, we stripped bark from trees and took it home. Mother boiled it for a long time, and we ate it. It was not good, but it filled our stomachs. We hoped we could find something better the next day or that Mother would be given rice or corn as payment for her work. My grandparents did not live that far from us, and sometimes I would walk to see my grandmother when I was extremely hungry. She always managed to give me corn powder, vegetables, or some other small thing to eat. We did not see our relatives much because it meant they had to share food, and they never had extra to share. Like most families, our whole family kept to themselves and did as we were told. My parents attended the mandatory community meetings held several times per week, where they were educated on how to be good North Koreans and sang songs praising our leaders. Na-mu, Lil-ho, and I learned these same things in school, and we all knew the words to the songs about Kim Il-sung and the royal family. We vaguely knew but did not talk about forced labor camps where thousands of people were locked up—a place we never wanted to go.

We did not see many people dying of sickness and starvation until after The Great Leader, Kim Il-sung, died in 1994 and his son, Our Dear Leader, Kim Jong-il, came into power. In the 1990s, there were several years of drought, and the mountain lakes, rivers, and crops began to dry up. The factory where Mother worked paid her with less and less food, leaving us kids to scramble for more food in the mountains. The mother of a childhood friend of mine came to our door one day asking for food. We were pals as children and enjoyed playing ball and collecting wood from the mountains together. Our family did not have any food to spare, but my mother gave the woman some corn. The woman was extremely grateful. She and her children died of starvation not long thereafter. Their deaths hit me extremely hard, as it was the first time I saw ordinary people just like ourselves die in this manner. That night, Na-mu, Lil-ho, and I lay on our blankets and talked in whispers about how it could be us who died in the same manner as our friends.

As a teenager, I saw dead or dying people in the streets daily. They were extremely skinny, with big stomachs and flies all over them. The sight and the horrendous smell of their decomposing bodies made me very sad and scared.

We kids, our parents, and all North Koreans had learned and believed in our strong Korean character and the belief that we were living in the best country under the fabulous leadership of The Great Leader, Kim Il-sung. We did not learn or understand The Great Leader's ideology of "Juche." Later I learned "Juche" incorporated the ideas of Marxism and Leninism with the North Korean character that strongly emphasized the individual, the nation-state, and its sovereignty. This intense adherence to the belief that North Koreans were independent and self-reliant would not allow North Korea to accept food, handouts, or aid of any kind from other countries. And most certainly not from the United States, even during this extreme period of famine. I later learned that nearly three million people died of starvation or diseases brought on by poor nutrition during the famine, and I felt extremely lucky that no one in my family had died during this time.

❀

One day, when I was twelve, my uncle knocked on our door. He lived about six hours away from us, and we did not see him often. After my mother and uncle hugged and caught each other up a bit about their families, he said, "Where is Seng-il? I need him to help me. He is twelve now and nearly grown."

"Yes, he is a big boy now," my mother replied, "but what do you need him to do for you?"

"I need Seng-il to help me collect herbs and mushrooms in the mountains so we can sell them for money. Isn't that what he and your other boys do, anyway?"

It was true; that is how my brothers, other older children, and I spent time in the mountains gathering things to eat as a supplement to the vegetables and food our parents provided. Uncle explained that my job would be to help collect and then carry them in a backpack onto the trains to deliver and sell. At that time, the authorities stopped grown men, demanded their identification papers, and asked many questions, while a kid could just jump on board with no problems. I thought, "Why not?" Uncle was to pay me in the best currency—food. And everything revolved around getting enough food to eat. I did not go to school after that but spent my time in the mountains searching for edible mushrooms, ginseng, and other herbs desired by people, then delivering them wherever my uncle wanted.

I worked for my uncle for about a year, and I learned a lot during this time. But Uncle had never helped our family in the past, and now he was not quick to pay me. He was honestly not welcoming to me whenever I came to his house. I saw many people in the mountains collecting herbs and mushrooms. Many men and women had small children with them who ran around playing in the mud, mostly getting dirty. The women would be bent over, collecting this or that, then pause to stretch their backs while glancing around to check on their children. Many kids—a little over twelve—were there to contribute to the family's income.

Simply put, we needed to help get enough food so we would not starve. Everything revolved around food and whether you got enough for the day. Our parents and all grownups, no matter their capabilities, were required to work on government-owned land. However, they never let us keep more food than necessary to get from one day to the next. They took our "surplus" for the military. They said, "It was to keep North Korea's military strong and ready at all times." If anyone kept food hidden, the punishment would be swift and savage. We learned not to waste anything.

The mountain people, as I called them, talked while they worked together. Since we did not have many other types of entertainment, it was our social time and a time to catch up on the local gossip. I was bored some days but did learn a lot from people, and I was also secretly proud that I could contribute and help my family. I was becoming a more valuable family member. After getting up early and walking for thirty minutes, I would be in the mountains as soon as the sun came up and I could see the mushrooms. When my backpack and the other bag I carried were full, I started down the mountain to the train station. I would quickly slip onto the train, sitting a few rows from the door. Sitting here allowed me to get on and off easily without people staring at my bags. They were hungry after all. I usually did not get home until it was almost dark, and I was both tired and hungry. Mother always had a small bowl of corn or vegetables waiting for me. It was not much, but I ate a few mushrooms to appease my hunger on days when the vegetables were more plentiful. After I ate at night, I would curl up in my blanket in my corner of the house and quickly go to sleep. I knew I had another day ahead of me, starting early the next morning.

❈

Some days, the young guys would talk more. I had been doing this for several years when, at sixteen, I met another guy just a few years older, and we began talking together. Nam-heck Yoo was short and stocky but strong. He had a funny red mark on his left cheek that made him look like he was very rugged and mean. He was not mean, but he was a little slow intellectually. Nam-heck began to tell me about his uncle, who lived in China, and showed me some pictures of his uncle and his family. His uncle sold many of the herbs that the Chinese used in their medicines for "good prices"—certainly for a lot more than we could sell ours for.

Nam-heck's uncle wanted him to come to the border with more herbs. The problem was that the border with China was far away. To make it pay, he wanted to take many herbs. Would I go? I thought about going with Nam-heck for many days—maybe even a week—before I made my decision. I knew what was here for me in my small village in central North Korea, living with my parents and brothers, almost stealing from each other trying to get by, and always hunting for mushrooms to sell. This would be my future here. This new prospect sounded exciting and promising. Because Mother would not want me to go far, I chose not to tell her. So, one day, Nam-heck and I did not go to the mountains but instead set off for the North Korean Chinese border to meet his uncle. I was excited to be going two hundred miles, mostly by train and by walking.

Nam-heck asked, "What did you bring?"

"Just the clothes I have on, a jacket, a knife for digging vegetables, and my backpack."

"Got any money?"

"No, where would I get any money? Do you have any?"

Nam-heck shook his head, no, and we silently started our journey. It took us nearly ten days to get to the border, eating what vegetables we found along the way before we boarded the train. We also ate anything we could find wherever we got off the train during the all too frequent stops in the middle of nowhere. We were always protecting our herbs. Nam-heck had been to China once before when he was in high school, so he was "experienced" by my standards. That train ride was hard because we had no money for tickets, so we rode on the roof of the train. It went under bridges or close to trees, and we could be knocked off the train. But the worst part was that due to the frequent electrical power outages, the train would sometimes stop in the middle of nowhere for anywhere from a few hours to twenty-four hours. Then it would start up again with no notice but with loud pops and surges of electricity coming out of the wires. If you were standing up, you could get hit by the electricity, thrown off the train, or even electrocuted. I solved this problem by tying a rope over my head to a train vent. These precautions prevented me from waking up and raising my head into the power lines, and they also kept me on the roof as the train rumbled along. People came to the railroad stations or the tracks and sold corn, potatoes, or rice to people who had money. The police did not search for or catch people on the train roofs.

We decided to get off the train and walk the remaining twenty-five miles to the border. We did not want to attract attention or have any hassles, but we needed a place to stay and also needed to find Nam-heck's uncle.

We asked several people, "Hey, I'm looking for my uncle. He lives in China but comes to the border often. He was supposed to meet us here, but we have not seen him. His name is Min Kyu-li, and he is about five feet, seven inches tall, and looks a lot like me. Have you seen him?"

No one knew or had seen Nam-heck's uncle! We looked in every nook and cranny along the border and around the customs area and asked everyone who was there selling goods across the border. We even asked brokers, who were, in truth, local farmers but who knew every detail of the border and would, for money, help North Koreans make their way into China. Some were honest, and some were not. Many of these brokers needed money, so they would help young Koreans get across the river. The not-so-honest brokers would take the young men's money, help them cross into China, and then turn them over to the Chinese authorities, who deported them back to North Korea. This was not considered good as the North Korean authorities did not like people leaving and usually beat or shot the men once they were back home since they considered them "traitors" to Kim Jong-il. They treated the young Korean women just as badly. China had had the one-child policy for so long, and most Chinese families wanted sons over daughters, so they aborted many girl babies. Thus, many young Chinese men could not find wives. Because they wanted wives so much and because Korean ancestry is such that they are very closely related to Chinese, these young men would buy North Korean women and marry them. Most of the women had no choice in this matter, as the unscrupulous broker, who seemed like just a nice person willing to help them leave, got the money. Also, the girls knew that they would probably starve if they went back home, and at least in China, they got food. It was human trafficking at its worst.

But Nam-heck's uncle was nowhere to be found! We searched for three days with no success. We were forced to eat some of our vegetables, and we dried the rest of the herbs and mushrooms. Finally, feeling quite depressed about it, we started looking for someone who could go into China legally. We needed them to go to the small town in China where his uncle was said to live and work and find him for us. It took us about twenty-five days to have people help us do all this searching, only to find nothing. Nam-heck eventually gave up looking for his uncle and decided to travel to China to find him himself. He assured me that he would return in no more than two weeks. Knowing I had no future in my small village, it seemed reasonable to stay and wait for Nam-heck. He knew more, and at that time, I had no intention or desire to go to China. I was there simply to get more money for our vegetables and herbs and, hopefully, help my family.

So, I waited. I was sure Nam-heck and his uncle would be back by the end of the promised two-week period and that we would have a good market for our herbs and mushrooms. I waited and waited...

CHAPTER 30

✣

I waited two weeks for Nam-heck to return. Not wanting to miss Nam-heck, I did not want to go into the mountains to camp or stay, but rather I wanted to be close by for his return. After all, we had a deal, didn't we?

No one had the money for hotels, so they stayed in the homes of local people. I decided I would ask some farmers if I could stay with them because I knew that sometimes they let people stay for a few days in exchange for food or help to complete a chore around the home. They did this for two reasons: times were hard, and the hotels had all closed during the long famine. I walked up to the nearest farmer's house and knocked on the door. At first, I didn't think anyone was home, but finally, a middle-aged man slowly opened the door and peered out at me with a blank stare. He was dressed in a pair of dusty pants and a shirt that looked too big. I figured that he had lost a lot of weight and that this was all that he had to wear. He looked tired, old, and worn out, partly because he did not have any teeth. Most North Koreans usually do not go to dentists. I am not even sure if they have many dentists in North Korea. At least I had never heard of one in my small town, nor had I ever seen a sign for one. When someone is hungry, they do not think about their teeth.

"I am waiting for my friend and need a place to stay. Could I stay at your house?"

At first, he just continued to stare at me. Finally, he took a deep breath and looked me up and down. He said, "Do you have money?"

"No. I don't have food, but I have herbs you could sell. Or I could work for you."

After sizing me up, he said, "I do have a heavy door that needs work. I guess you could work off your stay by helping me."

I nodded and moved towards the door, but inside, I wanted to jump for joy. The summer nights were cool, and I had only a light jacket and nothing to sleep on. Plus, I was hungry.

The man moved to the side, and I entered his modest home. The first thing I saw was the mandatory picture of The Great Leader hanging on the wall. His wife was sitting at a table, looking as old and tired as he did. I knew these people were having a hard time working the required amount of time the government stipulated for them to receive any food at all. The woman wore a faded pair of trousers and an equally faded and threadbare shirt. She was thin and had no more than one or two teeth left, but she smiled, gesturing for me to sit. I left the only remaining chair for the man and sat on the cleanly swept floor. I assumed that their children were grown and had left home to build their own families. These people were barely getting by. I hoped they would offer me something to eat before I curled up on the floor for the night. I would work on the man's door in the morning and assumed I would be doing all the work myself since the man was in poor shape. Ironically, that is what happened. I stayed a few days at this couple's home, first helping repair the door and then planting a garden for them that I doubted they would have the strength to care for down the road. They were kind and nice to me, but extremely poor. I wondered how long they would last as I left them to check again on Nam-heck's whereabouts. I sure wished he would get his butt back here. This was getting old.

✿

Over the next few weeks, I stayed with two or three other families there while waiting for Nam-heck. It was the same each time. Everyone had a modest one-room house with the mandatory picture of Kim Il-sung hanging for all to see. Every family member had a gaunt, blank face. If I did not have food or money, or if they did not need help, they would kick me out. By this time, I had sold almost all the herbs and vegetables I brought with me to the border. I was afraid of missing Nam-heck, so I did not spend much time replacing the herbs and vegetables. I kept asking around, but no one had heard anything from Nam-heck or his uncle.

During the next four weeks, I checked all the areas I thought Nam-heck might return to every day, hoping to find him. I had no word from him, and I was slowly becoming desperate. My options for staying with people were running out, and I had no money. I began camping in the nearby mountains and foraging for food. Finally, I went into the mountains, lay down, and looked up at the sky, and the wispy clouds. "What am I going to do now? I don't have any money and I can't wait any longer, but what am I going to do?" I had not seen any real opportunities for me to work or do anything this close to the Chinese Korean border. I had run out of food and had nowhere to stay. When I thought about going back home, I was equally depressed. There was nothing there for me. I had a family but no work, and I needed to contribute, or they would ask me to leave. Everyone had to make themselves useful. This is the North Korean way. I did not want to go back home and pick mushrooms and herbs to sell at low prices, barely getting by. I had not planned to go to China, and I had not told my mother I was going to the border. But now, after six weeks, I was beginning to think Nam-heck was not coming back, and in fact, I never heard from Nam-heck again. I wondered what happened. But I knew that I could not stay much longer here this close to the Tumen River, which also served as the border between North Korea and China.

All the things I had heard about China began to play up in my mind. They had lots of beautiful cars. Only government officials and people of high military rank had automobiles in North Korea. While we North Koreans always struggled for food, the Chinese always had plenty. We had always jokingly called the Chinese "Fat Cats" because they were so overweight compared to us North Koreans. There were rumors of plenty of work. And then there was the Yanbian Korean Autonomous Prefecture area. I had heard about this area when Nam-heck and I first started looking for his uncle.

One guy had said, "Well, he probably lives in the Yanbian Korean Prefecture area and shouldn't be too hard to find."

We both asked, "Where is that?"

"Well, it is an area in the northeastern province of Jilin, just north of the North Korean border. It's a pretty big area in China that Koreans both from North and South Korea migrated to in mass from the Korean peninsula in the 19th century. After they founded the Republic of China, a second wave arrived. Over a million people stayed after WWII and through the communist takeover. Some even fought in the Chinese Civil

War and after the war was over, the new Chinese government gave the Koreans an autonomous region in 1952."

"Why did they come?" I asked.

He answered, "I guess it was mainly because of the economic hardships and for political reasons after Japan annexed Korea in 1910 or thereabouts. China subsidized Korean language schools and publications in the autonomous region. The Chinese encouraged the Koreans to stay so the Russians would not come."

Since I was not going to China, the conversation meant nothing. But now, WOW! There was an area in China where they spoke Korean and where I could blend in. I wondered if I could find food, work, and success. I knew I was strong and prepared to succeed. Was this my opportunity? My excitement about going to China was growing.

I knew I had to have a plan if I were to escape to China. I walked to the top of the highest mountain to get a better view of the whole area and decide if, indeed, I wanted to escape. I saw border guards walking along the border and began to watch which way they walked and when. I timed them several times. I figured out when they changed guards and which areas were patrolled the least and when. I kept watching from my place in the mountain for three days. I knew the river was cold and had a swift current, but it was only two or three hundred yards wide. The small island in the middle would cut the current enough to make this a good point to cross. The trees were not close to the banks, making it dangerous because a guard would be able to see me easily once I reached the beach areas. My challenge was to get into the river, cross, and quickly hide in the trees without being spotted.

What did I need for the journey? I decided I needed to take the North Korean military uniform that I had bought some time ago on the black market. The uniform had not been hard to locate, and it had gotten me out of sticky situations in the past. I was glad I had it with me. I thought it might get me out of another tight spot, if necessary. I would also need a plastic bag to help me float if I got into trouble in the river. A plastic bag could save my life. I planned to put my clothes in the bag and swim across the river naked so I would be dry at least to go up in the Chinese Mountains, where I knew it would be cold at night. I would also take my small knife to dig herbs and vegetables to eat and to sell later for money. The only other thing I needed would be a rope to tie the plastic bag to my waist with.

I searched and finally found a discarded old piece of rope about five feet long. It was not good, but it would serve my purpose. I sat down to wait for darkness. I wanted to be able to see the Chinese shoreline while also being hidden from the North Korean guards. As I waited, it started to rain. My Lucky Day!!! A lucky day because it was darker, and the rain would cover many sounds down by the river, and I knew people tended to stay in when it rained. I thought the guards would be a bit lazier about going out in the rain to make their rounds. I hoped this was true.

Finally, it grew darker—almost dusk. While I waited, I watched the Chinese side of the river and saw a light come on. This would be my guiding light. It would help to keep me oriented. The time was now. I stripped off my clothes and put them in the plastic bag, then tied the rope around my waist and gave it a couple of tugs to test it. It was now or never. My heart was beating so fast, I thought it would jump out of my chest. Taking a deep breath, I ran as quickly as I could out from the cover of the trees and into the cold water. I plunged in and swam as fast and as hard as I could toward the other shore. I kept thinking, "Faster! Faster!" as I willed my arms and legs to swim harder, listening all the time for an unwanted shout. It took me only about ten minutes to swim across the

Tumen River, but it seemed like it took hours. Just as I reached the shore, a big light beamed right on me. My heart sank. A North Korean guard had spotted me, and it was he who was shining a big flashlight on me. Then I realized that I was now on Chinese soil and that no matter what that guard could do, I was ahead of him.

I grabbed the rope and plastic bag and ran as fast as I could into the cover of the trees. As I was breathing the air, I kept thinking, "I feel so different! It is so all so very different!!" I could not believe that everything, including nature, felt, and looked different to me. It was about 8:30 or 9:00 p.m. in August 2000. I had made my escape, and I was in China. I was so scared and excited, but mainly I was so happy.

CHAPTER 31

I was so happy to be out of North Korea and in a free country. A country where we thought everyone had a car, there were no food struggles, and we had not heard of any labor camps. I was in China! China, I thought, was a country where they allowed people to survive. Yes, the government owns the land, but people can lease it for thirty or fifty years. Life was going to be great! Or so I thought.

After resting for a few minutes and drinking in my new sense of wonderment and freedom, my new reality began to sink in. I knew that I had to move far away from the river and up into the Chinese mountains as quickly as I could just in case the police in North Korea decided to follow me. And while my understanding of China was extremely limited, I learned that the Chinese had come to North Korea in the 1950s and 1960s when they had been starving, and now the North Koreans have been immigrating to China since the 1990s for the same reason. I also knew we all looked very similar, so people would not know I was from North Korea if I wore Chinese clothes or did not speak. I knew I would be at a disadvantage until I got the proper clothes, and I needed to learn Chinese as quickly as possible. Nam-heck told me that we had to blend in because the Chinese would turn us into the authorities for a reward since we technically competed for jobs. They simply did not want us there. Knowing this information, I wanted to head toward the Yanbian Korean Autonomous Prefecture area. So, while it only took me ten to fifteen minutes to swim the river, it would take me five hours to reach a farmhouse where I could ask for assistance and some food. It was cold because it was night and high in the mountains. I did not know exactly where I was going or who was hiding in the mountains, so I moved carefully. There was no moon because it was raining and cloudy, but I pressed onward. I listened and watched for animals, as they are usually the first to sense that someone or something is near them. Sometime before sunrise, I heard a man driving his cow in the mountain grassland. He was on a small path near me. I hunkered down and watched the cow for signs she knew I was there. The cow lumbered forward, and I think it knew I was there. It raised its head a bit and turned towards me while slowing its walk a little. The cow then perked its ears up and bent them slightly forward as if it were listening. I was so afraid the man would see me, so I crouched down even further and held my breath. It was an eternity before the farmer spoke to the cow again and lightly prodded it to move forward. The cow responded and moved on. I finally could breathe. I stayed in that spot not moving for over twenty minutes before I finally mustered the courage to begin my search for a farmhouse and some possible food.

It took me a couple more hours before I saw what looked like a friendly farmhouse in the valley not far from the mountains, and I approached the door. I knocked and waited to see if anyone would open the door. After a few minutes, an old man with a grumpy expression appeared.

"Hello Uncle," I said. (Everyone calls their elders Uncle and Aunt.) "I am just traveling through, and I am wondering if you have some food and water to give to me?" At least this is what I thought I said in my extremely limited and broken Chinese.

He quickly shook his head no, muttering something about the Chinese authorities, and told me to get out of there. I left immediately, not wanting him to call the police.

❋

I continued to the second house, which was about a half-mile away, and again knocked on the door. An older Chinese man responded.

"Hello Uncle, I am traveling through, and I am wondering if you have some food and water that you could give me? I also need a place to stay."

This older man was clean-shaven and bright-eyed but moved very cautiously and deliberately, and there was a certain air of sadness about him. He smiled when he recognized my North Korean accent and replied, "Why, yes, son, I think I could put you up for one night." He held the door, and I walked into his house, which had very few possessions in it but was clean and orderly. He walked over to the table and gave me some leftover rice that he had from his dinner. "What brings you this way?" he asked as I began to eat the welcomed bowl of rice.

"Oh, I am on my way to visit some relatives," I answered.

I didn't know if he believed me, but then he started talking about himself. "I was married to a girl from North Korea," he said. "We raised a boy and a girl, and after they left, it wasn't very long, and the Chinese authorities came and took my wife. That was a while ago, and I haven't seen or heard from her since. I still miss her a lot." I thought he was going to cry, but he straightened and turned his face. "I help young people like you out occasionally because of her," he said in a soft voice. After a moment, he repeated that I could only stay one night. Later, I curled up on his floor, thinking I was in heaven.

The next morning, he woke me, gave me some rice in a plastic bag, and introduced me to a man with a scooter who was to take me back to the river so I could go back to North Korea. He hadn't believed my story after all! He had been sympathetic and compassionate but also frightened. He had decided that having his friend transport me to the river on the friend's scooter would attract less attention and suspicion about me being North Korean and why I was there. I wondered if it was my North Korean accent and silently vowed to get rid of it. I had learned that if a Chinese person was caught helping a Korean, they would be fined $5,000.00, and if the police did not find the Korean fugitive, then the Chinese person would have to go to jail. This man had already lost the Korean woman he loved, and now he had become too frightened to let me stay or even to help me in any other way. It was clear I was not welcome. I needed to go and not endanger this kind, sad man. Reluctantly, I rode behind his friend to the river. My heart was heavy.

I remember lying down in the grass in the protection of the trees along the river and looking up at the clear blue sky. How could I go back to North Korea and my home? I had no future there, and oh, the *shame!* I did not want to face my mother and the rest of my family. I would be disgraced! I knew I needed to help myself to help my family. In Korea, we have a saying. "Everyone must have a purpose. If a tiger dies, it leaves its skin, but if a person dies, he leaves only his name. A name does not have a benefit for others." I wanted to be more than just a name. I also thought the North Korean police would be "really hard" on me if I went back across the river and they found out that I had been in China. But I needed a plan if I were to stay in China. I stayed in the trees all day long, not far from the river's edge, trying to keep a low profile and not engage with anyone because I knew that could be dangerous. I thought a lot about myself, my family, and my future. My only food that day was the rice the old man had given me. I was unhappy and discouraged. "What had I gotten myself into?" I learned two things: first, I had to get into the Yanbian Korean Autonomous Prefecture area as soon as possible, and second, I had to work on my Chinese language skills and get rid of my North Korean accent.

❋

Late that afternoon, I took a different direction and moved along the riverbank, always staying in the cover of the trees. After walking for over three hours, I approached a small village of about ten or fifteen houses, which was located not too far from the mountains. The houses were like North Korean homes, and I picked a "friendly" one. When the older Chinese man opened the door, I began talking to him,

"Hey Uncle, do you have work for me to do for food?"

He eyed me carefully, and after a moment, he asked, "Ever worked with cows?"

I had not, but I had seen plenty in the grasslands and the mountains around our house, not that we ever got to eat the meat or drink the milk. How hard could this be? "Oh yeah," I lied. "A lot." I was very hungry!

"Well, we will see." He said as he handed me a bowl of corn. "I need you to help me feed my cows."

The man lived alone and looked about forty-five. He was an OK guy. He took me to a lean-to where he had three cows tied in a stall. I noticed the cows needed water, so, without being told, I took a pail and went to the river for water. He watched me closely as I watered and fed the cows a small amount of grain that he had there. He must have been satisfied that I knew what I was doing because he offered me a job.

"Early every morning, you need to take the cows to the mountains to graze and watch over them, so they are not stolen or wander off. At night, bring them back. I can't afford to feed them much of this grain every day. Think you can do that?" he asked.

My job would consist of getting up at 4:00 a.m. every morning, going to the man's home, eating a small bowl of rice, then taking the man's cows from his small farm into the mountains (about a thirty-minute walk each way.) I would sleep or forage for vegetables in the mountains during the day until around 3:30 p.m. when I would again herd the cows back to the man's house to get my second meal of the day. He would not allow me to sleep at his house, so I would return to the mountains again. For this, I received two meals per day and the equivalent of thirteen U.S. dollars per month. Koreans would get thirteen dollars per month, while the man would have had to pay a Chinese person the equivalent of one hundred U.S. dollars per month for the same work. I was happy, and I was free. I felt I was somewhat safe from the authorities because it would be harder for them to find me in the mountains, and I could earn some money for

Chinese clothes while I worked on my accent. I had food every day. I had a good life. I was surviving.

❄

There were other North Koreans in these mountains herding cows and doing this same type of work, and I spoke with them often. We talked about our pay, the type of work we did, and other available work. We spoke about our living conditions, safety, and rumors about what it was like in the various Chinese cities. After several days of working for this rather lazy farmer, I began talking with a man named Ji-rang Choo. Ji-rang was a forty-two-year-old man from North Korea who had been in the mountains tending cows and doing other farm work for a local farmer for nearly two months already. I never learned exactly why he had left North Korea, and I assumed that it was for more food and perhaps a better life, just like I had left. Ji-rang was a private guy and kept to himself a lot, but after seeing him in the fields working and always smiling and waving to him, Ji-rang began to let his guard down a bit, and we began speaking. We did not ever hear gunshots, but we did hear rumors of a North Korean man or woman being caught every few days and sent back to North Korea. There were stories about what they did to them and how they treated them, but none of these stories were pretty, and most were downright scary.

Ji-rang was getting nervous and anxious about staying in this area for much longer with all the rumors about so many North Koreans being captured. One night, Ji-rang and I were camping close to each other, sharing a fire and a meal, when Ji-rang's boss came into our campsite. He banished a knife in my face and threatened me, "Get out of here and take your ideas with you! Leave... Right now!" He was mean and upset and thought that I would talk Ji-rang into leaving with me. He would lose a good employee. I was unarmed and afraid of him, so I left. I returned the following day to see Ji-rang.

❈

"Hey Ji-rang," I called out to him once we were both away from the chance of anyone overhearing us. "That guy was mean last night! Is he always that way?"

"Yeah," Ji-rang laughed, "A lot of times, he is worse! Sometimes I practically beg for him to pay me my money. He knows I don't have too many options or know many people who can help me. I don't like him much."

"My guy is OK," I said, "but it is a dead-end job, and from what you and others say, we could get caught easily here. I do not want to go back to North Korea. Maybe it would be safer to move on together. We could kind of watch each other's back."

Ji-rang did not hesitate, "Yeah, we should head to Yanji."

Not knowing much about China, I asked, "Where is Yanji? Why there?"

"It's the capital of the Yanbian Korean Autonomous Prefecture region and a pretty big city. It has many ethnic North Koreans who have lived there for centuries and we could blend in easier. I think we could probably get better jobs there. But we need a few things first. Let's wait until we get paid, then leave right after that."

Ji-rang and I waited a few days until we both got paid. I got my money first, and the next day, Ji-rang watched both my farmer's cows and the cows he was to watch while I hiked into the village to buy us both some Chinese-style clothes to help us blend in better. Ji-rang managed to steal a large aluminum pan for cooking, and we stashed it away in the mountains. Our plan was underway. A few days later, Ji-rang got paid, and the next morning, we both brought our cows to the mountains like any other day. Ji-rang was grinning as he proudly showed up with a chicken that he had stolen from his farmer on his way to the mountains that morning.

"This makes up for me having to beg for the money we both agreed on every month," he announced. I just laughed. It had been a long time since I had tasted any chicken. There was no love lost for either one of our farmer bosses, but we did not want to hurt the cows and we wanted to get as far away as possible before they discovered we had left. So, after taking the cows to the mountains, we tied them to a tree near both water and grass and took off toward the city of Yanji.

We had only walked about three hours when we met a fifteen-year-old guy by the name of Yo-han Rim, who had also escaped from North Korea and was on his way away from the border and into safer territory. Yo-han joined us, and we continued our walk. He walked and talked with us for at least another three hours, telling us he was somehow connected with a church, but we had never heard of such churches. For some reason, Yo-han believed in a "Jesus story" and even tried to explain some of it to us as we walked along. His job was to tell this story to others as he traveled through the countryside. It seemed strange to us. North Korea does not have any state-recognized churches, and this concept was all new to us. The truth is, it was a crime to be talking about any religion there, but Yo-han felt comfortable and was not afraid to speak about it here in China with strangers. I glanced at Ji-rang. I knew Ji-rang was thinking the same thing as I was. "This is all well and good, but we just want to work, have enough food, and not struggle." At this point, the only thing I was interested in was surviving. I was not interested in a "Jesus" story. We didn't say anything, though. Yo-han was a nice guy. That night, we three cooked the chicken and rice I had purchased earlier. The next morning, Yo-han bid us goodbye and left, going off in a different direction. Ji-rang and I felt confident and optimistic as we continued walking toward Yanji. Several hours later, we saw what looked like a North Korean backpacker walking in the same direction that we were going.

❄

"Hey man," I yelled trying to get his attention, "where are you going?"

"Hi," he said. "I'm just going to the nearest village for some supplies. What about you guys?"

Ji-rang spoke up, "We are headed to Yanji. We hope to find some jobs. What is your name?"

"Do you work around here? I wanted to know more. I was still learning. "My name is Seng-il Park, by the way, and this here is Ji-rang."

"Yeah, my name is Jae-ru Guak. I work just a couple of miles from here doing construction work. It's pretty safe here as safety goes. We cut trees and clear the land mainly for roads but sometimes so they can build homes."

"That's great! Do you like the work, and do they pay you fairly?" I was suddenly extremely interested in this guy.

"Yes, the boss is a decent guy. The only problem is that you must work for a whole month before you get paid. And of course, we live out here in the mountains, but yeah, I like it a lot."

Jae-ru gave us his boss's name and address, telling us that he thought there might be more work here before he left. Life was looking up for Ji-rang and me! We could see Yanji off in the distance and settled down for another night in the mountains, determined to get up in the morning to find the general contractor and to ask for jobs.

We did, in time, find the contractor in Yanji who did have work for us, and he hired us both to trim trees and clear the land. The man gave us warm clothes and shoes and told us we had to work for a month before we got paid. We camped in the mountains not far from where we worked, and we were provided with food. We felt we could hide from the authorities and anyone else who might report us. Not bad. We had worked for this man for about two weeks when we had a horrible day. I never really liked crowds or having too many people around me, so I usually ate my meals a little away from all the others. On this day I was eating my lunch when suddenly about six or seven policemen pulled up with guns. Everybody scattered and ran in all directions, but the police managed to catch about twenty of my North Korean coworkers. I was lucky that I was on the fringe and ran like hell. I knew enough not to run in the same general direction as most of the guys and headed off in a different direction from the others. I was looking for a ditch or a pile of trees and branches that I could hide behind and not move until the raid was over. I found a place not too far actually and burrowed into the pile of debris. It was dark and dirty in there, and I hoped I would not run into any little animals, but I needed to be completely hidden. Everybody was for himself. That was the last I saw of Ji-rang. Later that day, hours after I thought the police were gone, I listened carefully for any sounds of people running around or any human life at all. After not hearing anything for a long time, I got the courage to slowly emerge from the pile. I was just dusting myself off and starting to orient myself when I spotted Young-sik Won, who was several yards away and looking about as confused as I was. Young-sik was about thirty-two and was a construction worker from North Korea who was also lucky enough not to be caught that day. The two of us went looking for a piece of plastic to make a tent with for the night and to see if we could salvage anything from the construction site. We knew that the work was over and that we would not get paid. We felt lucky that we had not been caught, but to tell you the truth, it kind of soured me on the idea of doing construction work. I felt a bit defeated. We went back to the construction site and poked around but did not find much, and we didn't have food or much of anything to camp with, so we decided to walk down into the little village next to Yanji. We chose a house and went to the door again, knocking and asking for food and a pan to boil rice in along with bean paste. They gave us some Kimchi, a Korean side dish made from fermented vegetables and seasonings. Some Chinese people were very nice.

❁

I wouldn't say that I was friends with Young-sik, but I felt that I had no choice, and we stayed together in the mountains, camping under a big plastic tarp that served as our tent for almost a year. Having worked on construction for several months and receiving good food during this time, Young-sik was in great physical shape. He was not very intellectual or friendly, but he was not mean, so we got along even though I would not say that we were ever very close. There was a restaurant owner in the closest town who would buy the mushrooms, vegetables, and herbs that we collected. We sold these items for money to buy salt and other food items, clothes, and shoes. We collected herbs daily in the spring by walking in different parts of the mountains where ginseng, especially, would grow. I learned to identify and collect these valuable plants while growing up. The restaurant owner was very particular about what shape the herbs and vegetables were in when delivered. I learned early on to hide a bag under some timber or bushes where animals and other people would not find them. By stashing them this way until I picked them up at the end of the day, they did not get beat up and remained fresh for sale the next day or so. To keep our minds occupied, Young-sik and I made games and competitions out of how many different vegetables we could find each day. On a good day, I could find a whole bag of vegetables and still have enough to eat that night for supper. In the summer, we mainly helped farmers in their fields plant and harvest rice, potatoes, and pecans. We had more contact with people in the summer, which made life more interesting, but I was always careful about what I told them about myself or what we talked about. I had learned to never tell anyone that I was from North Korea, speak about either the Chinese or the North Korean governments, or even say much about my family. Neither Young-sik nor I had the proper Chinese documents, and there were rumors that some Chinese, as well as Chinese Koreans, reported North Koreans if they didn't like you or if you had something they wanted. I was becoming adept at keeping conversations friendly but very superficial.

We again collected herbs and bracken (an edible Asian fern) in the spring and summer, and when fall and winter arrived, we helped people collect wood for heating and cooking. We both kept a low profile and did not interact much with people. We both knew we did not want to be caught and sent back to North Korea, and we were unsure of just who we could trust. I worked very hard learning Chinese and practiced every day to get rid of my accent. I had big dreams of someday being able to look and act like a Chinese person enough so that I could blend in and live a good life. In the meantime, I was surviving and learning so much.

Time passed, and one day while living in the mountains with Young-sik, I saw my old workmate, Ji-rang, working on another guy's farm. Ji-rang was no longer tending cows; instead, he and another young North Korean guy about my age, Yu-ri Moon, were planting potatoes for a local farmer. The three of us would get together, eat, drink beer, and talk about how we got there, the town, work, etc. Life was good. I had a home and food. I was free… kind of.

CHAPTER 32

✿

In 2001, we had a pleasant winter, spring, and early summer. It was one hot July day in 2001 when the three of us—Ji-rang, Yu-ri, and I—were in a café. We had become good pals and enjoyed each other's company. The café was a small restaurant where they served drinks and other food like rice cakes, roasted sweet potatoes, corn on the cob, roasted chestnuts, beef, and pork. Without warning, some undercover policemen, who we thought were just ordinary Chinese men eating in the restaurant, stood up and pointed their guns at us. It was our fault because we were smoking and had let our guard down, not being as careful or as watchful as we should have been. These Chinese guys suddenly transformed themselves into police, and we knew immediately that they were going to arrest us. Both Ji-rang and Yu-ri tried to run, but both were quickly overtaken by the bigger Chinese guys. They began beating both men over the head with their sticks. I started yelling, "I'm not North Korean! I'm not North Korean!" They manhandled and handcuffed us, knocking over some chairs and screaming all the time. It was chaotic. Three of the men took both Ji-rang and Yu-ri back to the Chinese police station. But because they were unsure about me, they were going to let me go, or so I thought. It turns out that they wanted to know the location of my and Young-sik's tent and then search it for evidence that we were North Korean refugees. They must have been listening to our conversation for some time to have figured out that Young-sik and I lived together somewhere in the mountains. We had been stupid to let our guard down so much. The other two policemen threw me into the back seat of their car and drove me back to where we had been staying in the mountains. They spent the next three hours searching through every item at the campsite. I was extremely scared as I waited and answered questions while they kept me handcuffed and my ankles chained.

"What did the two of you do out here?" the tallest guy asked.

"Nothing much, we just lived and collected vegetables and herbs to sell to the various restaurants in the village."

"How long were you out here?"

"Not long—just a couple months."

"Did you guys play hanky panky games?" The pudgy, shorter guy laughed a low, guttural laugh and, in a condescending way, nudged my shoulder. I did not like this guy at all. I was sure he had a mean streak in him, and I did not want to do or say anything to set him off.

"Are you from North Korea?"

"No, my parents died a couple of years ago, and I have been on my own in this region since then."

They kept asking me the same questions repeatedly, in slightly different ways, always trying to get me to admit I was a refugee from North Korea. I had to keep my wits about me and calmly answer every question. I could not let them get under my skin. Neither Young-sik nor I kept anything from North Korea and had even gotten rid of the clothes we had there. We wanted nothing on us at any time that would give anyone the impression that we were North Korean refugees. We were trying to always blend in and be taken for Chinese Koreans who had lived most of our lives in that region. But they still tore the plastic down, unfolded it, shook out both Young-sik's and my blankets, looked through our cooking pans and utensils, and looked at the few supplies we had. They even looked all around the campsite perimeter to see if we had buried anything. After about three hours, having found nothing of value or incriminating, they brought some lunch to the site. They kept saying, "This may be your last meal—eat whatever you want. You may not eat for a long time." I was very worried.

I was still trying to convince them to let me go. I kept saying that I had not done anything wrong and asking them if they couldn't just release me. "Let me go!" I pleaded. "I haven't done anything wrong. You haven't found anything here. I don't have anything wrong!"

Both men agreed; "If we let you go, we will lose our jobs. It's our job to catch guys like you, and we aren't going to lose our jobs." I could not convince them to let me go, no matter what I said.

❧

Finally, they took me to the Chinese police station, and I was locked in a cell with ten other guys. The cell was small—about five feet by eight feet—and had a cement floor. There was no furniture or beds in the room, and it smelled of dirt and urine. There was barely room to move when we all lay down to sleep. I hated being so close and touching others all the time. The Chinese fed us three meals a day of Chinese food, but I did not think it was very good. I had no idea how long they would keep me there, nor did any of the other guys. None of us knew what was going on or the exact reason we were being held here. Some guys had been there a couple of months already. One guy named Soo-jin was a decent fellow. He had been there only a couple of days and was a very small guy. He had silky black hair but very crooked teeth and a bad complexion. I guessed that his poor complexion was due more to poor nutrition than hormones.

"How did you get caught?" he had asked me shortly after I got there.

"A couple of other guys and I were in a café in Yanji when some undercover police overheard us talking and decided we were from North Korea," I answered, shrugging my shoulders like that was the end of it. I did not want to admit, even to Soo-jin or anyone else there in the room, that I was from North Korea. I hoped he would not ask me more questions, especially here in this tiny cell with so many ears. I learned that I should be cautious with everyone, even people in jail. You just never knew what could happen, and wasn't I there because I had been careless in the café?

Soo-jin continued, "I came from Pyongyang. My father was too sick to work the mandatory hours in the government fields, and he was taken away by the military police to one of those camps. The rest of my family has all died from starvation or disease. I didn't have much to lose by coming to China. I would have died there if I hadn't come." He turned his face away as he told me his story and fought back tears. I knew that Soo-jin was close to the breaking point. My heart bled for him, except that I was in the same predicament. There was a small window, and I looked up at the sky for hours on end. I kept wondering, "Why was I born? A bird has freedom. I do not. I'm no better than an animal." I was feeling so depressed, and in truth, it was an exceptionally low period for me. I was there for a week.

❁

The guards never talked to us and treated us like animals. I think they were waiting until they got enough guys to fill a transport vehicle to who knew where. I still do not understand why they called my name, but they came to the cell one day and called out five guys' names. Soo-jin and I were both called. They handcuffed and put ankle chains on us five guys and strung another chain so that we were all connected. As the guard bent down to secure Soo-jin's leg chains, I saw a look of absolute desperation on his face. I caught his eye and gave him a look desperately pleading with him not to do anything to get himself and the rest of us killed. They kept us chained this way as they loaded us into a small van and drove over the river into North Korea.

I was scared out of my mind, and I wanted to die. What shame for my family! I was so ashamed! How could I escape this hell? The guards were all armed and were quick to beat someone if they offered any resistance at all. There was nothing I could do. I always waited and watched for a chance to escape. I waited for them to make a mistake, but these guards were extremely cautious. They kept me in the first prison in North Korea for two weeks. It was better there than in the Chinese police station. There was more room in the cell, although I had decided all these gulags were the same and none of them were comfortable. They fed us North Korean food, though, and I was more familiar with it, so it tasted better. Soo-jin had been put in a different cell. I never saw Soo-jin again or heard what happened to him. I hope he survived, but I don't know... It was like my "life was being turned upside down." I had no idea what would happen to me or when or even if I would be released. By this time, I had learned that the very worst crimes that a North Korean person could commit were political crimes, such as talking with Christians, South Koreans, or

US citizens. I hoped they would think of me as a "rebel" only and classify my crimes as a betrayal or a minor crime of some sort that would not be considered so serious. However, I was very worried and was beginning to think I might be sent to a political prison camp for life.

❀

While we were in this first prison, they fingerprinted us and if we were clean and everything was in order (meaning our documents, I guess), then they called our names. Finally, they called my name, and I was taken out, chained together with fifteen other prisoners, and loaded onto a bus. No one knew what was happening or where we were going. Once we were on the bus and had sat down, they took our ankle chains off but left the handcuffs in place. They drove us about thirty minutes further into the North Korean mountains, and when they passed through the bus, they released our cuffs. This was my chance! I had to make a break for it now because they might pull the bus directly into a prison yard. There would be no way out if that happened. I looked at the windows and doors on the bus. I was in the middle of the bus, and there was no way I could get to the back door. And if I did make it, I thought it would take me too long to get the door opened. While I was fiddling with it, I thought the guard could and probably would shoot me. I waited until the guard walked up to the front of the bus and had his back to me. I jumped up, grabbed the small lever on the window next to me, and somehow got the window down enough to squeeze my thin body out of the narrow window. I planned to let go and fall to the ground even though the bus was traveling about fifty miles per hour.

I figured I did not have much to lose at this point, as I knew I would probably die in a prison in North Korea. I was about halfway out of the small little window, ready to give myself one last shove and let go, when a guard hit me as hard as he could with a bamboo club right across my left kidney area. How did he turn around and reach me so fast? I didn't have much time to think about all of this when he hit me a second time with a smart jab right between my outstretched legs! Incapacitating, end-of-the-world pain shot through my whole body. I gasped for air and tried to squirm away from him as he grabbed my shirt and jerked me back into the bus, dragging my thin body over the metal windowsills and bruising my flesh and bones all the way. One more blow to my head and I lost consciousness, which is probably a good thing because he continued to beat me.

❇

When I came to, I was in a hospital or medical place of some sort. I was covered in blood and had deep bruises and abrasions everywhere. I hurt like hell all over my body, and I had no idea how badly I was hurt. There was a lady (a nurse or a doctor) in a uniform with a name tag who was cleaning my face and my wounds. I was wondering why they brought me here. As the lady washed me, she kept saying, "You're strong! You are still alive!" I was afraid to answer her. I thought they might hit me or something. I was hurting all over, but I guess I didn't have any broken bones or internal injuries. I was lucky! However, I was extremely badly bruised, scuffed, and scraped all over my body. I was passing blood in my urine, and I had no idea how serious that was or when it would stop. While most of my wounds had stopped bleeding, they still oozed a clear liquid. It hurt like hell! My clothes had not protected me much and had been torn off me either in the beating or by the medical people. I was now wearing a thin prison uniform. I was cold, which I guess happens when you have these kinds of beatings, but I could not stand to have anything, including cloth, touch me on the side that had been dragged over the windowsill. I was scared and in a lot of pain. When the woman was done, they moved me to a small room or cell that was on the ground floor.

There were four other North Korean guys in this room, the size of an extra-small bedroom but not so swanky, of course. The North Korean guys all knew that being back in a North Korean prison was not good. We were all desperate to escape and get back to China. What we needed was some sort of plan. One thing I learned was that if you wanted to sacrifice for a better life, you could not be afraid of dying.

The five of us sat down and put our heads together to devise an escape route, with everyone contributing what they knew about the area and how best to get to the river, as well as where would be the best place to cross into China. I learned quite a bit about the area but was not at all keen on all five of us sticking together. To me, it seemed that five guys together would make far more noise and draw more attention than if we separated. But three of the guys felt it was best to stay together. I let the subject drop and kept to myself more by acting like I was in terrible pain, which was not far from the truth. In time, the guards brought us some water and some very thin corn soup. I managed to conceal a spoon and not give it back, and this would become my only tool. The room had a small window in it with a metal frame around it. We knew that the guards would hear us if we broke the window glass, so I began using the spoon to dig around and loosen the concrete around the metal frame. We hoped we could escape through the window. We all took turns working on the window frame, which they had installed from the inside, making it harder to loosen, plus we were trying to be as quiet as we could. Finally, it was loosened enough to remove, but we decided we had to wait until it was light enough to see which direction to go in. We all knew the plan, and we waited for the first crack of dawn.

�֍

When it got light enough for us to see, we knew it was now or never, and we all climbed out of the window. The other four guys all beat me out the window. I just could not seem to make my body move faster and was stiff to boot. Three of the guys took off in one direction, and one skinny guy who was about ten years older than me and I ran like hell in a different direction. At some point, we got separated, but I kept going. I had not had much food or good nutrition for so long, and I was extremely sore and lame from my recent beating. My body was in terrible shape. It seemed like my muscles and my entire body would not respond to my commands to go faster and faster, and I kept running out of breath. I was forced to make frequent stops in the shadows wherever I could. While I caught my breath, I would listen for the sounds of footsteps or the guards shouting. I did not know if they had caught any of the other guys, and frankly, I didn't care. I figured every man was for himself, and I was doing everything I could to get to the river as fast as I could go. I did not know that they had caught the older, skinny guy and forced him to tell them what our plan was and where we were going. All I knew was that I was in North Korea, that they were taking me to some other prison in North Korea, and that I had to get back over the border into China. I kept running and moving as fast as my body would allow me toward the river. I was almost to the river when five or six guys in military uniforms stood up with guns and yelled, "Hands up!" They had me surrounded. I thought I was a dead man. I was ordered to lie down with my hands above my head. I was so weak, tired, and out of breath. I lay down, and they kicked me several times, and one of them hit me with the butt of his gun and knocked me out. They tied my hands and then dragged me about three-fourths of a mile toward a car. They dragged me like an animal. I regained consciousness towards the last quarter of a mile and tried to protect my side and my head as I was pulled and bounced over the rough ground. They just kept dragging me. They no doubt knew that I had attempted to escape twice now, and they were not playing games. While I did not know exactly where they were taking me, I did know that my life could be over in an instant. I was almost eighteen years old. I wanted to live. I wanted to be free in China.

❀

I later learned I was going to an internment camp in North Korea, not far from the border between North Korea and China. The concentration camp or internment camp housed political prisoners, and I was now considered a political prisoner. I was thrown into a small cell with no food or water for the first five days. My whole body ached and longed for just a sip of water and something to eat. The different guards would come in two or three times a day and beat me up. They strung me up by tying my hands above my head with my toes barely touching the floor and beat me. One guard was particularly sadistic. In my mind, I called him "The Goon." He kept his head shaved but wore his military-style hat at a slight angle so that it partially covered a jagged scar he had on the side of his forehead. It had not been sewed up correctly, if at all, and was still discolored. When he got mad or exerted himself, the scar turned an even darker crimson. He was slightly on the fat side with fat cheeks, and his uniform always looked wrinkled like he slept in it. He was much bigger than I was and walked with his shoulders slouched with one hand fingering his belt. The first day, "The Goon" came in and just walked around me, then, in one swift move, gave the chain that was looped around my handcuffs a big tug. It was easy to yank me to my feet, and I was suspended in the air with my hands above my head and my feet barely touching the floor. He secured the chain on a hook on one side of the cell then walked around to face me. He grabbed a handful of my hair, jerked my head back, and spit in my face. "You pig traitor!" He shouted.

He then took out a baton made of bamboo and hit me on my chest and back, which hurt like hell. I hoped that he had not broken any ribs, and I was having a difficult time breathing. Every time he hit me, he shouted, "Pig Traitor!" or "You Pig!" He finally got tired of beating me and took a long swig of water from a bottle he had brought with him. How I wanted just a sip of that water! The Goon was not done. He walked around me, taunting me, but I was in so much pain in my wrists, where the cuffs were biting into my flesh, that it didn't matter what he was saying. He then did a couple of one-two punches into my stomach, knocking the wind out of me. I was fighting for my breath when he suddenly released the chain holding me in the air and walked out. It all happened so fast, I was not prepared to catch myself and just crumbled to the floor, gasping for air. At that moment, I hated the bastard.

The guards would come in at odd times of the day or night and always announce their arrival by kicking the cell door before throwing it open. This simple act sent chills down my spine, as I knew they were there to punish me in some awful manner. One of the guards would hoist me up by my hands and then practice the Korean martial art of Taekwondo. "Tae" means to destroy with the foot, "Kwon" means to destroy with the hand, and "do" means an art or way of life. I don't know how much of the "do" part he practiced, but he sure had fun with his feet and hands. I, of course, could do nothing but use my toes to try to swirl away from him to protect myself, which was not very successful. I did not like this bastard too much either. Sometimes they just used their fists. They broke my nose and kept on hitting me. My whole body hurt and ached all the time, and I desperately needed food and water. Sometimes they sat me down in a chair with my arms and hands stretched out on a table in front of me and beat my arms with a bar. While they never broke any bones, I did have welts and bruises on nearly every inch of my body. I did not know how long I could stand this or how long this would go on. No person should ever be treated this way. I never found out just why they beat me or what information they wanted from me. It never made sense to me—it still doesn't. I became like a zombie, and I think they finally realized they did not want another death at this place, so they gave me about three table-spoons of a thin, clear soup per meal, three times a day, with no water. It was enough to keep me alive, but barely.

It was while I was in that cell that I finally had to go to the bathroom. But when I used the hole located there in the cell, I passed 300.00 Chinese dollars. I had put it in a small plastic bag and swallowed it, and that was all the money I had. I kept stirring and stirring in that hole, looking for the money, but I never found it. I felt so bad about losing that money. This was an exceptionally low point for me.

❖

I was in this place for about two weeks when they needed workers to help build a storage facility at the prison and came to my cell to let me out for work. At least I got more food while I worked there, but they had guards all around with guns pointed at us all the time. They would come to the cell every morning and file us out, then make us walk the two or three miles to the work area. Once there, our job was to mix mud and grass and make bricks out of cheap and plentiful resources. Once the bricks were made and had dried hard, we started building the storage building.

The work was very labor-intensive and made us all burn extra calories, plus I was still a growing boy or was supposed to be. There were guards everywhere pointing their guns at us, and there was no way I could run, plus I was getting weaker and weaker. There was no way I could escape this place.

While I was locked up here, they were investigating me. Did I "talk Jesus," meaning was I getting involved with Christianity, which was a crime? North Korea does not sanction any religion, but Christianity is considered "Western," so it is particularly loathed. Did I have contact with the Americans or with any South Koreans? Did I meet with the Chinese authorities and give out any information about North Korea? They beat me repeatedly to get me to answer these same questions. I wondered how they all had the energy to keep beating us because there were so many men in the prison. I decided that beating us was their main "workout." It was disgusting.

They especially concentrated on the "talking Jesus" questions. "Do you believe in Jesus?" They would ask repeatedly and then sock me in the stomach.

"Jesus who?" I would ask. Sometimes, they hit me so hard that I would vomit or have a hard time breathing. It was tough.

"You know! Jesus God!" They would yell. This would go on and on until they got tired of that question and switched to another.

"When did you go to China? Who did you go to China with?"

"No! No! I'm Chinese Korean!" I would respond every time. "I lived in the Yanbian Korean Autonomous Prefecture all my life! I am not North Korean." I was extremely desperate but did not want to break and say what they wanted me to. I knew it would be my death sentence.

"Where in North Korea are you from? Who is your mother? Your father? Who is your brother? Your sister?" They continued to beat me. "What is your Korean address?" Sometimes I lost consciousness.

At times they threw water in my face to make me come around. And they continued to yell at me, "Did you meet any South Koreans? How about meeting any American Bastards?" They spit in my face and yanked my head back. Sometimes they stuck their faces so close that they almost touched mine as they screamed, "Do you know anyone in North Korea who went to church?" I had no idea how long this would go on. Would they ever let me go? I was losing all hope.

"You're from North Korea, aren't you? You want to go back to your home here in North Korea, don't you? You want to see your mama?" I wanted all this to stop. I hoped I could hang on and not "break," but I just did not know. I worried about my family. I longed for them to leave me alone and just let me work. Working hard for extremely long hours while being starved was easier than this interrogation process.

❀

I must have been there for about a month—the days kind of ran together. After the investigations were over, they decided to send me to another state security department "collection" center, where I stayed for another month. There must have been about fifty people in this collections center, but they came and went. They fed us crap food like animal food, only worse. We were used as farm labor, weeding, and planting crops. Guards with guns were everywhere, and they were brutal, always trying to entice us to say or do something that was "punishable." If we did something they did not like, they would beat us or, at times, shoot guys for no reason at all.

Some days we talked in our cell, and I got to know a man who was about thirty-five years old. He was so skinny and weak, but he worked hard every day. He told me he was afraid they would kill him if he did not do "his share." He was probably right. One day, this guy couldn't take it any longer. He must have felt that he was going to starve if he stayed here in prison, so why not try to escape? He watched the guards, and when most of the guards had wandered over to the shade of a nearby tree, he hit the guard closest to him. The guard had turned his back for just a moment, and the man hit him over the head with a small shovel. The guard was completely surprised and gave out a low cry before falling to the ground. I did not know if the guard was dead or what, but the thirty-five-year-old prisoner quickly grabbed his gun and ran as fast as he could toward the edge of the field. He did not get far when two or three of the guards standing together in the shade all opened fire on him with their guns. They shot him in the back. That all happened so quickly, and it was extremely sobering to see. We all knew it was best not to attempt an escape and to get right back to work.

Some days I could hear men screaming, groaning, or crying. Some were being "investigated," which was another word for being beaten. We were crowded together, with no room to stretch out in the cell. I was always touching someone, and of course, no one got to bathe. We all wore dirty clothes and stunk like hell. In a way, we got used to this over time, especially when the main desire was for food. I wondered if I would ever have enough to eat.

❀

We worked long hours every day for crap food. Then one day they called my name, along with five others. They put us on a train to what I now think was the Chongjin State Collection Center, but we did not know for sure where we were going. Chongjin is a lifetime prison controlled by the state security agency. It is in the city of Chongjin, in the North Hamgyong Province of North Korea, and is for political prisoners. North Korea does not have special buses or cars to transport prisoners, so we went by regular train in handcuffs and chains. It was while I was on this train that I spoke to some ordinary people. I spoke to one woman and two different men.

"Can you help me?" I asked the woman who kept looking my way. Maybe I looked like her son or a brother who had disappeared. I don't know. "I need your help to contact my mother." I pleaded. I looked at her and made a gesture as if to write something down. At first, she looked away, but then she looked down at her purse and dug out a scrap of paper and a small pencil. She looked around to make sure no one was looking or paying any attention, and then quickly handed it to me. I wrote down my mother's name and the small village where she lived. I wrote "Help! I am dying." under this information. Shortly after that, when everything looked clear, I handed it back to her. She briefly looked at the note as she put it in her purse, and a sad look came over her face, but she did not say anything. I know she knew I was not lying, but she stopped looking at me for the rest of the trip. I hoped she would deliver my note.

I was also able to connect with two men while I was on the train that day. One guy was about forty but looked older. I caught his eye after about an hour on the train and was able to whisper to him. "I need you to do me a favor. I am in poor condition and dying. I don't know if I will last much longer, but I need you to let my relatives know where I am. Please help me, mister."

This man thought for a moment, then nodded and drew a piece of paper out of his pocket, and the man he was with gave me a pencil. This time I printed the names of my aunt and uncle from another village on the paper before handing it back to them. "My name is Seng-il Park." I told them, "And I'm unsure where they are taking us, but it can't be good. Thank you for letting my family know what is happening to me."

I do not know which one of these people was successful in getting the message to my family. I knew that it was best to give them more than one relative's name in the hopes that if someone in my family heard about me, they would tell my mother or brothers. The thought of dying without anyone ever knowing anything about me was very depressing. That train ride was long and tortuous, mainly because I felt it was taking me to my last place to live.

I knew that I was getting weaker and that no one cared in the prisons. I was sure the guards had been trained to think of and treat us as subhuman. When we got to this state security collection center, they did not process us at all but simply herded us into small, overcrowded cells. These cement cells did not have windows, and we slept on the floor with no blankets or pillows. The smell of urine and excrement was overwhelming. Other inmates in the cell made the cell hot, but I supposed they would also keep us warmer in the winter (if I lived that long.) When we got there, I found that the food was better, but the work was more demanding. The prisoners were used for cutting wood and farming corn, potatoes, and other vegetables. The guards at this facility acted and treated us very much like the guards in all the places where I had been locked up previously. They all had blank, vacant faces showing no emotion, just going about their work of guarding us and treating us like animals. I later learned that North Korean guards were encouraged and even rewarded for hurting and killing prisoners. Some guards were rewarded with being allowed to attend college, and some received other benefits for "keeping us in line." I did not know this at the time, or I think I would have been even more discouraged and worried. No one talked much in my cell. I think they all felt like they were bound to die here, and what was the point, anyway? There were about one hundred prisoners where I was now, and it rained a lot. I was miserable and alone.

❊

While I was there at this camp, many people died of starvation and poor nutrition, and I helped to bury three of them. We would make simple boxes out of cheap wood if we had any wood at all; otherwise, we would wrap them in a blanket, and the person would be buried without ceremony or fanfare. But there was one young man who died who left a huge impression on me. His name was Jang-rhee, and he was only about five years older than me. Jang-rhee had probably been exceptionally good-looking at one time. I can still see his face—his hair had grown thin and gray, his skin hung from his bones, and oh, his eyes! He was so skinny, and his eyes were sunken and dull. It was a rainy day, and we had been talking.

"Life is…. no really…. like a little fly. Hit once and gone," he had said earlier.

Now the young man gripped my hand and held it tightly. Or at least it was as tight as he could considering he was dying and had no strength. I looked into his brown eyes, which I knew had been so vibrant and alert not so long ago but were now hooded, very dry, and so dull. He licked his dry, parched lips and opened his mouth to speak. After a false start, his voice came out in a low horse whisper, "Don't die." I leaned in closer so I could hear him speak. "You must live! Don't… Don't die like me." He again attempted to lick his lips with a tongue that was so parched—I had never seen anything like it before. I wanted to pull away, but his eyes bore into mine and held me to him. "Don't die like me... like trash! Just don't die!" He slowly closed his eyes, took a long, tortuous breath, and was gone.

For a moment, I just sat there holding his hand. I did not know what to think. It was certainly not the first time I had seen death. Jang-rhee would be the third man that I helped bury in the last three weeks. I had seen death all around me as I grew up in famine-torn North Korea. Death from starvation and illness had been all around, and I saw dead people in the streets nearly every day. And I knew what it was like to be hungry myself. Boy, did I know! But somehow the death of Jang-rhee truly rocked me. Perhaps it was because he was my age and I realized it could easily have been me lying there with no life left, with none of my family knowing if I was alive, dead, or even where I was.

Jang-rhee's words, "You must live!" came back to me loud and clear. "Don't die like me... like trash." It was then that the feeling slowly began to rise in my chest. It was a feeling of great anger—how could people be so brutal and cruel to other humans? How dare they be so "inhumane?" But it was also a feeling of great power and determination. "I'm going to live!" I thought, "I've got to live through this! By hook or crook, I've got to live through this! It will make me more powerful and stronger. I have just GOT to survive!"

❁

Some days later, I was outside planting potatoes in a field when one of my senior aunts appeared at the edge of the field. She had heard where I was and had come to give me some food. FOOD! I was so happy! At first, I thought I saw a mirage. I blinked and looked away, then looked over in her direction again. It *was* Auntie! I quickly hustled over to the edge of the field. Of course, it was against the rules, but she had bought off the guard with some cigarettes, and he just turned his head and pretended to be observing some other prisoners.

"Auntie, you know about me!" I cried. "You came, and you brought me food!" I hugged her quickly as she gave me some bread and vegetables. My mouth was watering, and I wanted to tear into the food right then. I knew I should save some food for later, but I was so hungry! And I thought that someone might steal it from me. No one was getting enough food.

Auntie was crying now, too, but it may have been because of the circumstances and the ghastly condition I was in. I am sure I was a shocking sight to see. I tore off the heel from the small loaf of bread and stuffed it into my mouth as I looked at her. I chewed that first bite so fast and asked her, "Does Mother know where I am? Does she know what has happened?"

My aunt swallowed back tears and just shook her head no.

"Please tell her…. tell her where I am," I managed to get out. Yes, I was so ashamed, but I was dying, and I knew it. I wanted to see my mother one last time at least.

I noticed the guard moving on the other side of the field and knew I needed to get back to work or risk a severe beating. Auntie knew it too and simply squeezed my arm before disappearing over the hill. I had no idea if I would ever see her or my mother again. But food! I had food to eat!

The guards knew I was dying. I guess they saw so many people die, and they knew the symptoms. Maybe they did not want such a young guy's death on their hands because the news that they were killing teenage so-called "political prisoners" could get out, and that wouldn't be good. I don't know if the guards contacted my mother or if my aunt contacted her, but after a week, my mother came with more food and to get me. They would not let me go. She was forced to stay with some relatives close to the camp and wait. I guess they had followed protocol and notified the local police in my hometown to come to get me. Well, the police did not have any money for this kind of transportation, so after about two weeks, they let me go with my mother.

I will never forget the day they let me go. It was just like in the American movies that I later saw. The guards came to the cell where they were keeping me and called my name. They said I could go. At first, I thought they might just be telling me a mean joke, but I slowly walked, half-dragging myself out to the gates where Mother was standing alone. She was crying when she rushed up and hugged me, "You are alive! My son, you are alive!" We continued to hug each other, both crying and rocking back and forth a little. She felt so warm and good to me. "You don't need to give me anything!" She said, "You don't need to do anything for me. You are alive!" We were both crying a lot.

We had not seen each other for well over a year. I think I weighed about thirty kilograms, or about sixty-six or sixty-eight pounds, and could hardly walk. Mother had brought a small cart like a wheelbarrow, and I lay down in it. Mother was not in great shape and was not strong. She struggled and stumbled a few times as she pushed me the whole way to the train station. I truly felt like I was going home to die, but *oh how great it was to hold my mother for one last time!!* We rode the train the whole way to my hometown, where my brothers met us. I learned on the train ride home that my father had died while I was in China. Mother and I cried for him.

I arrived home to heal and recuperate. My younger brothers caught tiny fish from the local river and fed me this high protein. I slowly began to heal and put on some weight. At first, I was so happy just to be at home with my family, but then the police began coming unannounced about two times a week to check on me. I began to think they wanted me to regain some of my strength but had not intended for me to be completely pardoned for my crimes. My family also believed that as soon as I was stronger, the police would arrest me and take me back to the collection camp. It was a fear that hung over us all. I told my mother about what I had seen in China. That it was so rich. There was plenty of food. There was work. She quickly told me to "Shut up! Someone might hear you!"

I was sad that I couldn't even share this information with my mother or brothers. I was unsure if they would believe me, anyway. After lifetimes of complete adherence and total belief in the greatness of the royal Kim family, anything else would be considered treasonous and dangerous. I knew I did not want to put my family at risk, so I stayed silent.

I stayed at home, slowly getting better and better. I was eating corn and the tiny fish that my brother caught, along with the vegetables that my family foraged for in the mountains. After I got stronger, I went into the mountains to visit my father's tomb. I pulled some weeds on his grave and mourned his loss, even though we had not been particularly close. I lay down on the grass in the mountains there staring up at the sky, thinking about my father, and after a while, I found a kind of peace. I stayed there, for a long time before slowly walking back to my home and to the harsh realities of living in North Korea.

During the previous year, I learned that there were several classes or layers of North Korean traitors. The first class was those people who escaped to China because they were starving, and there were a lot of them. In 1991, after the fall of the Soviet Union, Kim Il-sung implemented a "military-first policy." He believed that even though North Korea was a small state, he could stabilize the nation and make the country powerful and prosperous by growing the military. Consequently, the people were starving while most of the food was going to Kim Il-sung's army.

The second class of traitors was made up of North Koreans who "talked Jesus." North Korea is considered a secular state where public religion is discouraged. There are traces of Buddhism, Chondoism, and Confucianism, but for the most part, the "cult of the Kims" was what was studied and believed. That and the doctrine of "juche" (the belief in the self-reliance of the whole country) predominate. The large-scale destruction caused by the massive air raids and the suffering experienced by the North Korean people during the Korean War helped foster hatred of Christianity as being the "American" religion. Therefore, it is a crime to "talk Jesus."

The third classification of traitors, and perhaps the worst, was the class of people who defected to South Korea or the United States, North Korea's worst enemy. While I was considered a first-level traitor in North Korea (I had left simply because I was starving and scared), I was still a traitor, and the authorities would not let me go free.

As I was recuperating, I began to think about the many North Korean facts and realities that I had not known before I left. All those years, our leaders deceived and lied to us! It was eye-opening and something that I was sure would make it harder for me in North Korea, even if I were permitted to stay and work outside of prison. I could not even share the information with my family! After all, there is safety in ignorance. I also learned more about "Songbun," the "class structure," or a sort of "hereditary caste system," which is said to be a combination of Confucianism and Stalinism. No one ever talked about this system or truly knew where they stood in it, but we did know that your classification went back at least three generations and was even influenced by the actions of relatives today. No one wanted to be the one who caused his or her family and extended family for three generations (your generation, the one ahead of you, and the one that came behind you) to be sent to an internment camp with no way to escape ever. All this was not officially published or precisely defined, but it was "out there," and I was worried.

❋

I now realized that I could no longer stay and live in North Korea and that I had to leave. It simply was not safe, AND I had placed my brothers, my mother, and my grandparents in danger of being punished or killed since they were now associated with a "traitor." I believed they would be safer if I died or disappeared. All this plus I had seen that life was better outside of North Korea—that there was more food available and a person could find work. How could I stay in North Korea now that I had seen the outside and had learned so much? I did know, however, that I would have to leave soon if I wanted to leave at all, and I needed to go before I was arrested again. I wanted to go back to China. My family and I all knew I would die if I stayed here, was arrested, and taken back to prison. My mother cried especially when I told her, "I can't promise you my life. I don't know what will happen."

My mother cried and cried and finally said, "You owe me nothing. I don't need your help! Don't worry about me. You must go. Stay alive." She gave me $1,000.00 in Korean money (a lot of money for her) and twelve ears of corn that she had cooked and packed in a plastic bag for me.

Mother was very thin and tired-looking on that last day as I prepared to leave once again. We both knew that this might be the last time we ever saw each other. My heart was heavy, but I was so afraid of dying alone there in a North Korean prison. Her face was tear-streaked, and I knew she had not slept that night. My brothers each hugged me hard and then shook my hand before turning away, choking back tears. Mother hugged me as if she were hanging on for dear life and then released me slowly, knowing it was the only choice we had. She raised her hand and waved me goodbye. My mother's last words to me were, "Go, Son! Stay alive!"

On a warm, sunny day at the end of September, I left by train for China.

CHAPTER 33

❀

Once again, I took the train, but it was easier this time. I not only knew the way and just what I needed to take but also the challenges I would be facing. I also got lucky. There were not as many power outages, so we had fewer long stops in the middle of nowhere, taking only about three to four days to reach the final train station. I knew the train station was about twenty-five miles from where the best spot to cross the river would be, so I got off and started walking toward the city. My goal was to cover the twenty-five miles while keeping a low profile. I also knew I needed to prepare for my escape by going into the mountains to the highest point and again observing when and where the North Korean guards patrolled the river. I had my clothes, boots, a plastic bag, a rope, and of course, my knife ready to go. I just needed to select the proper conditions and timing for my crossing.

So again, I climbed to the highest point in the mountains to observe the guards. I made note of where they were patrolling the heaviest and timed them as they made their rounds. From this knowledge, I selected my exact crossing point on the river and timed my entrance to that point. This time, I made it across the river around 9:00 at night without any problems, hurried into the trees along the bank, and changed my clothes. Once in China, I was walking along the road when an old Chinese man passing by, waved, and called out, "Hey, where are you going?"

"Oh, I'm just going home." I kept walking. Not running because that might cause suspicion. I kept walking about five hundred more yards when I got off the road a quarter of a mile away and lay down in the grass. I had this funny feeling that the Chinese man might have called the Chinese border patrol. I lay in the grass for about an hour watching the road when I saw a car come down the road going kind of slow. It got to a crossroad area, pulled over, and shut off its lights. I thought they might be coming to pick me up at that point, so I stayed low and waited not moving. How well I remembered the beatings and torture I had gone through the last time I had been captured and repatriated back to North Korea. I was taking no chances of being caught this time no matter how long I needed to wait there off the road. I knew exactly what I was up against and I was determined to make a better life for myself outside of North Korea. I had promised my mother I would survive and by hook or by crook, I intended to do just that. After about two hours, the car turned on its lights again and turned around, and left. I lay very still there in the grass for another hour before crawling very slowly forward. I was so cold and hungry before I saw a residential area with about fifteen houses. I decided to stay away from them because I was afraid dogs would bark and alert the people. I was taking no chances as I went deeper up into the mountains and kept walking toward the city of Yanji (the center of the Yanbian Korean Autonomous Prefecture.) I wanted to be in the area with the largest concentration of ethnic Koreans. It was the place in China where I thought I could blend in easiest and I had heard there were more job opportunities there. I reasoned that I should live in that area for however long it would take me until I could assimilate readily with the native Chinese.

That night I crawled into the plastic bag I brought with me and slept until sunrise. I still had more than a three-hour walk to get to Yanji. I had learned that there were fewer hassles when traveling alone and that the more men, the more dangerous it was. I experienced this lesson the hard way.

❋

I still remembered the construction contractor who had given Ji-rang and me work in the mountains the first time I had come to China. I set out to find his house in Yanji and knocked on the door, not expecting him to pay me for the work I had done last time before the police raid (after all, we had agreed I wouldn't be paid until I worked there for one month). Instead, I was hoping he had another job for me. It took a few moments for him to recognize me, and he was clearly surprised to see me, but then he said, "WOW! What happened to you?"

He invited me in for dinner and gave me some clothes. He gave me the telephone number for Young-sik (the young, rather self-centered thirty-two-year-old man I had lived and worked with after the construction site raid.) Since I did not have a telephone, he called Young-sik for me. Young-sik was happy to hear from me and came to the contractor's house by taxi and took me to his mountain campsite where he was staying. I started life again by collecting mushrooms, herbs, and vegetables to sell in the village. I began working and living the "mountain life" that fall until the mushrooms were gone for the season. In truth, Young-sik was using me, and while he did give me food, he kept all the money from our harvesting. It was not the best arrangement, but all the time, I was learning to read and write Chinese and how to live in Chinese culture. I listened to a small radio we had when I wasn't working or studying. I wanted a future in China, and I knew I had to learn the language perfectly with no accent for me to fit into society here.

❃

Sometime in December, Young-sik and I met Gaun-il Long, a sixty-two-year-old Chinese man, who convinced us to leave our tent home and go with him by train to the other side of the mountain close to another village not far. He had a friend who allowed Gaun-il the use of a small house there in the mountains, and Gaun-il wanted us to work for him collecting roots. That meant that Young-sik, I, and Sun-ru Dong, who was a thirty-eight-year-old North Korean man already working for Gaun-il, would all live and work together while Gaun-il went back to his home in the village. The house was extremely small, and we had to collect wood for heating and cooking, but we did OK together until February when Gaun-il was to pay us for our work. When Gaun-il refused to pay us, Young-sik beat him up. Young-sik beat him up darn good and then threatened him, "If you call the police, I will find you and kill you!" Then Young-sik went his way and Gaun-il went back to his home in the village.

I continued to live together with Sun-ru there in the small house foraging for root vegetables and collecting wood and later the seasonal herbs and vegetables until I decided I honestly didn't want to live like this anymore. I liked Sun-ru and staying in the house, but I was extremely restless and wanted to be on my own. I had the nagging desire to have a better life in China. I knew I wanted to blend in with the Chinese people, work, have plenty of food while advancing myself, and perhaps even send help back to my mother and brothers. I did not want to live in hiding from authorities, always looking over my shoulder for a possible betrayal. At the bottom of all these feelings was the knowledge that I would never again be able to survive life in a North Korean prison camp. It was a cold hard realization that I always carried in the pit of my stomach.

❈

I took the bus to once again meet up with Young-sik, who now lived in the mountains; only this time I did not live with him. I wanted to be completely on my own. I found a plastic tent, collected a stash of herbs, mushrooms, and root vegetables, and kept all the money myself. It was rather nice. I later helped the village people harvest rice, corn, beans, and cabbage. I met and grew to like many Chinese Korean people as I worked with them. I disciplined myself to learn at least a hundred new Chinese words per day and was getting better at both reading and writing the language and I practiced pronouncing the words without an accent. I was learning and making money, and it was a relatively safe environment. I was comfortable and happy if not completely content.

❈

It was the fall of 2002, and after the harvesting was done that year, I again became somewhat impatient with my life. On a whim, I took the bus back to the little house in the mountains where we all had lived together last winter. Or perhaps I liked the idea of spending the winter in a house even though it was small rather than a tent. I was surprised to find Sun-ru Dong still living there. He told me that it was cold, he didn't like the snow, and he had no other place to go, so he was staying there and working for Gaun-il Long. A fifty-year-old North Korean man now lived with Sun-ru and they invited me to join them. I readily accepted on the condition that we all work together, share expenses, and that each of us got to keep whatever money we made individually during that winter. It was agreed, and the three of us settled down together until the fifty-year-old man decided to move on. It seemed like there were always people coming and going in the Yanbian Korean Autonomous Prefecture region. North Koreans had come for centuries to live and work here before they either fully assimilated with the Chinese or moved to another region of China. China seemed to have mixed feelings about having the North Koreans there. On the one hand, it discouraged the Russians from getting any ideas about taking over this region of China, but on the other hand, the North Koreans were illegal migrants and not wanted at all. No one was very stable there for long. Once again only Sun-ru and I were alone in the small house.

❃

It had been a sunny but cold day in mid-February when all hell broke out. It was a horrible day. I had gotten up, gathered some wood for heating and cooking, then told Sun-ru that I was going to the village for some meat, salt, and other necessary items that we needed. I bid him goodbye and walked down the mountain to the nearest village where I completed my shopping and errands. I was on my way back up the mountain carrying my packages when I noticed several cars in that area. This seemed strange as I had never noticed *any* cars around these parts before. I slowed down and looked all around but did not see anyone. I could see our house and I saw the small candle in the window, and thinking that Sun-ru was there, I continued walking.

A Chinese man stepped out from behind a tree and called to me, "Hello Brother." Before I could even answer him, three policemen tackled me. They wrestled me to the ground and handcuffed me. They grabbed my bags and went through them, throwing away a few items but keeping most of the stuff for themselves. They took my wallet and all the money I had saved that winter.

They shouted at me, "You won't be needing this food or money when you go back to North Korea!"

Man, I was so mad and so angry, but I was becoming more scared underneath it all. I did not want to go back to North Korea under any conditions. There was nothing I could do against these guys. They drove me to the city police station. They had taken all the money I made in the last few months, and now I was being taken to jail on top of it! All the time I was asking, begging really, "Why don't you release me? I haven't committed a crime."

Their response was, "It's our job." Once at the police station, I was thrown into a cell and was surprised that my cellmate was none other than Sun-ru. We suspected that someone had turned us in but did not have any idea who it was or why.

We spent the night in that city jail, and the next day, we were loaded into a car and driven to a different prison. That prison was not all that bad—the food was OK. I was in the same cell as Sun-ru who was growing more agitated and frightened with each passing day. I learned he was terrified because he had beaten up a North Korean police officer during a previous arrest for some other crime. He knew if they sent him back to North Korea, he would not survive. Remembering how they had treated me and what had happened before, I doubted that I would live either. We did not want to be transferred from this prison and at all costs, wanted out.

I watched the guard's every move and waited for them to make a mistake. They made no mistakes. I was getting more depressed. Then they brought in two more North Korean guys that they had rounded up and put them in our same cell. With four prisoners, they now had enough to transport us to a border patrol station prison. The four of us were hand-cuffed and chained together then driven for two hours in a small van by two police officers. They pointed their guns at us the whole time. There was no chance for an escape.

❋

Once we arrived at this rather small prison, the new guards checked our bodies all over, then took our jackets, shoes, and belts and put them on a shelf in the room where they tended to sit a lot. The four of us were together in the same cell for five days while they waited for more guys to schedule a transport vehicle to North Korea. The cell was about ten feet by ten feet and did not have any windows. It was stifling hot in there, but we could stretch out on the cell floor, dirty as it was. They fed us rice and pork, which was not so bad. We talked about what was in store for us once we were returned to North Korea, and man, I did not want any part of this! To be honest, I was terrified. I continued to watch and listen for any mistakes by either of the two guards.

This small prison was not unlike the jails or prisons that Americans see in their Western movies. Our cell door was metal with a small opening in it through which they pushed our food each time they fed us. They never completely opened the entire cell door for any reason. Then down the hallway a little way, there was another steel door with vertical bars on it. This door would always remain locked and led out into a couple of rooms where the guards had shelves, a teapot, and a table with chairs. The two guards talked, ate, and played cards there. One night, after bringing our supper to us, the guard shut the small trap door to our cell (they never locked this window door as it was so small) and then left after shutting the main steel door. He must have been in a hurry, though, because the door did not lock completely. Was this our chance to escape?

We waited until about 3:00 a.m. and everything was quiet. I was the youngest and the skinniest guy, so the plan was for me to try to shimmy out the small trap door. I convinced the others that if they pushed my butt through the trap door, I would get the keys and let them all out. It was a real struggle and the guys all had to push a lot. I really did not know if I would be able to make it, and I got pretty scraped up but finally, I was out. I quickly rushed to the steel door, quietly pushed it open then tiptoed out into the main room. The two guards were sleeping, and the keys were right next to one of them. I did not hesitate. I knew I had promised the guys I would get the keys for them, but it was too dangerous, and THIS was my chance! I kept on tiptoeing till I got to the outside door, quietly opened it, and ran like hell! There was snow on the ground, and I did not have a jacket or shoes, but I ran and ran. My life was on the line and I knew it.

I ran as fast as I could in the snow for about thirty minutes. I was freezing and my feet and lower legs were numb with cold, but I was so afraid of being caught that I just kept going until I saw a house a short distance away from all the others. I pounded on the door and it seemed like forever before an older Chinese man with a slight limp, but a kind face answered the door and let me come in. I saw no alternative but to tell him the truth about how I had just escaped and that I desperately needed his help.

❋

The Chinese man listened to me and after a couple of minutes invited me in. He limped away and brought me a pan of warm water to soak my feet in to get them warmed up. I was freezing and so grateful! He also gave me some rice and a cup of hot tea. Then he found some old clothes for me including a jacket and shoes. They were too big for me, but hey, I needed them badly and did not complain. This man was kind to me and let me stay two days to get very warm and rest up. He did tell me that first night that I could not stay long, and I knew he was right. It just was not safe for him or for me to stay in this town. I had no money or any resources of any kind, and yet I needed to get to a larger city away from here where I could blend in and be safer.

I sat there in that man's small house rubbing and wiggling my feet, trying to get the circulation back into them and get them warmed up. I was shivering all over. I began to think of who I could call for help. I could think of no one. I could not say that I had any friends. No one has friends when your primary goal is simply surviving, and I viewed everyone as either a competitor or someone who might turn me in. Finally, I thought, "Why not call the guys I used to sell my herbs and vegetables to at the market? Surely one of them will help me."

The old man let me use his phone and I started calling them one by one. Each time, I explained my situation, where I was, and why I needed their help. By the time the third person had turned me down with a resounding "no," I began to get extremely worried. I felt so alone and vulnerable. I stayed at the Chinese man's home that night, but I could not sleep because I was busy wondering just who else I could call for help. I knew I needed to leave the next morning and I sure needed someone to help me. Then I remembered Kimi Zhao, a man about my parent's age, whom I had known when I had lived in the house in the mountains. While living with Sun-ru and Young-sik, I used to go to Kimi's home occasionally where we watched television together and he sometimes made me dinner. We talked a lot, and I liked him very much. Kimi was an intelligent Chinese man who was always fun to be with and we had some laughs together.

The following morning after a light breakfast, I again used the telephone and called Kimi to explain my dire circumstances and ask for help. I was very anxious and nervous and was in a cold sweat as I carefully explained the situation to Kimi. I was hopeful but so scared that he would not be able to help me. If Kimi turned me down, I did not know who else I could call. I honestly had no other plan. When I stopped talking, Kimi did not respond right away. It seemed like an eternity before he took a long breath and said, "I will help you, son. You are like a son to me and it is not easy, but I cannot deny you. I can help you this one time but no more."

If I live to be a hundred years old, I will *never* forget Kimi. He helped me when I was in an extremely dangerous situation. I know he saved my life. Even now, I think about him, and I wish I could go back to China to thank this man. But every day he is growing older and I do not know....

Kimi asked me to find a taxi that was willing to take me to his home in the mountains and told me he would pay the taxi driver. That is what I did. With the Chinese man's help, we found someone to take me on this over three-hour ride. I was exhausted but relieved to be leaving this town where it was so dangerous.

❋

When we finally got to Kimi's place, he was nowhere to be found! I knocked several times on his door and there was no answer! I walked all around the outside of his house and even looked in a shed out in the back. He was not there! The taxi driver was waiting for his payment. After a few minutes, the taxi driver got upset and demanded to know what was going on. Where was your "uncle?" I did not have an answer. I did not know what to think or what to tell the driver. I kept looking in the windows and all around while I was genuinely beginning to panic. Would the taxi driver report me to the police because I couldn't pay him? After what seemed like forever but in truth was only about one hour, Uncle started walking towards us. I do not know where he had been or if he was just being cautious, but he came up and gave me a big hug, then paid the driver, who left immediately. It was about three hundred Chinese dollars and that was like a half month's pay. It was a lot of money for him!

Once Kimi learned that I had been caught in the mountains, and not in a village, he told me that I had to leave immediately. He thought the police would come looking for me here again in these mountains. I was still in grave danger. He gave me another 150.00 dollars and told me to take the bus to any big city in the Yanbian Korean Autonomous Prefecture. I knew he was right. In my haste to escape, I had not thought about how I was placing this man in great danger if I were to stay here. We hugged again, and I thanked him over and over. This rescue of me had not been easy for him. I took off walking out of the mountains down to catch a bus for Yanji (a city of about 350,000 people) where I hoped I could get a job, any job, and keep a low profile. I needed to blend in.

CHAPTER 34

✦

It was close to sunrise when the bus pulled into Yanji. I was still afraid, and I knew I was not safe. I was an escapee and wanted by the police even though I had not committed a serious crime. I had to be smart. Not scared—smart! I had to be careful all the time, and I watched every one. It was not a good feeling. I instinctively knew that the mountains would be safer again soon, but I also wanted a future. And what future was there living in the mountains? I still had no identity, no papers, and no passport. Without these, I was stuck.

It was shortly thereafter that I remembered that I had some relatives in China who had come here after WWII. It was an aunt and uncle on my mother's side, and they had three daughters who were young when they left North Korea. I had never met them. No one in our family had been in contact with any of them since they had left North Korea, but I hoped they could and would help me. It took some time to do the research, but I found that they were living in the city of Jilin.

I bought a bus ticket to Jilin. The bus ride was about six or seven hours, but I got there and eventually found their home. I learned that while my uncle was still alive, my aunt had died, and their daughters were all married with children of their own who were about my age. Two of the daughter's husbands had passed away. They were good people, but extremely poor. One daughter agreed to let me stay for a little while, but we knew the Chinese authorities were looking for North Koreans and that it was incredibly dangerous. My cousin's son had married a North Korean woman, and they had children. Later, the son's wife was taken away, never to be seen or heard from again. My cousin was now helping her son raise his small children, and everything was hard for them. While they were now naturalized citizens, they had no money, and she did not know a safer place for me to go. They were not able to help themselves, let alone help me. My cousin did not want me to stay or endanger them anymore than I had already done by coming there.

But where should I go? There was nowhere to go, and I knew no one to ask for help. I felt so alone! I was truly out of options and felt vulnerable and more than a little frightened! But I had to survive. I wanted to live!

❋

I decided to go deeper into China, where it was more populated. I did not want to stay in the mountains any longer because I had learned it was dangerous there too. I knew I could survive and get by, but there was no future in collecting herbs and vegetables. I would always be looking over my shoulder, afraid of being arrested and sent back to North Korea. I had a deep hunger for something else that I could not explain. I just wanted to have more of a life. After thinking about it for a long time, I decided to go to another city. I had heard about Dalian, which was a long way away. It was along the coast on a peninsula that jutted into the Yellow Sea. Maybe there would be some South Korean ships going to South Korea. My cousin had given me 150.00 Chinese dollars, told me her daughter lived in Dalian as well, and gave me her telephone number. At least this was something to hang on to, and it gave me some hope! I bought a train ticket with the money she had given me, and I rode the long route as a regular passenger.

Once I arrived in Dalian, I tried calling my cousin's daughter, who answered the first time but did not answer when I tried calling her a second, third, or fourth time. I think she was afraid. I walked down by the waterfront but did not see any South Korean ships at all! It was depressing down there. I stayed for ten days but did not have money for food or any way to make money. I was begging for money, digging in trash cans for scraps of food, and sleeping on the stairs of apartment buildings. I never saw any South Korean ships. I was miserable and disheartened. It turned out to be a wasted trip and a hard life. In the end, I resorted to stealing some bread and other food. I figured that I had to go back to Jilin to my cousin's place.

I wanted to clean up, get some food, rest for at least a couple of days, and thank her. Deep down, I believed there must be a way I could fit in near my cousins. The family had fit in years before—couldn't I somehow do the same? Dalian was so strict. No money equaled no train ticket and no train ride. I was a long way from anywhere or anything, and I had to walk about 150 miles north of Dalian to a small train station, hoping to get on the train somehow. There was no way to ride on the roof of trains in China as I had done in North Korea, or I would have tried that. I spent a long, lonely night there at the train station.

I got the idea to look for old, used train tickets and found several lying on the ground. I started looking for a cleaner-looking used ticket and finally found one, hoping to disguise it in some way long enough to board the train. The conductor did not even check anyone's ticket, and I was able to ride the train for about two hours. When I noticed that they were starting to check tickets, I decided to get off at the next stop. It was a small village, and I stayed there for three days, trash digging and stealing. It was not a good way to live. At one point, I hung out with some Chinese homeless men, who gave me some of their food. I even pretended to be deaf, so I would not have to talk much or reveal that I was, in fact, a North Korean. There were lots of homeless people in China, so this did not draw attention to me especially.

After three days, a Chinese policeman came up behind me and poked me on my shoulder. I still pretended to be deaf, but they took me to the local police station, where they questioned me. After a bit, they wrote down the questions.

> Question:"Where are you from?"
> Answer:"Yanji"
> Question:"What is your name?"
> Answer:"Chen Lee." I made up a fictitious name.
> Question:"Why are you here?
> Answer:"I'm looking for a relative."

The police did not believe me, but one of the homeless guys spoke up and said, "I know him for a long time. He's deaf."

The police let me go. Truthfully, at that point, I *did* look exactly like what I was—a homeless person. I went right to the train station and again looked for a nice-looking used ticket, then boarded the train for

Jilin and my long-lost relatives. They had helped me before. Perhaps they would help me again.

✳

When I got to Jilin, I went directly to my cousin's house and knocked on the door. She was slow to come to the door but finally answered it after I knocked several times. She probably figured that whoever it was wasn't going to give up. When she opened the door, she looked at me like I was the last person in the world she would ever want to see. She asked, "Why did you come back?"

I looked at her in a way that probably looked as defeated as I was feeling. "Can I stay one night?"

She took a deep breath, let it out slowly, and replied in a soft voice, "Yes."

I stayed with my relatives again, but for only one day. The way she had greeted me, I knew she did not want me there and that it had been a mistake to come here a second time. I just felt completely crushed at that time. The next day, my cousin gave me another fifty dollars of her hard-earned Chinese money. I felt so bad taking it from her, but she insisted. You cannot imagine how alone and vulnerable I felt at that time. I bought a train ticket to get out of her town, and as far as I could go with the money that she had given me. Several hours later, when I got off the train in a small village, I walked away from the village because I did not want to go to a residential area where dogs might alert the police. I kept walking for about five hours before I saw a small field with a small house at the edge of it.

✳

I walked up to the house and knocked on the door. A man about forty years old answered the door, and before I could say anything, he shouted, "Who are you? Do you need help? Are you from North Korea?"

I quickly said, "No!"

But he continued, "You look North Korean!"

I asked him for some food, and he gave me some rice and potatoes, but while I was eating, he must have called the Chinese police. They arrived before I was done eating and put handcuffs on me. I told the man, "I am not North Korean, and I will come back to pay you back for what you've done to me!" I do not think he believed me at all. I was so angry, but what could I do?

They took me to their local police station. It was small and, of course, had no heat. They took me into a backroom that had only one small window high up on one wall and no furniture at all. They started questioning me.

"Who are you and where did you come from? North Korea?"

I told them, "I am a homeless Chinese kid, and my parents died years ago. I don't have any relatives, and I have lived on the streets for four years. Please just let me go. I have not hurt anyone or done anything wrong. Just let me go!" I begged them.

They did not believe me and started to slap me all the time, asking the same questions repeatedly. Then they started to get tougher and beat me harder as time went on. My hands were still cuffed when they started taking turns hitting me with a piece of cane. I spun around and around so the cane would not hit me in the same spot twice. They would hit me as hard as they could, and it stung me terribly. Each time, they would yell, "You're from North Korea, aren't you?" I did not admit anything. I just kept begging them to let me go. Finally, I asked them for some water.

This must have made them extremely mad, and one of them got a rope. They tied the rope around my ankles, hoisted me up by my feet, and tied me to a hook there in the ceiling. I was upside down, and they continued to question and berate me. I kept trying to raise my head and body at least as high as my waist, but they would grab me by the hair and shout in my face. "You are North Korean! Just admit it!" One guy would do this for a while, then let me down for a few minutes before the next guy would come back into the room and take over. The second policeman would again hoist me up and continue trying to get me to admit that I was from North Korea. This went on for nearly five hours, during which I was not given any food or water. I did not know how much longer I could go on when they finally got an ethnic Korean from someplace and brought him into the room. They asked the Korean, "Does he look like a North Korean?"

The Korean guy looked at me and then walked all around me a couple of times before he said, "No, he doesn't look like a North Korean. See how he is dressed—not like a North Korean." I just wanted out of there. I was exhausted and so thirsty.

The Chinese police finally knew that I was not going to admit I was from North Korea, and this other man didn't think I was North Korean, so they decided it was enough. They took me out to the car and drove me out in the middle of nowhere, and pulled over to the side of the road. They told me, "Go to Yanji and never come back!"

❁

At first, I did not know where I was, and it was dark, but I didn't care. The police had let me go. These men had put me on the side of the road going to Yanji, thinking that was where I would go. But I thought I am going to go back to that forty-year-old man's house and prove to him that I'm Chinese and that he was wrong about me. I felt Chinese, and I had been in China for several years by now. I never wanted to go back to North Korea, no matter what. I guess it was just my stubbornness coming out, and besides, I had nowhere else to go.

So, I walked and walked. It took me half the night to get back to the forty-year-old man's house at the edge of the field. I did not want to beat him up or anything, I just wanted to prove to him that I was Chinese. I knocked on his door.

It took him a moment, then he said, "What the hell?" I do not know when he did it, but he called some Chinese gangs. These Chinese gangs were, in fact, small-time thugs who would beat up somebody for money. Twenty guys pulled up in Mercedes cars. All I could think was, "Oh my goodness, I didn't expect this!"

Thankfully for me, I had done some boxing when I had been living at home and kind of knew how to protect myself. But against twenty guys!? Now, this called for some negotiation. I did get hit a couple of times, but I asked them to let me tell my story, then they could do their business. I told them, "Look, I don't have a weapon." (Weapons are illegal in China.) "And this guy thinks I am North Korean. He called the cops earlier today, and they came and took me to the police station. The police let me go. I am Chinese." After a few minutes and a few more questions, the guys believed me. They believed me enough that they felt bad about trying to beat me up, and one guy threw me a twenty-dollar bill, then some others gave me money too!

Long story short, the next day, the forty-year-old man ended up giving me a job, but it was impossible to complete. I was given two hours to go into the mountains and get wood and bring it back to him. I was given no tools other than a rope. So off I went to the mountains, but I could not get wood because I didn't have any equipment and there was no wood lying on the ground. When I went back to the man, he said, "I told you. You can't do anything." I stayed that night and then left the next day. There was nothing for me to do, and I just wanted to get away from that man.

I took the train to Tonghua with the money the gang had given me, arriving at about 6:00 p.m. that night. I only had forty dollars left, but it was extremely cold outside—it was winter after all. I paid thirty-five dollars for a motel room for a warm night's rest and a hot shower. The next morning, I spent the last five dollars on breakfast and then started walking the remaining three hundred miles to Yanji. I only had a light jacket and was forced to sleep out in the elements. The farmers were drying corn by hanging the ears by their husks on clotheslines, and I stole some of these ears to roast over a small fire. I melted snow to drink and washed my face in the snow. Along the way, I saw some fruit farms. They had already harvested the fruit, and the workers were gone, but I did find an occasional piece of frozen fruit to eat. At night, I would build a small fire and snuggle up close to it. I could sleep for about an hour before the fire went out, and the cold would wake me only to start the process over again. It was the best I could do at the time, but I made a vow to myself that I would find somewhere or something better than this. This, I decided, was simply no way to live.

I had been walking like this for about a week, always keeping a low profile and never engaging with anyone much, when I decided to cut down out of the mountains onto a small road that I had spotted. I thought it would be easier to walk and a bit faster. This walking in the mountains in the snow without paths was hard work! I had walked a good number of miles when I saw a small piece of paper by the side of the road. It had the color of Chinese money. Could it be money? I ran up to it and quickly grabbed it out of the snow. It WAS money—a one-hundred-dollar bill! What a gift! I just clutched it to my chest and hopped up and down, whooping my lungs out. After I had done my private little victory dance, I thought, "I've got to thank somebody. But who do I thank?" I thought for a few moments, and then I remembered hearing about this Jesus guy. Maybe I should thank Jesus.

"THANK YOU, JESUS!" I screamed as I sank to my knees. I was so happy! I knew exactly how I would spend my windfall. With renewed energy, I walked on to the nearest village and got a hot meal, then bought a train ticket for the rest of the way to Yanji. Yanji was my destination because it was the capital and a big city in the Yanbian Korean Autonomous Prefecture. With more Chinese Koreans and Koreans living there, it would be safer, and easier for me to blend in, and hopefully find work. I had hope!

✻

I planned to find a home where the people would let me stay for a few days while I looked for a job. I found a place without much trouble, and the couple let me stay on the condition that I paid for their food. I immediately started my job search. While searching for a job there in the city, I ran into Ji-rang. Ji-rang was the forty-two-year-old man that I had been caught with inside the restaurant that first winter I was in China. I had not known what had become of Ji-rang or Yu-ri after we had all been caught. I called out to Ji-rang, "Hey Brother, what's going on?" He was just as surprised to see me as I was to run into him.

We talked for a while, and I learned that both Ji-rang and Yu-ri had been let go after a Chinese relative of Yu-ri's paid off the guards for their release. They had never been sent back to North Korea. He did not know where Yu-ri was now. Ji-rang was genuinely saddened to hear about my beatings and how I nearly died before being released to my mother.

"But hey," he brightened up. "Things are much better here now." He went on to explain that he was not doing farm labor anymore and that he was working at a motel restaurant now. While there were few jobs available, he worked one day every few days for about twenty dollars per day in Chinese money. Ja-rang was permitted to sleep next to the boiler that heated the motel and restaurant. Ji-rang invited me to stay, and I stayed with him for about five days. It was safe and warm there, and I was able to work for a couple of days for some money. But times were not easy, and it was the winter of 2003. I did not have much of a future, always being on the run, keeping a low profile, and working to just get by and survive. I was quite discouraged.

❁

One night in the boiler room, Ji-rang told me about a forty-eight-year-old Chinese man he knew who might be able to help by having some work for me to do. He gave me the man's name and address, and a day or so later, I bid Ji-rang goodbye after thanking him, and I bought a bus ticket to go find the man. After all, I had to keep moving—to keep on surviving.

I found Tao Zhang living alone in a small house in Yanji and he invited me in as soon as I mentioned Ji-rang's name. Tao was short and thin, but the most noticeable thing about him was just how weathered and old-looking his skin was. He looked and moved like he was much older than forty-eight, and I wondered if I had heard Ji-rang wrong when he had told me Tao's age. I could tell that he had spent his youth working hard out in the harsh Chinese weather. He brought me some hot tea, and we talked for a while before he offered me a job. I learned that Tao lived in the city during the winter but lived and worked next to the Buerhatong River in the spring until it got too cold in late fall every year. He was a fisherman and spent long hours fishing during the day, but he would bring his catch into the local villages to sell every few days. Tao told me that he was getting older and that it was getting harder for him to do all the work himself. He offered to let me stay with him in his house for the rest of the winter if I promised to work with him in the spring, fishing the river. Tao was a very charming, pleasant man, and I readily agreed to this arrangement even though I did not know much about fishing. After all, it wasn't like I had several jobs and a warm home just waiting for me elsewhere in China.

That winter, Tao and I spent hours talking, and I grew to like both him and his sense of humor. He demonstrated how to catch the fish and showed me what I would be doing once it got warm enough for us to be on the river. We waited for spring and for the weather to get warmer. While we waited, he showed me how to fish through the ice, but it was so cold and never as productive as fishing in the spring and summer.

Finally, it was time, and we moved and carried our gear, such as it was, to the river. Tao had no boat but used a couple of huge old tractor inner tubes that he had patched and blown up with air. He tied a rope in a crisscross over each inner tube, and we each sat on the rope in the middle of a tube with our feet and legs in the cold water while we maneuvered our fishnets, catching any kind of fish we could find. We stayed in a tent that we pitched next to the river and cooked our meals every evening. I had intended to stay only one season working with Tao, but I grew to admire and enjoy being with him more all the time. Before I knew it, four seasons had passed! It was safe, and I was surviving. I might have stayed even longer with Tao, but one day, while fishing, he met a woman close to his age who was doing the same kind of fishing and living close to the river. They started talking, comparing notes, etc., and it was not too long before I noticed that there was an attraction between them. I knew right then and there that I had better prepare to be replaced. I could not offer Tao what this woman could.

I had been learning how to hide my identity better, and my Chinese was surprisingly good by this time. I was proud that I had lost most of my North Korean accent when I spoke the Chinese language. Winter was coming again soon. I thought that I was more than ready to enter society with my experience in China and all the work that I had done on myself. I wanted to travel around the country freely now that I had been in China for over six years. I thought I fit more into the Chinese way of life all the time. I admit that I still thought a lot about the police catching me and sending me back to North Korea. I wondered if I could ever truly relax about this. I wanted to live a normal, everyday Chinese life, working and blending in. I started listening to the little radio that we had, hoping to hear of a job in the city that I could do. I knew the time had come for me to move on. I thought I was ready.

CHAPTER 35

✳

I moved back to Yanji and got my first job in the city, working at a public shower. It was essentially a hotel and restaurant that had multiple departments. I was assigned to work in the massage department. I met and greeted the clients in my job and explained the prices and services for massages given by the young girls in private rooms. I collected the money and then assigned a girl to a particular client. I was making about $600.00 per month—the most I had ever made, so it was not a bad job.

The problem was that it cost so much to live. I needed some roommates to help share expenses. I met a couple of guys, and we decided to share a studio apartment that was $400.00 per month, and we split the costs. It was great living with these guys, but the $600.00 per month sure went fast. Chinese people love karaoke, beer, and just having a good time. It all cost so much money, and after getting paid every month, all my money would be spent within a few days. I would be left with nothing and need to figure out how to get enough to live on until the next payday. The two other guys both had parents they could call to bail them out if they were ever short on money. Not me, though; I had to go without or somehow stretch my money.

✤

One of the roommates had a friend who was retired from the military. One night, this friend offered to take all of us guys out to a restaurant bar for dinner and drinks. Then he wanted to do some karaoke and have a few more drinks at the bar. When the guys asked him about the bill, he told them not to worry; he would pick up the tab. So, the group continued drinking and having a good time without thinking about the bill. We looked around towards the end of the evening, but our military friend was nowhere to be found! Who was going to pay? We sure did not have the money for a bill this big. The bar operators were about to call the police when one of the guys managed to get a hold of his sister, who brought the money down to bail us out of this horrible situation. We had to chalk this up to experience, even though it was hard on us all to pay back the sister.

✤

In April, I had an issue with one of the young girls who was giving massages. I took an older guy's money for a massage and assigned the girl to do it, and they went back to the private room. I never knew exactly what happened, but she burst out of the room screaming that she would not give the guy his massage. He came out screaming that he got ripped off, and now they both were screaming. It was chaotic and not a relaxing environment for our other guests. I was scared that I might lose my job over this, so I tried to calm them both down and asked the girl to just quickly finish up the massage. I was trying to appease both the guest and the girl. I don't know when she did it, but the girl must have called her boyfriend. Suddenly the boyfriend and two other guys burst in, mad as hell. The guest took off, and I went outside with the three guys to discuss the situation calmly. The three of them attacked me as if I were the one who did the hiring, set the rules, and forced ugly conditions. They hit me a few times with their fists while yelling at me the whole time. A crowd formed, and someone must have called the police. I had been beaten a lot worse before, but no beating is worth the pain. I just wanted out. It turned out to be a bad situation, and I did lose my job over the whole affair. I needed money to live and felt like I was due some compensation for the beating I had taken. It was a struggle, and the money was tight, but in the end, the boyfriend's mother gave me $600.00.

I had learned that I could now fit in and function within the Chinese community, but money was always a hassle. Without the proper documents and ID, the jobs I could get held no future, and I was stuck. Still, it was fun living with these two roommates, and I continued to live with them while I looked for another job.

CHAPTER 36

✾

I looked and looked for a good job—one that would pay more than $600.00 per month, which had been on the low side by Chinese standards. Plus, my living expenses and keeping up with my two roommates always kept me broke. I needed a job that made more money. Finally, at the end of April, I saw a computer job advertised in the paper. Of course, I had never seen a computer and did not know how to type, but I sure needed the job.

I went to the office and spoke with the man about the job. He asked me if I could type and if I knew a bit about computers. I was forced to lie and said, "Yes."

He looked at me intently and said, "Good. Come back tomorrow and prove yourself."

I went immediately to the closest internet café, where for two dollars per hour I could rent a computer and go on the internet as well. I stayed there the rest of that day and all night, teaching myself how to use the keyboard. I practiced and practiced typing and would ask other people questions about the internet when I needed to. The next day, I went back to the office and started work.

My job was to do online gaming. It was not actual gambling, but people did make money this way. Gaming is international, and South Koreans and some Chinese love marketing games. They loved a game called "Giants," where a person went online and created a character. That character would go to imaginary villages and figure out how to make imaginary money. You would get points for the imaginary money, and my boss would then cash in the points and pay me a salary. I think in America, they have a game called "Second Life" that might be similar. He had lots of guys working for him, and I found that I could do all right. I started out making about $1,500.00 per month working twelve hours per day doing this online gaming. Over time, the games kept changing, and I'd have to learn each new game. I changed games and bosses frequently, always making increasingly more money. They even paid my rent as part of the deal as I got better at it.

I worked at online gaming for the next year and kept doing better, working up to making between three thousand and four thousand Chinese dollars per month. I was living a good life. At times I lived with Chinese roommates, and other times I lived with girls. I had two or three different Chinese girlfriends during this time. Other guys had girlfriends, and it was only natural for me to have relationships as well, and it helped me fit in better. None of these relationships were successful because I never really wanted them to work out. Some girls complained that I didn't listen to them. Looking back, I think I was protecting myself at their expense. I was always hiding my identity and was never completely honest or truthful with anyone. I did not feel I could ever reveal anything to anyone as I knew one slip, just one mistake, and I would be sent back to North Korea. I did not know if I could survive the harsh treatment that

I knew would be doled out to me. I had always wanted to do better and keep improving my life. I could see that I was getting older, and that life was moving forward. Here I was living like the Chinese, but I could not get a job with a real future long term without identity papers. Although I was doing better as time passed, I also began to understand just how truly limiting China was for a North Korean like me. I was living an illegal life, and it ate at me a lot.

The last girl I lived with was pretty and nice and had a lot going for herself. I genuinely liked her a lot, but she was beginning to ask me more questions. She wanted to know more about me, and she was beginning to pressure me to marry her. I had no dreams of marriage. I just wanted to survive.

CHAPTER 37

✿

Having no one to confide any of this with and no one to discuss options
with, I began going down to the internet café to do computer research
about the prospect of leaving China. I was alone mentally during this
period, and it was downright lonely. I spent a lot of time weighing my
options and determining what was and was not feasible. I researched at
the café and sometimes while I was at work, but I told no one. My first
choice was to go to South Korea because they would take North Koreans
and because I knew that many Chinese dreamed of going to that country.
They said they wanted to go there to make more money, but all the time I
had been in North Korea, we had always been taught that South Koreans
did not have a particularly good life. Besides, I did not have any contacts
there, and I had no one who could help me in either China or South Korea.
If it were so good in South Korea, I should have gone a long time ago.
Meanwhile, my girlfriend was making things extremely difficult for me.

I did not think about trying to go to the United States because I
believed and had always been taught that the United States was the worst

country in the world. I must have searched hard for about six months, and I decided that I should go to any country that was in NATO. I researched South Korea, England, Canada, Australia, the United States, and a host of other countries that would consider North Koreans as refugees. It was all very overwhelming.

✿

But no one can research forever, and I decided I had to act. But act, doing what, how, and where? It was the summer of 2008, and I had been in China for nearly eight years. Some of it had been good, and some of it not so much. One thing was for sure; if I wanted to have a "real" life, I needed to leave China. These thoughts and questions about how to leave kept going around in my mind. Finally, I decided my best move would be to travel to Beijing because all the foreign embassies in China are located there. But first I wanted to say hello and goodbye to my relatives in Jilin. After all, it had been several years since I had seen them, and my cousin and one of her daughters had helped me when I needed it even though it had been extremely hard for them to do so.

I took the bus to Jilin and went to my cousin's house. I knocked on the door, and after a few minutes, one of her sons slowly answered the door. He was plump and sloppily dressed, and I thought he had been sleeping in the middle of the day. He was not excited to see me and promptly told me that his mother no longer lived there! He was ready to close the door, but I stopped him by asking more questions. He reluctantly told me that she had gone to visit his sister—the one that I had tried to see and who would not answer my second call when I had been in Dalian. My cousin and her daughter had then gone to South Korea. He had not spoken to them since they left China and didn't know anything more about them. He gave me this information in a detached manner, then almost closed the door in my face. I got the message loud and clear and knew it was useless to talk to him and probably best to leave him alone. I walked down to the train station and bought a train ticket to Beijing.

It was a long train ride, and I had to get off the train before I got to Beijing because of all the added security. Security police were all over China because of the 2008 Summer Olympics scheduled to be held in Beijing later that summer. There were more police on trains and in the train stations than there were in the bus stations. I thought this would be a good place to get a haircut and freshen up before taking a bus further into Beijing.

Once I got to Beijing, it was apparent that I needed to wait until the Olympics were over and things settled down before making any moves. I got the idea to call the South Korean news teams to see if they would help me. What a total dead end this turned out to be! They were not interested in either helping me or hearing my story. I was alone and had to figure out how I could help myself. So, I rented a cheap motel room, and while keeping a low profile and not engaging with anyone, I started checking things out. I found the area where all the embassies were together in a big compound. Since I had no identity papers or documents of any kind, I knew I could not just walk in. I was looking for a United Nations Embassy with weak security.

I walked and searched every day for over a week. I needed to be one hundred percent certain that things would work out for me. Ninety-nine percent would simply be too dangerous. I learned that they had erected two walls around each embassy, one inside the other, and each was about five meters or over fifteen feet high. The first wall was made of cement, and the second wall, about five feet inside the first wall, was always a heavy metal fence. Security guards were at every gate and opening imaginable.

There was a shopping district about a block away, consisting of mostly men's and women's fashion clothes for sale and a few restaurants. People were walking all over this area, and even more security guards patrolled the region.

Today, years later, people ask me how I chose to come to the United States. I didn't. Circumstances chose for me. While I was walking around trying to figure things out, I still did not know which embassy would be best to go to, although England, Canada, Australia, South Korea, and the United States were my first choices.

CHAPTER 38

❇

The United States was building a new embassy to replace its old one, and it was currently under construction. Was this my opportunity? The exterior guard walls were already constructed, but there was no security guard in front of the gate, and there were Chinese workers everywhere. My interest in this embassy took a dramatic increase, but again, I had to be sure. I continued to walk around the area and found a place not far away where I could observe the embassy without being noticed. From my hiding spot, I watched who was coming and going at all hours of the day and night.

I decided that I needed a large hook and some rope comparable to what mountain climbers use, and I purchased these at a hardware store. The guy at the store bent several pieces of metal into curves for me, and I was able to attach a long rope to these metal prongs. I put them in my backpack and waited until after dark when the number of people walking around the shopping area and the embassy had died down. I walked to the place where I thought no one could see me and stood there, making sure it was safe. Once I was certain no one would see, I heaved the metal prongs attached to the rope up over the exterior cement wall. It cleared the top of the wall easily, but would the prongs bite enough to support my weight? I tugged on the rope a couple of times to test it then hurriedly scrambled up and over the first wall. You would be surprised at how fast you can move and how much energy you have when you are afraid of being caught!

The second wall was a simple but strong metal fence and was easier to climb. I believed I could hide and sleep among the construction materials and debris until morning when they opened the embassy. Curiosity drove me to go to the doors of the embassy under construction and give the door a pull. Much to my surprise, it was not locked! I went in, noticing they were almost done with the construction on the outside. The inside was still being worked on, and they had new furniture—desks, chairs, and filing cabinets—stacked in what looked like what would become a reception area. Back in one of the rooms were a bunch of boxes with new computers, printers, wire connections, and other office materials. They had paint and other supplies sitting around as well. I walked around from room to room, but no one was there. On the side of the lobby or reception area, I saw a locked, glassed-in area that looked like it might be a small convenience store. It had food, wine, cigarettes, and drugstore-type supplies there and probably was open during the day to serve the construction workers. I was so hungry, but of course, I did not go near that store. I thought about sleeping in the embassy but decided I did not want to be surprised and woken up there. That just would not look good for me. They would think I was a trespassing bum, for sure. So, after exploring around inside for a while, I went outside to find a place to nest for the night. I did not want anyone to discover me until I was ready. I remember lying down on the ground that night with my backpack under my head and thinking, "This was so easy!" I was surprised at how easy it had been to get in. I thought, "My dream has come true! My nightmare is over!" Someone from somewhere had given me a cigarette, and I smoked it as my victory celebration. I was looking up at the stars and feeling so happy. Didn't they look a lot brighter now that I felt safer than I had felt in such a long time? I hardly slept that night. I kept going over and over in my mind what I would tell them in the morning. I was so excited! I was so hungry but so emotionally high.

�֎

Early the next morning, I woke up to the sound of the arriving construction workers coming into the compound and starting to work. I looked just like them and mingled with them until I saw some of the US Army guys walking around patrolling the area. They paid no attention to me. I watched the soldiers for a while and then picked the most kind-looking one. I walked up to him and tapped him on the shoulder, and when he turned around, I said in Korean, "Hello, can you help me? I am from North Korea, and I really need your help." Of course, he did not understand me, and I thought I saw him grip his rifle a little tighter. I repeated it in Chinese, but he still did not understand me. I think he heard the "North Korean" part, but he still looked suspicious and called out to another Army officer who came over. I kept repeating that I needed their help and that I was from North Korea. Finally, the second guy pulled out a metal detector, and they motioned for me to hold out my arms and spread my legs. They ran the metal detector all over my body and checked everything in my backpack until they were satisfied that I had no weapon or a bomb. Keeping their rifles pointed at me, they motioned for me to walk toward the old US Embassy.

Once we reached the old embassy, they took me to a small security room. Since they did not have a Korean interpreter, they got a Chinese interpreter. Then the questioning began in Chinese. I was not afraid at this point, but they kept asking the same questions repeatedly in different ways. They asked,

"Who are you?"

"An Yong-kwon"

"Where are you from?"

"Pyongyang"

"When did you come to China?"

"August 2000"

"How many are in your family?"

"Three"

"Mother?"

"Yes"

"Father?"

"No, he has been dead since 2001."

"No brothers or sisters?"

"No." I was afraid to tell them about my brothers. I was worried about a North Korean spy in the embassy.

It became clear that they did not believe I was from North Korea. They had different army and state department guys come in to do the same questioning. They asked me to draw a picture of North Korea and include the major cities and rivers. I answered questions about the North Korean leaders, Kim Il-sung and his son Kim Jong-il. I even tried to answer questions about the North Korean government and its policies. And finally, I sang the songs we had learned as children to honor the royal Kim family.

While the Americans were nice to me, the questioning went on and on for days. They brought me water and a menu from a Korean restaurant, and I ordered real Korean food. The Americans had never had a North Korean defector come to that embassy, and they did not quite know what to do with me.

❀

They brought me a cot to sleep on in time, and still, they asked questions about everything and everyone. They compared the notes they each had taken to see if my story had changed. Was it consistent, and could they trust that I was from North Korea and was defecting? Since the Americans did not have extra personnel to guard me, they sent for more guards from Washington. In total, six different guys were assigned to guard me, and I was there for nearly a year. One day they brought me an Xbox. I had never seen an Xbox or any of these electronic games before. They showed me how to play, and I became somewhat friendly with two or three of the guards. Every morning they brought me the menu from the Korean restaurant, and I ordered what I wanted to eat. It was during this time that I began learning English and trying to read the newspaper. I practiced every day with some guards. I guess they were processing me like they do all refugees before they admit them to the United States, and this all takes time. My whole world was this tiny room in the embassy because they had nowhere else to take me. I did not know how long they would keep me here. It seemed like forever. Yet it was warm, I had food and a place to sleep, I was safe, and I was learning English. I even read the Bible, or tried to—it was hard. After about a month, they brought in a person from South Korea, and he questioned me too. He asked the same questions, and I gave him the same answers. Then he asked,

"Where do you want to go?"

"Where can I go?"

"Anywhere."

"I choose the United States. I do not know English, but I can learn, and I want to see the North Korean enemy. Are they as bad as we have learned? I want to know who they are. Are they really our enemies? So far, the Americans have been good to me. I have learned that our leader, Kim Jong-il lied to us about other things. North Korea is not the greatest country. I want to go to the United States."

I had also heard about the new American president, Obama. He sounded fair, and he even came to China to speak.

The Americans were not mean, but after about a month or six weeks, they finished construction on the new embassy, and everyone moved into the new place. However, they kept me in the old embassy with only the guards. As the days turned into weeks and the weeks into months, I had a lot of time to think. I was playing the Xbox, reading newspapers, and learning and practicing English with the guards. But it was a lonely time, and I spent hours thinking when I was alone.

I learned and changed a great deal while living in China. I learned that human life is not just one big dream. It is many dreams. I had dreamed of coming to China, and now I was going to leave China, my home for almost nine years. Where they would send me or when I did not know. And I did not care if I could have my identity and all my freedoms. I learned that freedom is <u>not</u> free in China! You sacrifice! You want freedom, and you might sacrifice your life! China is not free—China would send me to North Korea, where they would torture me again and probably kill me this time. I realized that I was lonely and that I longed for companionship, even if I had never truly had friends. I yearned to be somewhere where I fit in, had shelter and plenty of food, and where I could let my guard down and not worry so much about betrayal or someone reporting me to the authorities. I was beginning to understand how much I had changed in the past nine years. I learned that surviving was not enough for me any longer. I now understood that I wanted to "live" and not just "survive."

A new identity in China was impossible for me. China is communist. They don't care about me or my life. I had heard about North Koreans who had been successful in obtaining Chinese ID cards. Sometimes there were car accidents, and before the police came, they switched the identity of the dead body to that of a North Korean. Then the North Korean had the dead person's ID. These activities were illegal and done on the black market. Unfortunately, I knew no one who could help me with this.

My guards did not know how soon the process would be completed. I was in a holding pattern. At times, they would bring in South Koreans who would question me to find out if I were, in fact, a Chinese person of Korean lineage who just wanted to go to the United States for the "American Dream." Many Chinese knew about the American Dream and wanted to go there. But for me, the American Dream was simply to go somewhere where I could have an identity. Someplace where I could fit in, find work, and be free enough to live a normal life without constantly looking over my shoulder, waiting for someone to betray me. I wanted to be safe from being arrested, tortured, or killed. To me, this would be freedom.

Day by day, I was under a lot of stress—I was still in China! I did not feel physical discomfort, but China itself is dangerous, and I knew it. Is this ever going to end? I could not communicate with any of my family, and at this point, I just wanted to leave. The guards brought me an English dictionary and I diligently practiced speaking English without either a

North Korean or a Chinese accent. Sometimes I would help the American guards and act as an interpreter when they needed someone to speak Chinese to a taxi driver or whatever. I tried to exercise and sometimes played a type of soccer with the guards. I had good Korean food from the Korean restaurant, but I was still very thin. The mental stress of just being there and not knowing what would happen was taking its toll. I still had severe nightmares every night. They were always the same. The police would be chasing me as I ran and ran. Sometimes they caught me, beat me, and sent me back to the North Korean concentration camps where they tortured me. It was awful. I was so alone.

❀

Finally, U.S. Immigration came and took pictures of me and took my fingerprints. I thought it would be soon. By now, my English was getting better, and I spoke only English to the guards. Still, no one told me when I would be leaving or where to, for that matter. But every day I waited for news, and I started marking off days on the calendar. It took almost three months before they told me I would be leaving China for the United States on August 5, 2009. I had been there at the embassy for almost a year. I did not need to know or feel anything about where I would be going in the United States. I was just excited about leaving China!

❀

August fifth finally arrived. I was given a new set of clothes and told to leave everything behind—no Xbox or anything. I did not mind. I was so ready to leave! But then there was a problem. An embassy car was ready and waiting to take me to the Beijing airport, but the airport authorities would not accept me until and unless the documents were all signed by the Chinese authorities. A Chinese lady about thirty years old came to the embassy and kept calling the Chinese authorities, trying to get all the documents in order and signed. Finally, they were ready, and the Chinese lady, Lian Hsu, came with me in the embassy car to the airport. We had to hurry, and the plane waited for about ten minutes for us to get there. We rode on an electric cart to the gate and boarded the plane. I had never ridden in an electric cart or been on a plane before, and I was happy to learn that Lian was coming with me the entire way to the United States. It was a great day for me. I was not afraid to be on a plane. All I could think was that I was finally taking off from China! My dream was finally coming true! "I've made it." I thought as I breathed out a long sigh and tears rolled silently down my cheeks.

As the plane circled over Beijing, I looked out of the window and silently vowed that I would come back someday. "I will be back—someday when I have a passport and an ID, I will come back legally."

I still want to go back to China. While I did not miss North Korea in any way other than for my family (certainly not the poverty and starvation), I do miss China. I had some good times there, and they have a lot of good people—people like Kimi Zhao who gave me money and helped me. He is getting older, and I would like to see him before he dies to thank him for everything he did for me. I also want to take some pictures of some places I saw and visited. While I was in China, I never took pictures because I needed to travel light. I did not want anything to tell a story about where I had been or where I was going. Maybe someday, I do not know…

CHAPTER 39.

✳

It was an extremely long airplane flight, but I was already in heaven for the most part, so it was not so bad. Lian told me we were going to Chicago, Illinois, and would catch another airplane to Louisville, Kentucky. I had no idea where either of those places was, so she showed me a crude map that she got out of the pocket in the seat in front of us. I wondered what my life would be like when we got there. It all felt a little unreal.

At one point, Lian turned to me and said, "You are going to the United States. You had better have an American name. Do you like the name, Adam?"

"Adam," I repeated.

Lian smiled and said, "Yes, you are Adam, but you have no Eve. You can go find Eve in America."

"Adam, I like that, Adam. I know about Adam and Eve. I read about them in the Bible in China when I was learning."

"So, you should be Adam," she said with a certain finality, and the subject was dropped. And so, I became Adam mainly because I did not want to become a James, Frank, or Richard—the people in the United States all seem to have the same names. People called me Adam, but at first, the name seemed unreal to me and did not seem to fit accurately at all. After all, I was not anything like the "Adam" in the Bible. I did hear other American names and thought about changing my name a lot, but nothing seemed to fit with me. Later, I met a guy about my age who came into the store (where I would later work) several times a month and who everyone seemed to like. It turns out that the guy's name was Adam, and when his buddies called his name, there was a certain kind of care and respect in the way they said it. I liked that, and gradually, Adam started to sound good to my ears, and I began to identify more with the name. I truly became Adam.

Lian and I arrived in Louisville, Kentucky, at about 10:00 p.m. the following night. I was dead tired but so excited to be in America. Things seemed so bright and busy even at ten o'clock at night. Things were happening fast. Three guys stepped out of the crowd and walked up to me. One of them stuck out his hand and said, "Welcome to the United States." He was speaking Korean! All three guys had been sent by the immigration department and were North Korean! Holy Cow! I never expected this! They introduced themselves and told me they were there to take me to "our" apartment.

Lian broke in and announced that she was leaving me. She gave me a brief hug and said, "Good luck, Adam." And she left. I was in shock! All of this was turning out to be much better than I had imagined! This United States was some enemy!

I could not believe it! I learned that one guy had been in the United States for only six months, another for one year, and the third guy had been here for two years and lived in a different apartment complex not far away. The three of us would live together in a two-bedroom apartment with two bathrooms. Unbelievable! It was a far cry from my family's outdoor toilet, which was just a hole in the ground. The four of us would later become good friends and have Korean BBQs and drink beer together.

The next day, one of the guys took me down to the Refugee Community Center, run by Catholic Charities, where I started the process of getting settled. I was given fifty dollars in cash, a social security card, an ID, and an insurance card. They told me I could go anywhere with these cards but not to lose them. What freedom! However, the main thing on my mind was that I needed to get a job. My English was good enough, so after a couple of days of searching, I got a job as a cashier at a South Korean convenience store there in Louisville, selling beer, wine, and cigarettes along with other "convenience" items. I liked it there in Kentucky. There was a big river nearby and farms. I had a job, and eventually, five guys and a couple of women became good friends. We would get together to tell stories about how we escaped, what we needed to do here in the United States to live, where to go, and where to shop for reasonable prices. We cooked good Korean food, laughed at our mistakes, and taught each other what we learned about our new country.

Another thing we did together was to celebrate the day that each of us came to the United States—the day our new lives began. For me, August 6, 2009, was the day I arrived, and is still the biggest holiday of each year. I still celebrate it every year. The main thing was that I was no longer alone. I began to relax a bit, but I was still having nightmares and bad dreams about being chased, caught, and sent back to North Korea.

PART IV

Adam and Sophia

CHAPTER 40

✿

I had been in Kentucky for about two years, living and working there and learning more every day, when the church community came to us with an invitation. The invitation was for a convention of North Koreans living in the United States. The convention of North Koreans is held one time per year and is always held in Chicago, Illinois, and lasts for four or five days. It sounded like a wonderful opportunity to us Korean guys, and we all wanted to go, but none of us had the money for such a trip. But not to worry; the church had taken up donations, and they would pay our way. What a gift! Traditionally, North Koreans keep to themselves and do not socialize or interact much with other groups. Now we were all to be sent to Chicago to learn how to live better in the United States and how to integrate more into U.S. society.

On Labor Day in 2011, the four of us all took a plane to Chicago to go to the convention and to meet North Koreans from all over the United States. There were about fifty people there; some were married with children, some had married U.S. citizens, and some were single like the four of us. We sat and talked about our lives here in the United States. We listened to people explain rules and laws, rights and freedoms, places to go, and things to do. It was an exciting time.

On the first day, I noticed a small, pretty Korean girl with long black hair who kind of kept to herself, but I did not speak to her. By the second day, I was feeling a little more comfortable being there, and at the lunch break, I walked up to her. She was looking down and did not even look at me. I did not really know how to talk to a North Korean girl very much. After all, I had been only seventeen, fighting to survive first in North Korea and then in China for so many years. When could I learn? But finally, I found the courage to speak to her.

"Hi, my name is Adam. What is your name?" She did not respond or even act like she knew what I was saying. So, I tried again, this time in Korean.

"Hi, my name is Adam. What is your name?" She still did not look up or answer, so I continued, "Are you hungry?" Still, no answer, and I thought she looked like she just wanted me to leave her alone. So, I walked away and went to the buffet table, where I got two plates of Korean BBQ food. I came back to her and shoved one plate toward her. She had to look up, and I nodded my head toward a couple of seats at a table close to us. She took the plate of food, followed me to the table, and sat down beside me. Still, she did not speak and just picked at the food. I ate my food silently for a while, then I looked at her again and said, more forcefully this time, "What is your name?"

This time, she answered me. "Sophia Soon."

I smiled at her, but inside I felt like I had scored an enormous victory. Sophia was so shy and was slow to warm up to me, or to anyone for that matter. Over the next few days, I learned that this was her first time at the North Korean convention and that she had come from Phoenix,

Arizona. She liked it in Phoenix, where it gets hot, but she had come from the mountainous region of North Korea and so did not mind the heat. I did not push her; she was like a little bird, and I did not want to scare her away. Also, I was unsure about how to proceed with this boy-girl thing American-style, or even Korean-style, for that matter.

I had a good time at that first Korean convention, and I spoke to Sophia several more times over the next couple of days. At the end of the convention, I gave her my address and phone number and asked for hers. She took a long time to write out her information, but when she gave it to me, she agreed that we should keep in contact.

※

I went home with my apartmentmates to Kentucky feeling incredibly happy and quite upbeat. I felt like I had met a lot of good people and that I had learned some valuable things about living in the United States. I had hope for the future, and... there was Sophia.

When I got back to Louisville, I went right back to work. I continued to work long hours at the convenience store and learn everything I could. And I thought about Sophia. After more than a week, I called her. We talked for a long time on the phone. I thought she kind of liked talking to me. That was a new feeling for me. I did not know what it all meant. We spoke on the phone many more times, and I learned that she was three years younger than me. Sophia had first gone to China in 2002 and then come to the U.S. in 2010. She arrived a year after me. She was beginning to talk more all the time. Finally, I asked her if I could come to visit her in Phoenix. She shyly said yes, and in November 2011, I flew to Phoenix, Arizona, to visit her and look around.

I liked Phoenix, the wide-open spaces, and the mountains. I had not seen dry deserts before, but they were interesting and quite different. I was also beginning to understand and like Sophia more all the time. I went home and thought about it all. I talked with my roommates about how my life was going in Kentucky. Would it all be that much different in Arizona, I wondered? Sophia had said she liked it, and I knew there would not be many North Koreans there, but then there were less than two hundred in the whole USA! She also mentioned that there was a small community of South Koreans close to where she lived. It was not long before I decided to move to Phoenix and give it a try. I was always looking for a better future and a chance to better myself, so I said goodbye to my Korean apartmentmates and flew to Phoenix.

I stayed with Sophia during the two weeks it took to find a job. She was working as a restaurant cook, so we got along financially. I finally found a job as a cashier at another small convenience store. I had dropped out of school when I was in sixth grade to work for my uncle, and with no diploma, I could not even work in one of the larger name-brand convenience stores. It was the best that I could do, *and* I was surviving.

CHAPTER 41.

❀

Time passed, and I continued to live with Sophia in her small apartment. I liked my work and felt safe there. Gradually, I got to know my boss and coworkers a little. However, old habits are slow to break, and I did not engage a great deal with others. I guess I was still being extra cautious and careful to obey all Arizona and United States rules and regulations. Again, I was trying hard to fit in and blend in the best I could. I had learned in Kentucky how to go to thrift stores and get American clothes and shoes so that I looked like everyone else. Life was good.

I was still having a hard time believing I was living in the very country that I had spent my whole life believing was evil and bad. In school, I learned how to shoot those "American Bastards" with a mock gun. And now the "American Bastards" were treating me kindly and fairly and helping me adjust to *their* country. I felt like my North Korean teachers and the Kim leaders had lied to me.

Something that surprised me was that one day I noticed that when I woke up, I was not painfully hungry at all. And I was not dreaming of food so much. What a change! I had nightmares often, but they were getting better. Now, I would wake up, go to the bathroom, have a drink of water, and go back to sleep. The dreams no longer lasted throughout the night. I also noticed that Sophia, who had been so shy at first, was beginning to be more open with me. I think she saw that I was kind and helpful to her, and she was beginning to trust me. She also saw that handling money was, in fact, easier with the two of us living together and sharing expenses, and she could depend on me to help her. Sophia and I were never "best buddies" in the way Americans think of it. She never raced home to tell me of something interesting or exciting that she had seen that day but was always quite quiet and reserved. Hey, so was I! North Koreans are all that way—we want to be certain things are OK and safe. That is the way we learned to be under our leaders in North Korea. That is how we learned to survive!

❀

After a long day at the convenience store several weeks later, I came home and went into the bedroom. I knew Sophia was on the late shift at the restaurant where she worked, and I was bone-tired. I had decided to wait for her and planned to have supper together later. As I lay down on the bed for a quick rest, I saw a blue cloth on the night table. I wondered what it was and felt its dampness as I picked it up. It was not made of nice material and was quite rough to the touch. I shook it out, finding it misshaped and non-descript. It did not look or smell like a cleaning cloth. What in the world? I wondered why Sophia would have such a cloth.

Later that evening, I asked Sophia what the cloth was. Tears welled up in her eyes. She looked down and whispered, "I was missing my little girl today, and that blue cloth is what we used to signal where I was so she could always find me."

That is why the cloth was wet! Sophia must have been crying a lot to have the cloth remain damp for so many hours! My heart ached for poor Sophia! She missed her daughter years later. "Well, we must put the cloth where she can find you." I picked the cloth up and took it outside to hang it on the mailbox next to our door. I hoped this would make her feel better. The truth was, we did not know when we would see her daughter. It was the best we could do. We had to survive.

❋

One day shortly thereafter, Sophia worked extra-long hours while I got off at my regular time. I decided to surprise her and have our supper ready when she walked in the door. I will never forget the sound of her slow, steady footsteps on the stairs outside of our small apartment door—I knew she was dead tired. She slowly unlocked the door, knowing she needed to make a meal for us both. Her face lit up when she smelled the Korean BBQ that I had somehow managed to put together.

I looked at Sophia, who was smiling. It was clear; she was happy she would not need to make supper. Her immense relief and hunger were showing. I could also tell that she was excited that I had chosen Korean BBQ and Kimchi for the meal. As the minutes went by, I started to feel something I had never experienced. Her obvious pleasure and delight made me feel good! I began to think that I liked this feeling of sharing and being with another person. It was all so new to me. I had not trusted anyone or anything my entire life! Sophia looked so trusting, shy, and vulnerable all at the same time.

Was this love? I did not know. I admit that I was unsure of what love meant. No one had ever spoken or explained the concept to me. I had known only survival, and so far I had managed to do OK with it. By this time, I had been around enough other guys in the United States to hear their boasting stories about women. They talked about their sexual exploits, where they went, and what they did with women. It was confusing. None of this fit with what I was feeling. I knew I felt a sense of responsibility toward Sophia and more than a little attraction toward her, but love? I really did not know. I did know I liked Sophia and being around her. I was beginning to feel safe and excited about the future. I knew I wanted to discover and explore these new feelings. I wanted to stay with Sophia. We could face whatever life brought us together. We were surviving!

PART V

January 2020

CHAPTER 42

Phoenix, Arizona

✳

Adam would be the first to admit that this past week had been an extremely long one, what with working about sixty-five hours and always thinking about Sophia and their life since they had gotten together. It had been a stressful period. They had spent nearly ten years together and had built a wonderful life here in Arizona. Of course, they had their issues, and things were not always easy. They had a home and children and were comfortable. Neither of them was ever hungry like they had been in their previous lives, Adam's nightmares had stopped, and they were living a life neither of them had ever even imagined. Adam was able to provide for his children and to be a better father than his father had been to him and his brothers, which made him feel immensely proud if he were honest.

Adam did not understand Sophia. It had been tearing him apart long enough. It was clear they needed to talk, and he wanted to clear this up before it went on further.

Entering the house, Adam knew what he would find. Sophia would be sitting in the dark bedroom crying and clutching the blue cloth while the children would be outside entertaining themselves. Both the kids and the house would be dirty, and if he guessed right, the children would also be hungry. He hoped he was wrong but doubted it. With a sigh of resignation, Adam marched straight to the bedroom and turned on the light. Stepping close to Sophia, he touched her shoulder as he knelt and gently took both her hands and the blue cloth into his.

"Sophia, look at me." He commanded. "This has to stop. The house is a mess. The kids need you, and I need you to be a wife and a mother. You cannot just hide away and wish you were with Yoon-ha. We need you to be with us a hundred percent."

Sophia moaned and tried to withdraw her hand, but he held it firmly and continued. "Sophia, Yoon-ha was seven years old when you left China, and you have been in the U.S. for nearly ten years now. Yoon-ha is undoubtedly a young woman now with a child of her own. You know that Su-lin would have taken care of her and loved her dearly. She's had a good life, Sophia. Now Kimi, Elayne, and I need you here to be a good mother."

"I don't know! You don't know!" Sophia cried.

"You are right. But everything points that way. I tell you what, let's save our money, and once we have our citizenship and passports, we can go find both Yoon-ha and Su-lin. We can travel to China and find them. Sophia, we can do that."

With that, Sophia sobbed more. Adam stroked her hair and patted her head as he continued. "Sophia, nothing is easy! But it is the *only* way! All we need are our documents and enough money. Our documents will be here soon, and we can start saving money right away. I will ask my boss for more hours tomorrow, and you are good at saving money. We will do it together. Come on." Adam held her tight. It was clear to him that Sophia did need to see Yoon-ha again so she could move on with her life. Right now, their children needed her here to be a fully functioning mother, and if he were honest, he needed her as well. She could not go on this way, and he was determined to keep his family safe and together. They had to survive, didn't they? He had no idea how or when they could travel to China, but he knew it was vital for them to at least attempt to find both Su-lin and Yoon-ha. Adam nuzzled the top of her head and continued to hold her for a few minutes as her sobbing gradually lessened.

Later that night, after Adam had fed the children, bathed them, and put them to bed, Sophia climbed into bed next to Adam and sighed. "I still miss her so much."

"I know you do, Sophia. And I wish it all would have been different, but you are needed here more than ever. I know we will find her. You must believe that. We have a plan, and we will find Yoon-ha."

Sophia did not speak immediately. A small smile gradually began to appear at the corner of her mouth. Sophia had not smiled all week. Adam felt both warm and relieved.

"We do have a plan, Adam. Yoon-ha, Yoon-ha...." She murmured as she snuggled down close to Adam in the bed.

"Yes," Adam thought, "we will find Yoon-ha. We do have space for love." He tightened his hold on Sophia.

THE END

QUESTIONS FOR DISCUSSION

1. What do you think Seng-il meant when he said, "They don't give you the space to love in North Korea."

2. What did you feel towards Ha-na's father? Was he a monster or simply following North Korean/Chinese customs?

3. What do you think of the "one-child policy?" Would that policy work in places where they do not favor boys over girls?

4. Did Ha-na do the right thing by giving up her child? Under what circumstances could or would you give up your child?

5. How do you think Ha-na and Seng-il's past traumas would affect their lives in America?

6. Do you think Ha-na/Sophia and Seng-il/Adam will ever get back to China? Will they find Yoon-ha and Su-lin?

A special request from Ellen —

If you enjoyed this novel, please leave me a review on Amazon and write to me at: Ellen@EllenMason.com.

I appreciate all feedback.

ACKNOWLEDGMENTS

I have many to acknowledge and thank for their help with this book. First, I must acknowledge Adam Park and his wife, Sophia, because I could not have written this book without them. I knew I had to tell this story when Adam told me, "*In North Korea, they leave you no space for love. I don't know love—is it a bowl of rice?*"

I began researching North Korea and China in earnest and interviewed Adam (~ 80 hours) before writing this novel. Adam's story closely follows his genuine journey, while I could not make Sophia relive her horrible time in China. Sophia left not one but two daughters behind. Therefore, I gathered true stories and accounts from women who had escaped North Korea and entered China (most were sex trafficked) and then wrote a composite story for Ha-na. I thank each of these women for having the courage to come forward with their stories.

I picked up the story of Adam and Sophia from the time they met in Chicago and followed the true story of their settlement in Phoenix. In full disclosure, I must tell you that both Adam and Sophia changed their names again as they started their lives in Arizona. However, they do not want to reveal their actual names, and I have honored their wishes. I wonder if they will always play their cards close to their chests, keep their heads down, and keep a low profile.

I would also like to thank the first readers of my novel, who gave me invaluable feedback on both the characters and the writing. These include my sister Jeanie Murphy, my sister Penny Murphy, my brother Ron Mason, and my friends Lisa Miller, Beverley Rowley, Sabena Norman, Meilee Smythe, Jan Smith, and Jeff Smith.

I must also send a huge hug and say thank you to all the other friends and neighbors who kept cheering and inspiring me as I moved through this process. You know who you are, and I will always be grateful for your encouragement.

And to my husband, Roger, who was there and encouraged me the entire way. He is my most ardent supporter, my best friend, and the love of my life. His belief in me is what keeps me going. I am so fortunate!

ABOUT THE AUTHOR

Born and raised in Iowa, Ellen Mason grew up in a family/town where things were not always perfect. She was always interested in why and how people who came from difficult backgrounds survived and often thrived in the world.

After obtaining her education, getting married, and entering the medical world, Ellen remained fascinated with the struggles many Americans and especially immigrants overcome in their quest for success on their own terms.

Later, as a personal life and business coach, she met Adam, who told her, *"In North Korea, they leave you NO space for love. I don't know love, is it a bowl of rice?"* Ellen was rocked by the raw emotion of the gut-wrenching story of how these two teenagers, suffering from starvation and oppression and who had never known or understood what freedom was, came to realize that was exactly what they wanted and needed.

It was then that she knew she had to tell the story of Ha-na and Seng-il's internal struggles, betrayals, and heart-breaking choices, as well as the deep friendships and kindnesses they enjoyed as they each navigated the harsh realities of life in the most oppressive societies of North Korea and China to life in the United States. After witnessing their personal growth, she felt other Americans should hear and experience the desperation that many immigrants to the U.S. have gone through to have what we so chauvinistically take for granted.

You can learn more about Ellen at her website: EllenMason.com You can also follow her on Facebook, Goodreads, and by joining her mailing list. She loves to talk about her past careers, traveling, reading, writing, and her love of freshwater and saltwater fishing!

Email Ellen at Ellen@EllenMason.com